A Day For Bones

Books by Dale E. Lehman

Howard County Mysteries

The Fibonacci Murders
True Death
Ice on the Bay
A Day for Bones

Bernard and Melody Capers

Weasel Words
Rooftop Sonata

Science Fiction

Space Operatic
The Belt
Penitence

Short Story Collections

The Realm of Tiny Giants
Found by the Road
Manifest Secrets

A Day for Bones

A Howard County Mystery

Dale E. Lehman

RED TALES

Chase, Maryland

A Day for Bones
Dale E. Lehman

Copyright © 2022 by Dale E. Lehman

This is a work of fiction. All the characters, organizations, and events portrayed in this book are either products of the author's imagination or are used fictitiously.

Cover art by Proi
https://99designs.com/profiles/proi

Book design by Dale E. Lehman
Book set in 11-pt. Calluna
Chapter headings set in 18-pt. Imprint MT Shadow

Published by Red Tales, 2022
Baltimore, Maryland
United States of America
https://www.DaleELehman.com

Trade paperback: 978-1-958906-00-2
Ebook: 978-1-958906-01-9

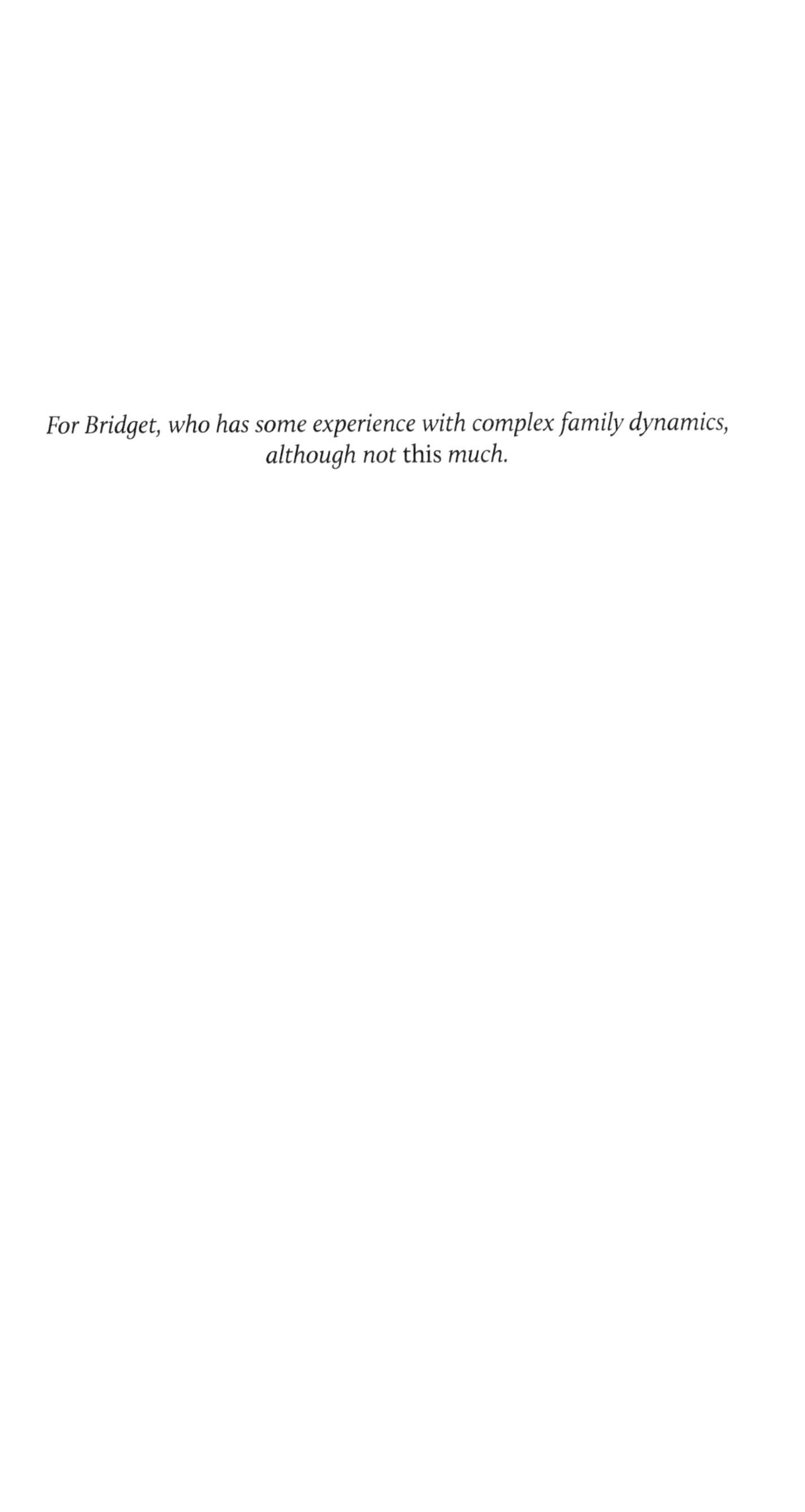

For Bridget, who has some experience with complex family dynamics, although not this much.

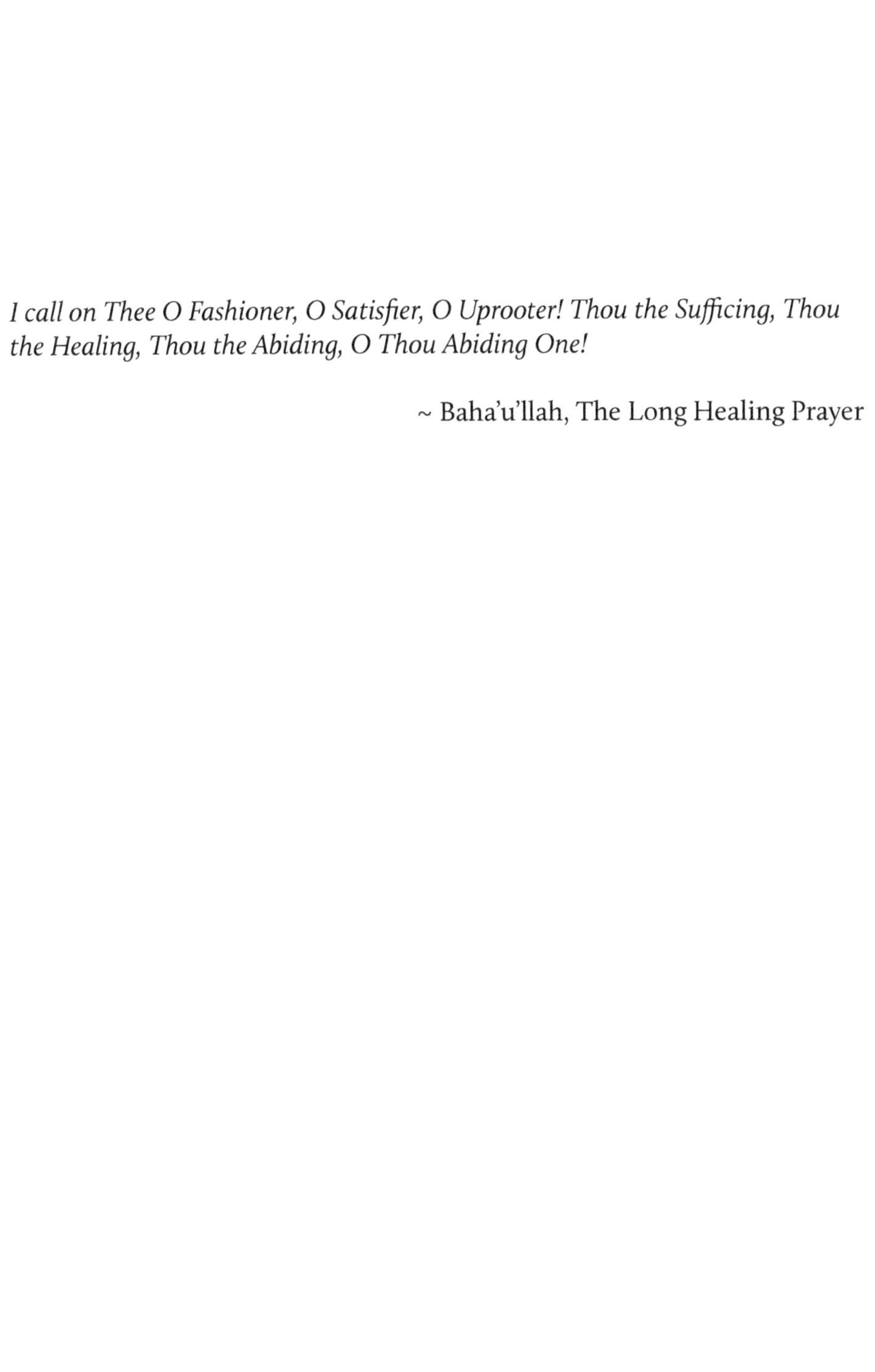

I call on Thee O Fashioner, O Satisfier, O Uprooter! Thou the Sufficing, Thou the Healing, Thou the Abiding, O Thou Abiding One!

~ Baha'u'llah, The Long Healing Prayer

Chapter 1

Helpless, he watched from his second floor living room window above the bakery. Water surged down Main Street below, hurling branches and wreckage and even cars through the darkness. Mother Nature, the most efficient of brooms in hand, was sweeping the town clean.

A strange phrase, he thought, *sweeping clean*. A friend's grandmother had once spoken in those terms: the 1937 Ohio River flood, she said, had swept their house clean away. But this wasn't clean. The water raged muddy brown, full of tumbling shapes torn from buildings. Nor did it pass with the quiet swish of a broom over a floor. Its predatory rumble signaled satisfaction as it feasted on its kill.

What had the flood ripped from his own business two floors below? He could only imagine. The old oak door with its rich red grain highlighted by dark, swirling knots? The glass storefront with its Old English script, smashed into a million lethal shards? Splinters of wooden tables and chairs where once customers gathered for food and companionship? Cakes and cookies and pastries still warm from the oven, dissolved in the night, their commingled aromas diffused on the wind?

He might have wept had he seen it. Tomorrow he would see and weep. Tonight he could only watch the street boil.

Behind him, a whisper of movement announced his wife. She came into the living room from the kitchen, dinner over, dishes done, and stood beside him. She took his hand in hers. They watched together, silent, he tall and slim, she short and slim, while water rushed down the street and sirens wailed in the distance and frightened people cried in the terrible night.

"Will it be okay?" she asked.

He shook his head, not knowing.

She squeezed his hand.

"Yes," he decided. "This is what insurance is for."

"Insurance can't fix everything, Jim."

"No."

Denise lifted her round face to him. A lock of her long, dark hair crossed it, and he pushed it back from her hard eyes. "Water is a shovel," she told him. "It digs up everything."

It had crossed his mind, too, this *everything* of which she spoke, the dangerous secret whose exposure she feared. But a torrent of decades had rushed by. It could hardly matter anymore. The here and now filled his thoughts. Lost business. Lost customers. Lost heritage. His bakery was more than a store. It was four generations of Ferrings. James Ferring IV hoped someday to pass it to James Ferring V, little as his son cared. In time, maybe, James the younger would remember his heritage, and the bakery would be waiting. This wasn't the first Ellicott City flood, nor would it be the last. They would rebuild, reopen, recover. People always had, always would.

"Say something."

Jim regarded Denise with dull eyes. When she was twenty-seven, she had been the most beautiful woman in the world. Now, at twice that age? He didn't know. She wasn't unpleasant to look at, but as she gained in years she'd lost something else. A sparkle had slipped away when he wasn't looking, leaving her cold, cynical, the self-appointed watchdog of the modest Ferring empire. He took her into his arms and held her close. "I wouldn't worry about it," he whispered in her ear.

Together, they stared into the darkness.

She watched the water.

He watched the water.

"I would," she said.

Years later, when his grandchildren Susie and Andrew were old enough to understand the word, Detective Lieutenant Rick Peller would describe the night of Tuesday, May thirtieth as one that should have been euthanized. The flood was bad. What it unearthed was worse. And to add insult to injury, he ended up soaked, bruised, battered, and only by the grace of God alive. He began at the scene of a gun shop burglary.

The call came as he trundled home in his F150 following a day of senseless if non-lethal violence and its attendant paperwork. Crime never took time off. That day, it had been a drug dealer shot in both kneecaps by a disgruntled client, a knifing at the Columbia Town Center over a botched fast-food order, and a betrayed girlfriend tracking down her ex's lovers and inflicting heavy damage on their cars with a hammer. Peller was a bit sorry they'd caught her but proud that his team had scored one hundred percent that day. Every perp had been apprehended by the time he left for home.

But May thirtieth wasn't over.

"What do they want with me?" he demanded of the dispatcher. Even with the current understaffing, routine burglary shouldn't be a job for an off-the-clock lieutenant.

"Geri wants you," the dispatcher said, as though crime scene technician Geri Franklin outranked them all.

"Why?"

"That's above my paygrade, Lieutenant. I just make the calls."

"Yeah, sorry, ten-four. On my way." Peller rerouted himself. He'd been looking forward to phoning his son Jason and the grandkids that evening. It had been a couple weeks since he talked with them, and he was feeling the distance. Fortunately, they lived two time zones west in Denver. With luck, he'd wrap this up quickly and catch them before Belinda tucked the kids in bed.

His destination was The Lodge, a store west of Ellicott City just off U.S. Route 40. It was hard to miss. A bright green sign upon which a twelve-point buck pranced identified the stand-alone building. A nearly dead light flickered inside the sign, supplying an illusion of movement. Fast food restaurants, a grocery store, and a pet supply store clustered nearby, screened from the gun shop by stands of tall trees. Maybe they were embarrassed to have The Lodge for a neighbor. It stood alone, like the last kid to be picked for a team.

He parked and went in, noting in passing the bars on the windows, the deadbolt on the front door, the alarm system controls on the wall inside. The storefront felt surprisingly roomy. The goods were arranged along the walls and windows, leaving the middle open. Glass display cases served as counters on three sides. Racks of guns, hunting bows, and fishing rods lined the walls behind the counters. Apparel and other merchandise hung on clothing racks before the windows.

The two responding officers huddled over one of the display cases, talking shop with the lone employee on duty. A sleek semi-automatic handgun lay on the counter while the employee pointed out its features with his meaty index finger.

When Peller entered, the officers snapped to something like attention. The employee tugged his untucked button-down shirt into position over his stocky frame. Heavily bearded, he didn't look like someone to be messed with, but his expression was that of a child caught stealing cookies.

Peller introduced himself.

"Chuck Ferring," the big man said. "I'm the owner."

"What's the story, Mr. Ferring?"

Ferring waggled a thumb toward a curtain covering the storeroom door. "Somebody broke in and made off with a dozen or so weapons. Mostly handguns. A couple rifles."

"When did this happen?"

"About an hour ago. I was helping a customer. I heard a noise and went back to check. By the time I got there, they were gone."

The senior officer, David Moles by his nametag, south-of-the-border by his face and accent, likewise motioned at the curtain. "The back door was unlocked and a few boxes knocked over. That's probably what Mr. Ferring heard."

Ferring cleared his throat and looked at the gun on the counter.

Peller could well imagine his embarrassment. Barred windows, deadbolts, alarms, and the burglars just strolled in. "When was that door last used?"

"Four days ago," Ferring said, "when we got a delivery."

An open and shut case, Peller quipped to himself. *They opened the door, took what they wanted, and shut it again.* An all-too-common story. Why weren't people more careful? "What about your customer? Did they hear the noise?"

Ferring shrugged. "He heard it. I guess he got tired of waiting. He left before I got back."

"How long did that take?"

"About ten minutes. When I realized stuff was missing, I checked over everything."

Trampling any evidence. "Did you know the customer?"

Ferring shook his head.

Peller figured it better than even odds the customer had been a distraction, allowing the burglars to work unnoticed. He turned to the officers. "So why am I here? Something unusual turn up?"

Moles made that thumb gesture again. "The tech is working the scene now, sir. And yeah, we found something unusual." The officers glanced at each other as though sorting out who should spring the surprise on him.

"Such as?"

"There's a note. She's bagged it for you."

After thirty years on the force, little surprised Peller anymore, but sometimes a sight, sound, or comment triggered a disquiet in him. He'd learned to pay attention to that feeling. "What kind of note?"

"A sort of manifesto. It basically says…" Moles looked at Ferring as though willing him to finish the explanation, but Ferring wasn't inclined. He gazed out the storefront and chewed his bottom lip.

"Says what, Officer?"

"Your people will die. That's the gist of it. All your people will die."

A few heavy drops of rain splattered on the shop window, rapping like a cane against the glass.

"Are you the only employee here, Mr. Ferring?" Peller asked.

Miserable, Ferring nodded.

"Then I guess you're stuck for a while. Make yourself comfortable. I may need to ask some questions."

Not waiting for a reply, he pushed his way into the storeroom. The curtain concealed a door that stood open at the moment. It, too, had a deadbolt on it. *All that useless security*, Peller thought. A set of well-stocked metal racks surrounded him. Neatly stacked upon them, scores of boxes bore clear labels identifying contents and quantities: rifles here, shotguns there, handguns across the way. Ammunition. Knives. Assorted hunting gear. Outdoor clothing. The place bespoke such organization and care that the unlocked door felt like someone blowing a raspberry at Ferring. Kneeling before the gray metal door, now open, crime scene technician Geri Franklin carefully lifted a fingerprint from the jamb. Rain splashed in the darkness beyond.

"Anywhere I shouldn't step?" Peller asked.

"You're good." Her eyes never left her work.

The door had both a lock on the knob and a heavy deadbolt. The windowless walls were painted battleship gray. Making a slow circuit of the shelves, he noticed nothing obviously out of place except a single box which had fallen about ten feet from the door. Crumpled along the edge that hit the floor, it hadn't popped open. Aside from that, he couldn't have said anything was amiss. The burglars hadn't trashed the place. They knew what they wanted and where to find it.

"I'm told the burglar left a note."

Franklin stood and hefted a small bag where she kept her tools and collected evidence. She was tall and lean with intense blue eyes. She looked a good five years younger than she really was. Her face should have been in high school, but her focus overmatched the most skilled of surgeons. Peller thought she'd make one hell of a detective if she were so inclined.

"Here," she said. "It's an odd one." She extracted a plastic bag and handed it to Peller. He tilted the bag to reduce the glare and read.

Your life will be destroyed. Your means will be taken. Your weapons will turn against you. The wronged will be avenged. The end has begun.

"Great. Another lunatic loose in Howard County. We've had more than our share these past few years." He handed the note back.

"Maybe it really is the end times," Franklin said. She sounded so serious that only those who knew her would know she was kidding. "Or a sick joke. It's too apocalyptic to be real, don't you think?" She returned the note to her bag without looking at it.

Thunder rumbled overhead. The rain transitioned from rattling on the roof to hammering as though trying to break in. It sounded like a thousand empty soda cans bouncing around up there. Peller looked at the ceiling. "Some people thrive on apocalypse. Let me know if anything turns up."

"Yep." Having finished with the door, Franklin closed it to keep the rain out and clanked the deadbolt shut.

Peller returned to the showroom, where Chuck Ferring and the officers had moved on to the subject of bow hunting. The trio slid into silence at the first glimpse of Peller's tight-lipped concentration. "You read the note, Mr. Ferring?"

Ferring nodded.

"What do you think?"

"Sounds like someone needs meds." Ferring appeared to need some himself.

"Does someone want to hurt you?"

"No, sir. I just run this little store and try to be a good neighbor."

Peller stared at Ferring long enough to make the man uncomfortable but got nothing more. "Whoever did this hates you. Maybe you should tell me who it is, before something ugly happens."

Ferring shrugged once more. Despite the rain, the information creek, barely damp to begin with, had run dry.

Peller tossed a business card on the display case. "If you change your mind, give me a call. Make sure you submit your theft report to ATF tomorrow."

Beyond the front window, rain worthy of a tropical storm battered the asphalt. He could have been home by now, chatting with Jason, Susie, and Andrew while the storm raged outside. He could even be having dinner with Joan Churchill if he wanted. She'd brave the weather to spend an evening with him, although he wasn't sure why he thought of her. Introduced through Detective Sergeant Andy Newton's well-intentioned meddling, he and Churchill had met a few times over the past four months, but only as friends. Peller didn't want more than that. Some days, today particularly, he didn't want that much.

He shunted her to the back of his mind and pulled open the door. A blast of cold wind drove a splatter of rain into his face. "Whoa. Looks like a night for flash flooding," he told the others. "Be careful going home."

Shoulders scrunched, he plunged into the downpour. Five giant steps carried him to his truck. He yanked the door open, dove through, and slammed it behind him. Clothing soaked, he turned the key and watched the windows fog. Once the defroster cleared them, he drove route 40 east and merged south on 29. As soon as he had, the police radio chatter swelled.

"Ten forty-six, St. Paul and Mulligan's Hill."

"Main Street's a river. I can't get there."

"Any units on New Cut Road, respond."

"Ten fifty-three on New Cut south of College. Big oak. Just missed the houses, thank God."

"Can you get through?"

"Only on foot. It'll be a soggy hike, but we'll get there."

"Ten forty-six, Main and Church. A woman with two children."

Peller could almost hear the terrified screams of the children trapped with their mother in the family car, water surging around them, maybe pushing them down the street toward the Patapsco River. He radioed that he would approach on Old Columbia Pike. Wipers running full steam, he took the exit toward Ellicott City's historic district as fast as conditions allowed. Likely he could do no good, but they needed police on as many sides as possible. The historic district lay in the bottom of a valley that wound down to the Patapsco. With sprawling development, the valleys and ravines feeding it had become asphalt rivers channeling rainwater inexorably downward. Flash floods could cut off most escape routes in less than a minute and hold the cavalry at bay for an hour.

Lightning seared the dark. He could barely see through the wall of water that his windshield had become, but he knew the way. Being the only fool on the road, he held to its center. A barrage of calls echoed in his ears: people trapped in cars, power lines down, trees down. He'd never seen a storm like this. Not even the occasional tropical storm rambling up from the Gulf of Mexico had ever struck with such fury.

Rounding a downhill curve, Peller felt his truck skid. He eased up the gas and fought the vehicle into line. Over the pounding rain, he heard a dull roar. It wasn't thunder. It rolled on and on, nonstop. This was the voice of water. Somewhere in the dark, rapids churned across his path. He slid to a stop just as his truck dipped its toes into the shore of a newly-formed lake. He clambered out. Simultaneously, the deluge transformed into a light spring rain that any other day would have brought to mind daffodils and tulips. But not today. Floodwaters boomed as he picked his way onto the sidewalk and down toward Main Street. There, a muddy froth rushed between the shops, carrying off branches and chunks torn from buildings.

Up the road to his left, a car faced into the torrent. Somehow it held its ground, but it rocked in the current and might at any moment be dislodged. Peller could just make out moving shapes behind the windows, small hands pounding on the glass. Standing just out of the water above the intersection, half a dozen drenched men looked on in horror. He ran toward them and called over the thundering rapids. "Let's get them out of there!"

One of the group, a stocky man with a military haircut, gave a thumbs up. "We made a human chain but couldn't reach. We're two people short. One, now you're here."

"We'll be enough." Nobody argued. Game for another attempt, the group reformed the chain, the first man anchoring himself to a lamppost in a foot and a half of water at the edge of the torrent and the rest hanging onto their neighbors, one by one gingerly wading into the street, feet planted against the current. Peller elected himself for the most dangerous position at the far end of the chain and within a couple of minutes had reached the car. He could see the people inside now, a woman in tears and two small children—a boy and a girl—crowding the rear window, screaming for help. He stretched out his arm and groped for the door handle. The water battered him, threatening to knock him down and carry him off.

Arm extended so far it hurt, his fingertips fell just shy of the handle.

"Stretch!" he called back, and each link of the chain passed on the message. The whole line stretched.

He got hold of the handle and pulled. The flood pushed back. He fought it, but the water was stronger, and the door wouldn't open. Inside, the woman rocked back and wailed.

"Stay calm!" he yelled, but she couldn't hear. "Lower the window!" He tapped the window with his fingernails and motioned downward, hoping the woman would understand.

She did. She pushed at a button on the door, but nothing happened. Peller's heart sank. The car's electronics had shorted out in the water. Without power, the windows couldn't be opened. The woman turned the key a few times and slapped at the steering wheel, then made a hopeless gesture at him.

Short of turning the car around so the rushing water would work in their favor, Peller couldn't see how they could get the woman and her children out. The flood hadn't risen much. Had it crested? Maybe car and passengers could stay put until it subsided. But no. Something slammed against his shin, and he nearly tumbled over. The object thumped the car. The vehicle shuddered.

Along the human chain, gritted teeth and locked hands urged him to try again. The men hadn't given up, but the effort to stand their ground wore on them.

"What's your name?" Peller asked the man next to him. He had to yell to make himself heard over the rush of water.

"Ron," the other replied.

"I'm letting go, Ron."

Ron eased his grip. Peller grabbed the door handle again, released Ron's hand, and yanked himself against the body of the car. The water threw him hard into it. Bracing himself just behind the door, he hauled on the handle with both hands and felt it move. It might have weighed as much as the entire car, but he pulled until he could work his thigh into the opening to hold it. Then, pushing with everything he had, he pried the door open enough for the woman to pass through. He couldn't help her. His whole body had to maintain pressure against the door just to keep it open.

"Hold onto the door," he yelled at her. "Reach for the guy at the end of the line. His name's Ron. He'll help you."

She shook so much, she could barely hold onto the steering wheel. Ron motioned encouragement. "My children!" she wailed.

Peller hadn't figured that out yet. "We'll get them."

"I can't do this!"

"Yes, you can. We've got you."

She forced down a sob, scooted into the opening, and gingerly dipped a foot into the water. "I'm scared."

Something thudded against the door. The impact nearly knocked the wind from Peller, and his feet slipped from under him. He hauled himself up and pushed on the door. *I can't take much more of this,* he thought. *I have to get her moving.* Fortunately, he got an idea. "Ma'am, I need you in the chain by the lamppost. With your help, we can get your children out."

That convinced her. Whole body trembling, she worked her way beneath Peller's arms and around the door, where she caught hold of Ron's hand. He pulled her to him, and Peller waited while she worked her way steadily down the chain. It felt like hours. She reached the far end and, clasping hands with people on either side, took her place. The chain shifted toward the car. Ron grabbed the door handle and pulled. The weight on Peller eased.

Peller motioned to the children. "Come here," he called. "I'll help you. Everyone will help you." The girl, about two years her brother's senior, took the boy's hand, helped him into the front seat, and gently pushed him forward. She was scared, but she put on a brave face for her brother. *Good girl,* Peller thought.

Keeping one hand on the car for a brace, Peller carefully picked up the boy and shifted just enough to get him in reach of the chain. Even with Ron pulling, the flood tried to cut Peller in half with the door.

"Climb over us," Ron told the child. We can't let go of each other." Shaking, the boy did as he was told.

Peller motioned the girl out and helped her into the chain. To avoid disrupting anyone's balance, he waited while the children made their way along the line and breathed a sigh of relief when finally they were in their mother's arms. Then he eased himself out of the doorway. Water pressure pushed the door shut as he went. He had to take care lest his arm be pinned, but finally he was free.

Holding onto the door handle, he began to turn so he could take Ron's hand. Just as Peller reached out, Ron yelled, "Damn!" and stumbled, barely keeping his balance. Something hard slammed into Peller's gut, knocking him off his feet. He flipped over backwards and went under. Cold, muddy water surged over him. He tumbled, tumbled, heels over head, hands scrambling madly for something, anything to hold on to. They found nothing. Unidentifiable shards scraped his face, his legs, his arms, his back. Just when he thought his lungs might explode, his head popped from the water and he sucked in a great gulp of air before being pulled under again. The flood tossed him five directions at once. He surfaced a second time, not knowing which way was which.

The water dragged him down again and battered him with every-thing it had collected. His body slammed against something unyielding. He clawed for a handhold and wrapped his arms around the object. Whatever it was, it stood its ground. He hung on while the angry torrent clawed at him. Water crashed over him, flooded his mouth and nostrils, but still he held on and got his feet wrapped around the object, too. Almost out of air, he clambered up whatever had saved him, surfaced, spat out water, gasped his lungs full of air. Above him, a blinding red glare pierced the night. The pole had thin, sharp projections on either side about at the level of his hips. He worked his feet onto them, hoping whatever they were would take his weight. As he pushed higher, metal buckled under him. He slipped, but his footholds didn't give way.

He hung there, body all but fused to the fluted pole. Above him, an old-fashioned traffic signal capped the pole. Gasping for breath, he straight-ened to get as much of his body out of the torrent as possible. He blinked water from his eyes and assessed his predicament. His feet and calves re-mained submerged. The flood ran nearly eight feet deep below him.

He looked up into the blaze.

"Red light," he panted to nobody, for nobody was there. "Means stop."

Chapter 2

Detective Theresa Swan liked the locale if not the assignment. A farm girl from North Carolina, she loved rustling trees, the rush of hidden waters, the chatter of birds, and cerulean skies. She could almost imagine this was the Howard County of fifteen thousand years past, where damp soil had never felt the touch of human feet and the twitching noses of deer and squirrels had never caught a whiff of humankind. She drove with the windows down, warm wind whipping her dark hair about her dark face and shoulders, scarcely believing that only last night a once-in-a-century storm had battered the region.

But the tranquility was short-lived. She had come to the eastern end of Patapsco Valley State Park, a fringe of greenery where Howard County abutted Baltimore County, to investigate a report of human remains. As she approached the scene, tension knotted her muscles. She had crossed paths with death just twice before. Her grandmother had passed five years ago, when Swan was twenty-three, and a friend from her academy days had been killed in a traffic accident a few months ago. That was it. She hoped this wasn't the scene of a grisly murder.

Don't get ahead of yourself, Swan told herself. Howard County wasn't Baltimore. Probably some hapless soul had been swept down the river in the flood and deposited here. Although, that wasn't much comfort. Death by torrent couldn't be pleasant. Rumor had it Rick Peller nearly became a statistic himself. She shuddered at the thought.

Swan followed River Road to a hill above a sandy shelf where the Patapsco bent slight north. A uniformed park ranger waited there, leaning on the rear of his official pickup truck, picking his fingernails and whistling to himself. She stopped her cobalt blue Chevy Cavalier fifteen feet behind his vehicle. He glanced up as she climbed out, then returned to his nails. When Swan introduced herself, he reciprocated, albeit stiffly.

"Bob Allen." He squinted at her face. "Didn't expect a pretty black lady. We usually get grumpy old white guys."

Was that a compliment? Sexist? Racist? All three at once? Whatever. Her superior and mentor Detective Sergeant Corina Montufar would have advised her to ignore both praise and slights. She was just a detective, here to do a job.

Swan catalogued Allen's appearance: average height, slim, probably in his mid-forties, gold wedding band on his left ring finger. A hint of a tattoo peeked above his collar on the right side of his neck without revealing the design. She suspected his hair was thinning under that ranger hat. What showed was dark brown with no hint of gray.

"So what's the trouble, Mr. Allen?"

"No trouble, really, just something strange."

"What kind of strange?"

"I supposed you'd call it human remains."

"Are we talking a fresh body in the woods or something you dug up with a shovel?"

Allen grinned. He had a toothy smile that made him look a bit manic. "I like a woman with a sense of humor. A skull. Come on, I'll show you." He led her off the road and down a tree-covered slope, judiciously placing his boots with every step.

Swan hadn't worn boots, just a comfortable pair of white flats. She hadn't expected a field expedition. Three steps down slope, she slipped and caught at a branch. She nearly slid into Allen.

He paused and eyed her shoes with some amusement. "This mud is slick. Better be careful."

Thanks for the heads up, she grumbled to herself. With the help of the trees, she picked her way down. Her shoes would be ruined by the time they reached the water, and her blue and green pantsuit wouldn't fare much better. Mud was already splattered halfway up her calves.

They reached the river. The flow gurgled by, carrying twigs and bits of bark downstream. "The water is up a foot or so." Allen motioned along the river's course. "Usually, this bar is about twice this size. Here's our friend." He led her upstream and pointed to a human skull stuck in the mud, two-thirds exposed, empty eye sockets gazing heavenward as though in prayer. A smooth expanse of mud surrounded it, untouched save by the water that had deposited it.

"That definitely looks weird," Swan commented.

"I've named him Carl." Allen flicked a smile her way. "After my college roommate. Carl spent more time lying around staring at the ceiling than anyone I've ever known."

She laughed. "What did he major in, naps?"

"That was his minor. He majored in women. He'd have hit on you for sure. He was white, but he enjoyed variety." He cocked his head at the skull. "Maybe naming it is premature. This could be a lady skull."

Exhaling frustration, Swan slipped her hands into her pants pockets. The fingers of her right hand brushed the grip of her gun, holstered there. *Give me an excuse*, she thought. But no. He wasn't worth the bullet.

"What do we do with this guy or girl, as the case may be?"

Swan withdrew her hands. "I'll call a technician to photograph and collect it for the medical examiner. Whoever it is, they've been gone a long time."

"Makes one think, doesn't it? Colonial settler? Indian? Confederate soldier? Escaped slave?" He smirked. "Could be a relative of yours. Or mine. I have ancestors on both sides of the Civil War."

They both knew what her ancestors had been. Swan refused the bait. "Is there an easier way back to the road?"

"That *was* the easy way."

"I don't know if I can make it in these shoes."

"Yeah, fashion isn't much good out here. But I'll get you back."

They returned across the sand bar to the hill. He took a few careful upward steps, made sure his feet were planted securely, and reached back to Swan. Reluctantly, she took his hand and started up behind him. He climbed judiciously and to his credit made sure she didn't face-dive into the mud. When they reached the top, he let go and accompanied her to his vehicle, silent, eyes flicking between the ground and her face.

"Something wrong?" Swan asked.

"You don't fit my idea of a detective. Not that I've ever met one."

"What, am I too skinny?"

He laughed.

"Or too female, maybe?" *Or too black?*

Allen declined to answer. He touched the brim of his ranger hat. "It's been nice, but I have to get on with my day. Come back and visit sometime." He climbed into his truck and drove into the park's interior, leaving Swan to wrestle with a tangle of anger, hatred, and self-doubt. He'd manipulated her far too well.

She pushed emotion aside and joked with the dispatcher as she put in the call, recommending the tech bring climbing gear. Then she immersed herself in the scenery, breathing deep and slow as jays and sparrows and cardinals flitted about. She listened to the hammering of an unseen woodpecker and the impressive repertoire of a mockingbird. The breeze licked her face like an exuberant puppy. She leaned her seat back, closed her eyes, and for a rare half hour did nothing but enjoy sound and sensation.

All too soon, tires crunched to a halt and Geri Franklin's voice intruded. "Overwhelmed, aren't you?"

Swan opened her eyes to find Franklin peering into the car, amused. She put her seat up and returned the smile. "I deserve a break. I slid the whole way down to the river in these." She opened her door and stuck out her left foot, muddy shoe and all.

Franklin shook her head. "Unprepared, Theresa. Shame on you."

"Some of us spend more time at our desks than in the wild. Being prepared means knowing our passwords."

"So have that man of yours take you camping and teach you some survival skills."

"Ken? They only thing he knows about the great outdoors is the lawnmower."

Franklin laughed and stepped back so Swan could exit her vehicle. "So, what's the deal?"

That was more small talk than most people got from Franklin. If she was more open with Swan and Holly Ross—the youngest detective on the force—it was only their shared generational bond. Otherwise, she was all business and particularly looked it now: jeans, a long-sleeved denim shirt, and hiking boots. She had a canvas bag stuffed with the tools of her trade slung over her right shoulder. She was all set for a jaunt through a soggy wood.

Swan pointed into the trees. "A park ranger found a human skull by the river. The flood probably washed it out of an old grave. Photograph and collect it and send it to the medical examiner. I'll show you the muddy slope of death. After that, you're on your own."

"After you."

Swan led Franklin to the top of the incline. "The ranger's name is Bob Allen. He won't likely come back, but he knows I called you. If he does drop by, try not to push him off a cliff."

Franklin eyed the mud and shifted the bag to her left shoulder. "Sounds like you don't like him."

"He's either a racist misogynist or clueless."

"Don't stress over it, Theresa. Mind over matter. If you don't mind, he doesn't matter."

Easy for you to say, Swan thought.

Franklin took hold of a tree branch and tested the mud at the top of the slope with her right foot. "For serious. You can't control anyone but yourself. Go back to your nap, now. I got this."

Swan watched Franklin negotiate the slope as though she'd been born on the side of a slippery hill. Returning to her Cavalier, she contemplated that nap but decided against it. She was on the clock, after all. Paperwork beckoned.

In her two years in investigations, Detective Holly Ross hadn't worked any big cases, just a parade of nuisance crimes: a break in here and there, an occasional assault, a bit of vandalism, and the guy they'd branded "the drive-by flasher." *There* was a case she'd rather forget.

Something this odd, though…it could be a game-changer for her career.

Of Cherokee descent, Ross had an oval face and a hesitant smile, as though she was never quite sure she was where she should be. But that smile belied her ambition. She knew where she wanted to be, and maybe because of that Captain Morris had moved her to Detective Sergeant Eric Dumas' charge in a recent "workforce rebalancing." The move presaged great things, making her part of a team the Captain regarded as special. And her first big assignment as part of that team was…

…this.

Two blocks up Main Street from the river, a block and a half north of where Rick Peller had by luck or miracle snagged a traffic signal pole the previous night and narrowly escaped death, a three-story building of deep red brick and black wood casings commanded Ross' attention. The building, home to the HorseSpirit Arts Gallery, had weathered the storm as well as could be expected. Her eyes played over three large arch windows overhead. Below to the left, a circular window surveyed the street from just above the door. A huge arch window occupied the rest of the storefront. All that glass, and most of it still intact.

Most of it. The lower part of the arch window had been smashed. Water gushed through and swept various *objets d'art* off an oak table. The table had been knocked off-kilter, but somehow it hadn't overturned. A waterlogged painting now lay flat on the tabletop alongside ceramic shards. More shards and scraps and water-logged paintings lie scattered about its feet.

None of that particularly surprised Ross. The flood had done worse up and down Main Street. Several basements had been clawed open and foundations eroded. Farther down, an SUV had lodged in a double door. Water was still draining from that store. The art gallery got off easy. Ross was only here because of the bones.

A collection of disarticulated human bones littered the table and floor. A femur had come to rest in the window, precariously balanced on the jagged glass. Ross identified a humerus, a tibia (or was it a fibula?), a pelvis, vertebrae, and a collection of ribs. She guessed they had they all come from the same body, yet they hardly made up one ex-human. The rest must be scattered along the street or washed down the Patapsco and out to the bay.

Police photographer Scott Sahin had arrived ahead of Ross and set to work documenting the scene of whatever this was. Not a drowning. This guy was long dead before the flood happened. Ross studied the street. Scores of people were clearing debris, talking to insurance adjusters and re-porters, lamenting the damage to their businesses and lives. That's all Main Street was: businesses flanked by residential side streets. The flood certain-ly hadn't dug these bones from a cemetery, so where had they come from?

"You good here?" Ross called to Sahin.

Sahin waved. "Give me half an hour."

"You got it. Did Geri come with you?"

Sahin pointed his camera. "She got another call but said she'll be along shortly."

"Good, she'll love this one." Ross returned to her car, slid in, and grabbed the microphone. "Dectective Ross. Got an unusual 10-78 for you. Send me enough officers to canvas the Ellicott City Historic District. We have a collection of human bones in a storefront. We need to find any others scat-tered around before they're hauled to the dump with the flood debris."

She could almost hear the dispatcher do a double-take. "Sounds like we need a ten-code for a joke."

Ross smirked. "You don't believe me?"

"Hell, no. It's not October."

"So pretend it is and send me some cops."

"And a bag of candy. Ten four."

Ross laughed. This was definitely going to be a day to remember.

"Good morning, Sherlock."

Slumped in a chair in the Howard County General emergency room waiting area, Peller opened his eyes, relieved to hear a familiar voice if not the moniker. The place, only a third full this morning, was as pleasant as an echo chamber overflowing with irritated lions. A chorus of subdued moans and complaints competed with a running argument between a middle-aged man and his blanketed girlfriend over his need to get to work. Overlaying it all, a barrage of celebrity gossip and pharmaceutical commercials flowed from wall-mounted televisions. The place had a terrible bedside manner.

Thankfully, Joan Churchill's brown eyes make him forget all that. She smiled, radiant in a pure white blouse and red ankle-length skirt. She had recently cropped her dark hair short. Peller found it unsettling, as though someone else had stolen Churchill's face. He was used to her with a pile of fluff wound on top of her head. Righting himself, he tried to return the smile. "Thanks for coming. I hope it wasn't too much trouble. I didn't know who else to call."

She waved away his concern. "No trouble at all. My boss is very understanding. Are you okay? How long have you been here?"

He pushed to his feet, a bit stiff but otherwise recovered from his tumble through the flood. The guy arguing with his girlfriend grew more strident as he catalogued every day he'd taken off since January first. "I'll tell you about it in the car," Peller said. "Just get me out of here."

Churchill took his arm to steady him, not that he needed it, and led him through the vestibule and into the warm morning. Peller blinked at the clear sky and felt the sun's warmth on his face. It seemed one age had passed and another begun while medical staff probed and sampled and imaged his body. Abrasions and bruises, they finally decided, nothing worse.

Churchill steered him to the car and opened the door for him. Had he felt more himself, he would have objected to the babying. Once she was in and the engine started, she asked, "Hungry?"

The word triggered either response or awareness; suddenly Peller was famished. "Yeah. What sounds good to you? I'll buy."

"You don't have to do that."

"You didn't have to spring me, either."

She gave him a curiously motherly look, something Peller wasn't used to receiving from anyone but his own mother. "You sure?"

"I'm sure."

"There's a little café and bakery on Broken Land Parkway across from the mall. I've never been there, but I'm told it's pretty good."

Peller leaned against the headrest and closed his eyes. "Works for me."

Churchill drove and allowed him some silence. At first Peller could only feel relief that the ordeal was over, but the eight-minute ride afforded him time to wonder about the woman and children he had plucked from the car and the other men who had put themselves at risk to help. They must all have seen the flood sweep Peller away, must have felt terrified and helpless. Defeat snatched from the jaws of victory. Did they know he had survived?

By the time Churchill pulled into a parking spot in front of the café, Peller had dug down to Chuck Ferring's gun shop. The note puzzled him, but more so did Ferring's reaction. The man must have known, or at least suspected, who had robbed him. So why the stonewalling? Ferring had no choice but to report the robbery. Failure to do so jeopardized his registration. Yet he seemed to fear investigation more than the threat left in his storeroom.

"Wake up, Sherlock, we're here."

He opened his eyes to find Churchill grinning at him. "That's going to remain a private name, right?"

"It has so far, hasn't it?"

"I sure hope so."

She winked and got out of the car. They entered the café and were inundated by the smells of baked goods and coffee hanging heavy in the air. She ordered a strawberry scone and a medium coffee, he two cinnamon rolls and the largest coffee available. The shop was crowded. The only available table sat smack in the middle of the action.

"More noise," Peller groused, but only loud enough for her ears.

"Don't like crowds?"

"Not this morning."

"So how did you end up in the hospital, anyway?"

While they ate, he related the whole story from daring rescue to treatment for minor injuries. "It's amazing how long you can sit in the ER feeling like you're dying before they pay attention to you."

She peered over the rim of her coffee cup. "Come on, Rick. Some patients *are* back there dying. Believe me. My little sister is a nurse."

"Oh, I know. I've seen it in the course of duty a few times. I'm just saying, the system isn't exactly designed for comfort."

"Ah, you want to experience your misery in stylish luxury."

Peller laughed. It made something in his left side smart. "Well, it would certainly be a change of pace."

She nibbled at her scone for a moment. "I'm glad you're okay. That must have been scary."

He studied Churchill's face. She ate, avoiding his eyes. "I didn't have time to be scared. Not consciously, anyway. When something like that happens, you're on automatic. It's only afterward you have time to think about it."

"What did you think afterward?"

"I don't want to think about it."

"I'm serious, Rick."

"So am I."

"You could have been killed. You could have been swept into the river and..." She set down the remains of her scone and picked up her napkin to delicately wipe off her fingers.

"I wasn't. All's well that ends well."

She lifted her coffee cup. Her hands were trembling. Good thing the cup had a lid on it.

"I'm a sworn officer of the law, Joan. Sometimes I have to go into harm's way. But it's no different than driving. Every time you start your car, you're taking your life in your hands."

Churchill watched the cup tremble. "It is, too, different."

Maybe. A little. Peller finished the first of his cinnamon rolls.

She managed a sip of her coffee. "Wading into a flood is a lot riskier than driving."

"I did it to help a frightened mother and her children."

"I'm not saying you did the wrong thing. I'm saying I don't want to lose you."

Peller's insides knotted up. He wasn't interested in romantic entanglements. Churchill knew that, even though she harbored dreams of more than friendship. This leak of concealed emotion unnerved him. "I don't, either."

Her eyes narrowed.

"I wouldn't needlessly throw myself in front of a train," he said, hoping that might placate her.

His offering's efficacy was hard to gauge. "I don't know how Sandra stood it."

He didn't, either. They'd never broached the subject, as though by not facing it they might avert disaster. Ironically, Sandra had died, not Peller. But he couldn't speak of it without ripping open the wound.

Her expression softening, Joan took his hand in hers. "Sorry. That was a stupid thing to say."

"It's okay."

"No, it's not. I don't want to hurt you, Rick. I know you won't ever be over it. I wish I could help you carry the burden. But I never even knew her."

Peller slipped his hand from hers and picked up his coffee cup. Before the rim touched his lips, he decided he didn't really want it and set it down again. He checked his wristwatch. "I should get to work, I suppose."

Churchill leaned back and brushed at her skirt as though it were overflowing with crumbs. "And I suppose you'll want me to drive you."

"Sorry. I left my truck illegally parked last night. They probably towed it."

She forced a smile. "And you a cop. Shame on you."

On their way out, they pitched the remains of their breakfast in the trash.

Chapter 3

The breeze toyed with the man's wavy brown hair. Standing beside his parked car, hands stuffed in his pockets, he looked down Main Street in stunned silence from just above the Historic District's west end. The place looked like a giant had raked the street with a huge club. There were gaping holes in foundations, smashed windows, debris and mud everywhere, even a couple of overturned cars. People swarmed the area, working to order the chaos. He tried to put himself in the position of those who lived and worked down there. He couldn't.

He didn't know most of the businesses crowded along the street, but he knew one, a red brick building at the close end of the district. That was the Colonial Bakery, a great place for breakfast pastries. He'd patronized it a few times, even met the owner once and learned a bit of its history. The bakery had been in the family for generations and had links to the mills that first put Ellicott City on the map.

Now, *that* could be a story.

He pulled his cell phone from his pocket, tapped his office number, and waited. "Hey, Bill, it's Jack Collins. Is Tanya in? Oh. Do me a favor and ask her to call me when she's free. I'm in the flood area. I have an idea for a feature, and I'd like to start on it while I'm here. Thanks."

Collins pocketed his phone before another thought struck him. He took it up again and tapped a different contact: Ella Montufar. "Hey, babe. Just wanted to let you know I might be late tonight. I know, I know. Call and see if they can push the reservation to, I dunno, maybe eight o'clock? No, I'm starting on a new story. The flood area, yeah. It's safe now, just a lot of clean-up going on. I will. I love you. Bye."

He tucked the phone away again and strolled down the street into the chaos.

Peller arrived at Northern District Headquarters to a round of cheers and an offer of a free cup of coffee from the office coffee machine, courtesy of Captain Whitney Morris. Peller waved off the applause with a good-natured smile and declined Morris' generous offer, since he'd tossed his last cup without finishing it. "Just find out what they did with my truck," he said.

Morris gave him a thumbs up. Corina Montufar gave him a hug. Eric Dumas pulled a quarter from Montufar's ear and handed it to Peller, joking, "Put it towards a candy bar."

Once the noise and tomfoolery died down, Peller settled into his cubicle and started the paperwork on the gun shop robbery. The responding officers had documented the building's security arrangements, noting locks, barred windows, and interior and exterior security cameras. Geri Franklin's initial report stated that fingerprints had been lifted from the door and other interior surfaces and were being processed. She'd found nothing else of note.

Once Peller had completed his own report, he placed a call to ATF's Baltimore Field Division office and was transferred to an available agent.

"Hi, Lieutenant, this is Special Agent Zee Mirlo. How can I help?" Mirlo spoke with a touch of a Mexican accent. Peller guessed he was second-generation.

"We had a robbery here last night, Agent Mirlo. I just wanted to make sure the shop owner filed his report."

"Sure, we can check on that. And please, call me Zee. It's actually Zenon, but not surprisingly, I don't put that on my nametags."

Peller laughed. "I don't think I've heard that one before. What's the origin?"

"Hell if I know. It crops up sometimes in Mexico. Online Spanish-English translators refuse to translate it. It's usually given as 'living' in baby name lists. I've done my homework, you see. I guess it's nice to be living, but people make funny faces when they hear 'Zenon,' so I just go by 'Zee.' Why should 'Zee' be more normal, you might ask? Again, hell if I know. 'Mirlo' means 'blackbird,' in case you're curious."

Peller leaned back and wondered if Agent Mirlo had aspirations to standup comedy. "Well, at least you found the origin of that one."

The rapid click of computer keys suggested Mirlo was working Peller's request. "Might've been better if I hadn't. The blackbird is apparently the symbol for a naïve person. Maybe one of my ancestors got taken for a long, scenic ride. Can you tell I like to research pointless subjects?"

"No comment, so long as you're equally good at meaningful research."

"Absolutely. Howard County, Maryland. The Lodge, owned by one Charles Ferring. He filed first thing this morning." Mirlo whistled. "Looks like somebody netted a nice haul."

"Through an unlocked back door of all things," Peller commented.

"Mr. Ferring obviously didn't read our brochures."

"He had a solid deadbolt. It just wasn't in use at the time. An oversight, I guess."

"Usually is. Anyway, we'll get on it. Does the store have security cameras out back or in the storage area?"

"It has them. I'll forward our reports to you. The robbery itself looked pretty routine."

"So why did they call in the big guns?" Mirlo asked.

"The thief left a bizarre note. Sounds like Ferring has a nemesis. What's your email address? I'll include the note along with the rest."

Mirlo gave it and waited while Peller sent the documentation. After it arrived, he took a moment to skim it. "Never a dull moment, huh?"

"And this is the quiet part of the state."

"Given circumstances, I'll post a reward on this one. I'll get the process in motion and let you know how it goes." His keyboard clicked furiously. "I see your tech got backups of the security footage. Want us to go through it?"

"I'll do it," Peller told him. "I want to track down a customer Ferring was speaking with at the time of the break-in. With any luck, the cameras caught his face."

"You think he was a diversion?"

"Wouldn't surprise me."

After they said their goodbyes, Peller sent an email to Geri Franklin requesting access to the security videos. He then dug into public records related to The Lodge and compiled an impressive list of interesting activity, which he organized in a spreadsheet. An hour and no reply later, he called and got Franklin's voice mail. He hung up without leaving a message. *Hurry up and wait*, he thought.

Montufar slipped into the seat by his desk almost before he was aware of her presence. "You look amazing for a drowned man."

He shrugged. "Once they wring out the water, it's not so bad."

"You didn't break anything?"

"Only my pride."

"Then you got lucky. What happened?"

Peller told the story, as best as he remembered it, starting with the gun shop robbery and ending with Joan Churchill plucking him from the hospital.

Montufar absorbed it all without interruption. Mercifully, she didn't comment on Churchill riding to the rescue. "And people think we spend our days asking annoying questions and saying, 'Book him.' You sure you're okay?"

"Abrasions and contusions," Peller admitted. "Otherwise, I'm sound."

"What about this robbery?"

"Glad you asked. You'll love this one." He showed her the reports and told her about the note.

"So Chuck Ferring has an enemy."

"But he won't admit it, which got me curious. According to public records, Ferring opened The Lodge in 1998. It's been the target of repeated vandalism and robbery over the years. They haven't been frequent enough to draw much attention, but if you put them together, they seem suggestive."

"How so?"

Peller turned his monitor so she could see it better "I've compiled a spreadsheet with the relevant data. See what you think."

Montufar read through Peller's list. The Lodge opened in March of 1998. One April night, its front window was broken by a thrown rock. In December of the same year, obscenities were spray painted on the front door in red, again at night. On July 4, 2000, Chuck Ferring went to the shop, which was closed for the holiday, to retrieve some paperwork he meant to take home the previous evening. While he was inside, someone took a sledgehammer to the trunk of his car. More red spray paint defaced the side of the building Thanksgiving Day that year, and in April 2001, another rock broke the front window. The shop's first robbery was reported in August 2001, with a second in October 2002. Neither raised much alarm as no firearms were stolen, only clothing and fishing gear. Another rock sailed through the window in June 2003. More red graffiti in February 2004. Last year had been quiet at The Lodge, until this robbery accompanied by death threat.

The investigating officers had been different every time. As the police reports piled up, indications appeared that Howard County's finest understood the store had been a target more than its share of times, but

Ferring always maintained he had no idea who had committed the vandalism, and the robberies seemed so petty as to be the work of teenagers. Who else, breaking into a gun shop, would steal only clothing and fishing rods?

Montufar leaned on her elbows and studied the list a second time. "The graffiti incidents sound like the work of the same person. Same paint, same foul language, same lack of coherent message. Personal insults, maybe, or pointless stupidity. The rocks through the window, ditto. The vandalism of Ferring's car, though, that's personal. Rage. Like the note."

Peller nodded. "Unfortunately, until somebody puts him in the hospital or the grave, we can't do much about it. He's quietly uncooperative."

Montufar pushed back from the desk. "Then you're off the hook."

That surprised Peller. "You know I don't work that way. Nor do you."

"Hey, I did my work for the day. I sent Theresa to check up on human remains in Patapsco Valley State Park."

"Human remains?"

"Turned out to be a skull, probably something old washed out by the flood. It's a day for bones. Eric sent Holly to the Historic District to check up on human remains found there, too."

Another of those disquiets stole over Peller. He masked it with a joke. "The two of you are overworked, aren't you?"

Montufar gave him a look of mock surprise. "Of course. We do have a wedding to plan."

"At taxpayer expense?"

Rising, she winked and hurried off, but not on matrimonial business. Peller knew she was as interested in the robbery as the bones. She'd be back, probably with Eric Dumas. She'd want his assessment of Peller's spreadsheet, so he kept it open and turned his attention to the photos in the vandalism report for Chuck Ferring's car. The investigators had counted twenty-seven impact points, mostly on the top of the trunk door but some on the sides around the wheel wells. There were also a number of rambling scratches and a few smaller ones. Peller inspected each photo, finding nothing remarkable except ...

He leaned closer and zoomed in on a set of scratches above the driver's side tire. There, small enough to be missed among the more serious damage, someone had carved two letters. They were crude, unsteady marks, but to Peller they looked like "DC." Had the vandal signed his handiwork?

As Peller predicted, Montufar returned with Dumas in tow. "Mind if Eric has a look at that list?" she asked.

Peller motioned to the computer. "Not at all, but look at this first. Is that what I think it is?"

Dumas squinted at the image. "DC?"

Montufar leaned in close to him and nodded. "Looks like it to me."

If they all came to the same conclusion, it likely was real. "I'll have to ask Mr. Ferring who he knows with those initials. Here's the list." He brought the spreadsheet to the fore and waited while Dumas read.

When finished, Dumas shoved his hands in his pockets. "A vendetta. Corina said there was a note?"

Peller brought that up on the screen next. "For your reading pleasure."

Wide-eyed, Dumas said, "That should have got Ferring's attention."

"Apparently not. He's still in denial. He had to report it, but I don't think he wants results."

Dumas gave Montufar a questioning look.

"Not enough data." She nudged him. "Why else would I bring you in?"

"Thanks. Okay, how's this for wild speculation? Ferring's tormentors know his dirty secret. If he turns them in, they'll expose him."

Peller tried to suppress a laugh but didn't quite succeed. "That's wild, all right. What would you call that? It's not exactly blackmail."

"I wouldn't call it anything," Dumas replied. "Vandalism is sufficient to arrest whoever did it. Find out who or what DC is, and you won't need much else."

But that, certainly, would be easier said than done.

Chapter 4

"Not now, Mr. Collins."

Light framed the ghostly figure in the half-open doorway. Collins squinted at her from the head of a long stair behind the Colonial Bakery. He stood in the building's shadow. Sun glare spilled from the apartment, nearly blinding him and rendering Denise Ferring a shadow, albeit a formidable one. She had the tenacity of a guard dog. Collins requested and pleaded, but she refused to let him speak with her husband James. Out of words, the newsman stood in humiliated silence, head bowed.

She finally took pity on him, or as much as she could spare. "I'm sure he'll talk with you later. Maybe tomorrow or the next day. If you have a card, I'll give it to him."

"Sure." He dug a business card from his wallet and passed it to her. "But if he could spare just a couple of minutes, just to capture the moment..."

She didn't look at the card. "Capture the moment? Did you see the damage?"

Collins nodded.

"That was his heart. He doesn't need a reporter capitalizing on his pain." She eased the door shut. The deadbolt clicked.

"I wouldn't do that," Collins objected too late. He turned to the long descent. "I wouldn't," he repeated. He wasn't a vulture. He wrote success stories. But nobody found success without some pain, some loss.

He descended to the sidewalk and circled to the front of the bakery. Police and cleanup workers swarmed the street like ants. Two buildings down, a photographer snapped pictures of something protruding from a storm drain. Collins squinted at it. Probably a branch, but it looked curiously like a femur. Weird.

He climbed the hill to his car.

As morning gave way to noon, the sun warmed Ellicott City into the mid-eighties, well above average for this time of year. The air steamed as the

Earth gave up the last of the flood waters while a small wave of cops washed down the pavement, searching for bones. They found them lodged in damaged door and window frames, stuck in storm grates, and wedged beneath car tires. The trail stretched up and down Main Street, with the HorseSpirit Arts Gallery the center point. Many bones had become entrapped there, but a few washed as far east as Maryland Avenue, the intersection where Peller had been rescued. Others made it only to Old Columbia Pike on the west, near the badly damaged structure of the Colonial Bakery.

Holly Ross walked the route three times, pondering how the skeleton had found its way here. The forensics report would reveal the deceased's age, but she didn't need it to know that this individual—Ross took to calling it Napoleon—hadn't died recently. Napoleon must have been buried in the flood's path, and the torrent exhumed him. Or her. That put the skeleton's point of origin at the bakery or upstream from it. She redirected the search uphill and along the side streets feeding into Main while Geri Franklin, who had arrived half an hour earlier, and two other investigators documented and collected the remains.

Two hot, tedious hours yielded nothing further. Ross returned to the bakery and studied the destruction. The flood had gouged a pit beneath the sidewalk, buckling concrete and asphalt. The brick foundation walls of several buildings lay exposed. Beneath the bakery, a section of wall had collapsed, leaving a gaping hole through which mud had flowed, coating the basement floor.

Ross dispatched a pair of officers to locate the bakery's owner and gingerly descended into the pit. She couldn't enter the basement without invitation or warrant, but the view through the breach suggested the shop's insurance claim would be substantial. Crates, boxes, shelving units, and equipment she couldn't identify had been thrown about, much of it smashed to pieces. The shadowy bulk of a boiler stood in back. Ross figured it would need replacement. A few broken floor tiles were scattered about, jutting up from the mud like daggers. They might be asbestos.

By the time she climbed out, the officers had returned to report that James Ferring IV would speak with her in his home above the shop. They directed her to the back of the building, where she found a long stair leading to the apartment door. She went directly up.

The beyond-exhausted proprietor admitted Ross to the apartment. He was built like a runner, tall and wiry, but his arms hung limp at his sides and his eyes suggested he'd just crawled out of a grave himself. His dark hair, graying at the temples, was mussed. Silent, he vaguely motioned the detective in. Ross half expected the living room to be as disheveled as its owner, but it had an elegant feel, expensively furnished in polished woods and gold fabrics. Family portraits hung on two of the walls, mountain scenes on the other two. A few potted plants accented the corners. The curtains hung open, so everything was bathed in the sun's ironic brilliance.

"Something to drink?" Ferring asked. His voice was quiet but even.

"I'm good."

He motioned Ross to the sofa and sat on a facing chair. Between them, a slender cherry coffee table displayed a few magazines: *National Geographic*, *Foreign Affairs*, *The Economist*.

"I'm sorry to bother you at a time like this," Ross said.

Ferring shrugged. "This isn't the first time. It won't be the last. "

"Maybe you should move to higher ground."

"Some of our neighbors are talking of leaving." Ferring stared out the window. "It's all this development. Floods are more frequent and getting worse all the time. Main Street is a disaster waiting to happen. Maybe the government will finally take action. Maybe it won't just be talk this time."

Ross put no stock in that fantasy. "How long have you been here?"

Ferring studied his hands as though counting on his fingers. "My great-grandfather opened the business in 1890, and my grandfather moved to this location in 1928. So that makes it …" He narrowed his eyes and shook his head.

"A long time," Ross supplied.

"Yes."

Ferring counted his fingers again and got the same vague answer.

"Mr. Ferring," Ross said. "I'm here because of something…unusual. Probably disturbing, too."

"I doubt anything could be more disturbing than what's already happened."

"We found human bones up and down the street. It looks like the flood washed them out of the ground somewhere near your business." Ross let Ferring draw his own conclusions.

He looked out the window and took a shot at it but came nowhere near the bull's eye. "Somebody drowned? Not surprising I guess."

In fact, he was so far from the mark that Ross suspected deflection. "We only found bones. This person died a long time ago."

"Oh."

Strange, his lack of interest. Either he was sunk in shock or hiding something. Ross made it plain for him. "Could someone have been buried beneath your store, Mr. Ferring?"

Finally turning his attention on her, Ferring shrugged. He showed neither fear nor surprise. "It's possible. This building was here long before my family moved in."

Neither confirm nor deny. Cagey fellow. "Do you mind if we poke around the basement?"

"So long as you don't get in the way of the cleanup. The insurance adjuster will be here in the morning. We'll want to start work the moment he's gone."

"With luck," Ross said, "we'll be done today."

Ferring turned to the window again. "Now there's a thought. 'Bakery haunted by ghost of man buried in cellar.' What a promo that would be." He tried to smile but looked the worse for it.

Ross took her leave without commenting on that. Back on the street, she called Geri Franklin over. The women and two other investigators ventured beneath the Colonial Bakery, flashlights blazing.

The moment Ross returned from the Historic District, Peller called the team together. They assembled in the conference room around the long table. The whiteboard at the head of the room was half filled with indecipherable notes scrawled by someone at the last meeting. Outside the window, trees glowed in the late afternoon sun. Dumas sat on the window side of the table with Ross, Montufar on the other with Theresa Swan. Peller settled in at the head of the table and leaned back. His chair squeaked as he did so.

"Somebody needs to tell the Captain to buy new furniture," Dumas quipped.

"Not me," Peller said. "I'd rather keep my salary. But on to bones. I hear we have a collection."

Ross folded her arms on the table before her. "All up and down Main Street. Geri Franklin estimated the skeleton was sixty percent complete. No duplicate bones, she said, so it's probably one individual. One thing we don't have is a skull."

Swan cocked her head. "Really? I've got a skull with nothing else. It washed down the river and came to rest on a sand bar in Patapsco Valley State Park."

"Convenient," Peller said. "The lab will let us know if they belong together. Meanwhile, do we know the skeleton's origin?" He looked to Ross for the answer.

"My money is on the Colonial Bakery, at the west end of the Historic District. Its foundation wall was breached and the flood made a mess in the cellar. All the bones were found downhill from there. None were above it, and we didn't find any likely source uphill."

Peller knew the lay of the land. He imagined how the bones must have been scattered along the street and concurred with her assessment. "What do you know about the bakery so far?"

"It's owned by James Ferring IV. It's been in the family since—"
Peller leaned forward. The chair squeaked again, hideously. "Ferring?"
Ross nodded.

"Odd. There was a robbery last night at a gun shop called The Lodge. The owner's name is Chuck Ferring."

Dumas leaned back, looking thoughtful. His chair squeaked, too. He grimaced but otherwise ignored it. "Definitely a strange happenstance."

"Happenstance?" Montufar shook her head. "I'm taking away your thesaurus."

Her fiancé grinned at her. "I'll still have my word-a-day calendar." He turned to Peller. "I'll bet they're related. Ferring isn't a name I've heard before."

"Not as common as Smith or Jones," Peller agreed. "The burglars left a threatening note for Chuck. His shop has a history of vandalism and minor thefts. Has the Colonial Bakery experienced similar trouble?"

"I'll check on it," Swan volunteered. "Until the forensic results are in, the bones don't mean much anyway."

"Yeah," Montufar said with a wink at Dumas. "That gives us time to find you a tuxedo."

"Not while the boss is watching, dear."

Peller gave them a pinched smile and turned to Ross. "Did James Ferring let you inspect the cellar?"

"He did. We didn't find any bones there, but Geri took some soil samples. She said they can be matched against any soil embedded in the bones."

"What did Ferring say when you told him why you wanted access?"

"Not much. Maybe he was just in a state, but I got the feeling he was hiding something."

Peller silently ticked off the coincidences. A skull without a skeleton here, a skeleton without a skull there. A crime at one Ferring business, a skeleton in the basement of another. Both Ferrings obfuscating.

The chair squeaked as he rose. "I think," he told the team, "I'll pay Chuck Ferring another visit."

Chapter 5

The glass door slid open with a quiet swish, and a white-clad woman carrying a small silver tray stepped onto the patio. She was young, late twenties, with light brown hair fluttering alongside her slender face. Her artificial smile suggested she didn't want to cause distress even though her task was unpleasant.

"Hey, Mr. Jim. It's that time again."

She touched Mr. Jim on the shoulder. Her fingers were light, like feathers, like someone else's fingers he once knew. He looked at her, mouth slightly open. "Bess?" She looked like Bess, somewhat, but no, that wasn't right.

"I'm Carly. You remember me, don't you?"

He didn't remember anything. He was old and didn't remember how he got that way. He was in a wheelchair and couldn't recall why. He was on this patio, corralled by a wrought iron rail, bathed in light from the lowering sun, looking over a green expanse of hills, and didn't know where he was. On his right, a small, glass-topped table held a folded newspaper, unread; a plate with a half-eaten turkey sandwich; and a glass half filled with a clear liquid, maybe apple juice or iced tea. Why was somebody's lunch here?

"That's okay," she assured him. "You'll remember me later. But now…"

She set her tray on the table. A cup of fresh water rested in the center of the tray beside a small paper cup, a ketchup cup he seemed to think, although he didn't know why she would bring him ketchup.

She hadn't. She picked up his left hand, gently opened his fingers, and dumped a small white pill from the ketchup cup into his palm.

"Midday meds," she said and handed him the water, which he took in his right hand. "Bottoms up!"

Mr. Jim popped the pill and lifted the cup to his lips. He made a face. He hated pills and would have spit this one out, but she was watching, eyes wary. She wouldn't like it if he spit it out. She'd make him do it again, damn her. He drank half the water and swallowed the pill.

"I wish all our residents were as easy as you," she chirped.

Liar, he thought. She busied herself stacking everything onto her tray, everything except the newspaper. He looked at her again, or maybe for the first time. "Bess? Where's Roger? He should be here by now."

The woman in white pursed her lips and shook her head. "I don't think we know anyone named Roger. Little Jimmy might come later. He called to say he'd try."

That distressed him. He wanted to see little Jimmy, certainly, but he wanted more to see Roger. It had been such a long time, such a terribly long time. Nobody had expected the war to drag on like that. But with it over, with everything over and done, with the fallout behind them...

"Roger needs to come. I need to tell him something." He slapped his hands on the arms of the wheelchair several times. "I must tell him."

She might not have heard. "Are you warm enough?" she asked. "I can get you a blanket if you want." A shadow fell over them. She squinted up at the clouds floating lazily over the sun.

He was plenty warm. Why would she think he was cold? "Call Roger. Tell him to come. It's important."

"Hmm." She picked up her tray with everything on it and cocked her head at him. There was that artificial smile again. He hated that smile. "Maybe if you tell me, I can pass it along."

He lifted a finger and tapped his chest. "*I* have to tell him! Now!"

"Okay, Mr. Jim. Just be calm. Remember your heart."

Why was she talking about his heart? There was nothing wrong with his heart! The whole problem was Roger. He had to fix it, soon, before it was too late. None of them were getting any younger. "Call him now," he insisted.

"I'll see what I can do. But just in case he can't make it, what do you want to tell him?"

Mr. Jim slumped in his wheelchair. The whole family had gone mad. It was all *her* fault, that woman, that French woman. None of them even knew her name, none but Roger, and he'd never see her again. What had he been thinking, running off like that? None of this would have happened if Roger hadn't been so brave, so patriotic, if he hadn't gone to war.

The woman shrugged and turned to go. Mr. Jim heard her open the sliding glass door.

"Please," he said. "Please call him."

She looked over her shoulder. She sure looked like Bess.

"Tell him to come home, Bess. Tell him all's repaid. No. Tell him all's *forgiven*."

Her smile slipped away. "Okay," she said quietly. She steadied the water cup on the tray. "I'll see what I can do."

Captain Morris located Peller's truck. It had been towed, but she secured its release and had it delivered to Northern District Headquarters in short order. Nevertheless, Peller didn't arrive at The Lodge until nearly five o'clock thanks to a nasty five-vehicle accident that snarled westbound route forty. He entered the shop to find Chuck Ferring talking with a young female employee, pointing here and there, giving instructions. Peller waited by the door until the owner turned to greet his presumed customer.

Ferring's face drooped when he saw who it was.

"Sorry to bother you, Mr. Ferring." Peller crossed the floor while Ferring twined his hands in front of him. "I need to follow up on a few things."

"No bother, Lieutenant. Happy to help."

Clearly, he wasn't.

Ferring rounded the display case and stood behind it, his big hands atop it as though to hold it down in case Peller tried to walk out with it. The barrier didn't calm his nerves. "I filed my report," he said.

"Yes, I spoke with ATF this morning. They have it." Peller looked out the window. Traffic was light here, backed up behind the accident as it was. The waning day remained warm and bright. "I suppose you heard the news about the Historic District."

"Yeah, bad business, that."

"One of my colleagues was down there this morning. A lot of damage, he said. The water took a bite out of several foundations. It particularly enjoyed chewing up a bakery. The Colonial Bakery. Ever hear of it?"

Ferring stood so still, he might have been trying to hide in plain sight.

"The owner's name is James Ferring. A relative?"

The answer was slow in coming, which suggested Ferring didn't care to admit it. "Yeah, a distant cousin. Third or fourth, something like that. I never could figure out how that works."

"Do you know him well?"

Ferring shrugged.

"Is that yes, or no?"

"Our sides of the family aren't close. Sorry he took a hit, though. That's rough."

Peller suspected Ferring was sorrier the subject had been raised, so he gave the guy a break. For the moment, it was sufficient to know James and Chuck were indeed related. "Back to your troubles. I was looking over some records this morning. Your shop's had more than its share of vandalism and theft over the years."

Ferring lifted his hands from the counter, then didn't seem to know what to do with them. After a moment of deliberation, he shoved them in his pockets. "Nothing we couldn't deal with."

"Doesn't it strike you as odd?"

Again, the shrug.

"You don't think so?"

"Every business gets hit sometimes."

"Not this often," Peller insisted. "Why would yours be targeted again and again?"

To fix the blame, Ferring gestured at the weapons in the display case. "You know how it is, Lieutenant. Maryland is a blue state. Anti-gun nutcases sleep under every rock. Every time some lunatic shoots up a school, honest businessmen like me get blamed."

Peller waited for Ferring to look him in the eyes, which he didn't. "I don't see a correlation, Mr. Ferring. Looks to me like the same people have been attacking your shop time and again, and not in reaction to mass shootings."

"Like I said, nutcases. I hope you find them."

"Who do you suspect?"

Ferring spread his hands in denial. "I told you, Lieutenant, I don't know. I really don't."

Peller, jaw set, gave Ferring the evil eye. The merchant grew nervous again and rubbed his thumb at a nonexistent smudge on the top of the case.

"I don't believe you," Peller finally said.

"I can't help what you believe, sir."

"What about that back door, then? Did you determine why it was unlocked?"

"We must not have locked up after that delivery on Friday." Before Peller could object, he added, "Or maybe the burglars knew how to pick a lock?"

"Who holds keys?"

"Just me and Bobby Grant. He's my assistant manager. At least one of us is on duty at all times. Nobody else needs a key."

"I'll want to talk to Mr. Grant. Is he here now?"

Ferring shook his head. "Tomorrow, Friday, and Saturday. You want his phone number?"

"Yes, please." Peller waited while Ferring swiped through his cell phone and supplied the number.

After logging a note in his own cell phone, Peller said, "One last thing. That attack on your car on the fourth of July in 2000. Photos show letters scratched into the side."

"Letters?" Ferring's surprise was genuine this time. Peller figured nobody had noticed before. The responding officers hadn't called out the marks, at any rate.

"D. C. Ring any bells?"

"District of Columbia?"

"I'm thinking they're somebody's initials," Peller said.

With another shrug, Ferring denied all knowledge.

"If you think of any possibilities, let me know." Without a farewell, Peller made for the door but turned before exiting. Ferring was watching him like a frightened squirrel. "What's worse, Mr. Ferring, these constant attacks, or telling the truth?"

Ferring neither moved nor answered.

"If you're afraid of retaliation, I can get you protection."

Suddenly defiant, Ferring waved his hand at his wares. "Look at all this stuff, Lieutenant. You really think I need more protection?"

Peller took his time looking, as though he didn't already know what Ferring sold: hand guns, rifles, shotguns, knives, archery equipment. Even the fishhooks could be weapons.

"Yes, Mr. Ferring," he said. "I do."

Peller had further protection to offer that evening, fortunately to someone who wanted it, unfortunately to one he felt powerless to protect.

South of Ellicott City, on a hilltop set back from one of the undulating roads that fed the Historic District, a cluster of low, connected buildings made a bold effort at cheering any who drove the tree-lined road onto its campus. Smaller trees dotted the grounds, interspersed with rainbows of flowers and islands of ornamental grasses. Peller studied the surrounding wall of old oaks and pines as he got out of his car. It was no more than a screen, really, behind which stood a new development of crowded single-family homes whose owners preferred not to think about what bordered their lands.

He crossed the parking lot to the main entrance, an unpretentious glass double door labeled "Eagle's Wings Clinic." A bald eagle, listing to port, hovered motionless over the name. He passed into the quiet of the lobby and signed in at the front desk, showing his driver's license.

The woman behind the desk, a young brunette with a friendly smile and suspicious eyes, watched him write. "And you're here to see?"

She should know by now. Peller had been here enough over the past four months. "Shania North." He held out his left arm.

The receptionist wrapped a green paper bracelet around his wrist and pressed the adhesive strips together. "Room two-thirty-seven." She pointed to Peller's left. "Down to the end, right, second corridor on the left. Take the stairs up to the second floor. Her room will be three doors down."

"Thank you." Peller hardly needed directions. He had the route memorized after his first visit.

The corridors had a look somewhere between hospital and apartment building, bright enough but cheerless and largely unadorned save a display of small gold plaques bearing names of the clinic's prominent donors and, beside them, portraits of leaders past and present. Peller ignored them. He already knew their faces: mostly white, male, and on the high side of sixty, dressed in formal business attire, all with rock-steady eyes that proclaimed they, certainly, never had need of their own services.

Unlike Shania, who had returned last week for her second detox. Opioids were the curse that kept on cursing.

Her door was closed over but not shut. Peller knocked.

"Come in," she said in her timid soprano.

She was sitting in a chair by the bed wearing a hospital gown. Her medical encumbrances had been unhooked. A blanket covered her from the waist down, and an open book snuggled on her lap like a sleeping cat. Her eyes lit up when she saw him. "Hi, Rick."

"How are you feeling?"

"Better. Just wishing I didn't have to be here."

"Hospitals do get old fast." Peller thought better of mentioning that he knew that from recent experience. She didn't need to know how close to death he had come. He pulled a chair from beneath the wall-mounted television and sat close, facing her. He didn't recognize the book's author or title. "What are you reading?"

She smiled, embarrassed. "A silly romance. I needed something to do. They have a library here."

"That's good. I like to escape into westerns, myself."

Shania closed the book and set it on the bedside table by the phone. "I'm getting a library card when I get out. I liked reading when I was little, until it stopped being fun."

"When was that?"

"High school." She made a face like a little girl spurning broccoli. "They made us read boring stuff. Momma never had money for books. Or time for libraries. She worked all the time." Nibbling on a fingernail, Shania looked at nothing. "It killed her. Work. You know?"

He nodded, although the experience was alien to him. "What did she do?"

"Emptied wastebaskets and cleaned toilets. They paid her like it was worth nothing. That's what she said. 'If I stopped, they'd think it was worth something,' she always said. 'Finish school,' she said. 'Do something better with your life.'" Shania wiped a bit of moisture from her eyes. "So, dummy me, I dropped out the year she died. Made good money dancing, though. Customers thought *that* was something." She spat out the last words with a sarcastic laugh.

"Well. It's never too late to learn a new skill." As soon as he said it, Peller found the platitude vulgar, but the advice refused to be contained. "You could get your G.E.D. and take classes at a community college."

"Maybe." Shania picked up her romance again and studied the tawdry cover. "Or find a sugar daddy and get hitched." She tossed it carelessly on the bed. "But you're the only decent guy I know, and you're married." She nodded at his wedding band.

"Widower," he corrected automatically. "Sandra was killed in a crash a few years ago."

Shania put a hand to her mouth. "Oh my God. I'm so sorry."

"It's okay. I never had reason to mention it to you."

She looked him in the eyes, seeking the pain of loss that had to be hiding in there somewhere. Peller never showed it to others, nor would he now. It was too private, an intimacy he could only share with Sandra herself. Nor could he understand why Shania cared to find it. Most people preferred to insulate themselves from his hurt.

You know why, he thought he heard Sandra whisper.

"It ripped my heart out," Shania said. "When Carnell died."

Carnell. She had never said his name before. Peller saw the scene again: the run-down house, the filthy, stench-ridden room, Shania on the floor wailing beside her unmoving companion who had died the ignoble death of an addict. Had Peller not arrived to ask Shania follow-up questions in the Bellamy investigation, she might have perished, too, by her own hand if not from inability to care for herself.

"I know," he said, unable to find any other words.

She folded her hands together and stared at them, expressionless. "Can't change it, though, can we?"

"No. But it changes us, for better or for worse. Sooner or later, we have to make peace with reality."

"There ain't no peace in my reality. People don't get over opioids."

"Some do," Peller said gently. "You will. You're stronger than you realize."

Shania smiled at her hands. "You got more faith in me than I do."

"That's why I keep visiting."

She snagged a tissue and wiped at her eyes.

"Any word on when you'll get out?"

"Soon, I hope."

"Then what will you do?"

"Don't know. I gotta make money, I guess, but..." She held her arms out and looked at them, turning them back and forth. They were still bone-thin. She'd hardly put any meat back on her frame. "I only know one job, and nobody'll pay for *this*."

"Does the clinic have career counselling or job placement services?"

"Yeah, but they don't know what to do with me. Got me into a little store last time. We sold books and candles and stuff. I wasn't too good at it."

"Did they let you go?"

"Nah, the owner felt sorry for me and kept me around. But business was bad, so she had to close. And here I am, again."

Peller wanted to say he'd find something for her, but the only careers he knew were in the department, and he didn't think she'd go for any of them. "Something will turn up," he offered. "Whenever I was in a jam, Sandra used to tell me to trust in God."

"I don't know how. Anyway, He probably doesn't want me."

Peller took her hands. They were cool to the touch and as bony as her arms. "He wants us all, Shania. Don't write yourself off."

She cocked her head, puzzled. "Don't know why." She pulled her hands away and adjusted her blanket. "Why do *you* care about me?"

Peller had never figured that out, but he had his suspicions. "I suppose you're the daughter I never had."

"Never knew my daddy. Momma said he was bad news." She chewed her lip and gazed at Peller. "I'd rather you be my uncle."

Peller felt strangely honored by the suggestion. "That works," he said.

Chapter 6

Peller left a message on Bobby Grant's answering machine at the dinner hour. Grant called Peller's cell phone midmorning on Thursday, June first, just as the detective opened a short email from ATF Special Agent Zee Mirlo. Mirlo had posted a five-thousand-dollar reward for information relating to the break-in at The Lodge. No tips to report yet, but as Mirlo put it, the Lotto tickets just went on sale.

"I appreciate the call," Peller told Grant. "You're Mr. Ferring's assistant manager?"

"That's right," Grant said. He was a baritone behind a bad connection, or maybe too nervous to keep his voice together.

"You have keys to the shop?"

"I do."

"Who else has them?"

"Just Chuck. Mr. Ferring. The owner."

Peller nearly laughed. "Yes, I've met him. You know the rear door was unlocked at the time of the theft?"

"That's what Ch—Mr. Ferring said. I didn't know."

"When was the last delivery made?"

Grant thought for a moment. "Friday afternoon, I guess."

That matched Ferring's statement. "Who received that delivery?" Peller asked.

Grant's voice dropped a few decibels. "Me." In a rush, he added, "I'm sorry, okay? I told Mr. Ferring I was sorry. I was sure I'd locked up afterward."

Peller wondered what kind of taskmaster Ferring was. "Don't beat yourself up, Mr. Grant. Accidents happen. But I wonder, are you sure? Or are you assuming?"

"I was the last one to unlock it," he said miserably. "I must have forgotten."

Assuming, then. "But thought you had locked it."

"I know!"

"I'm not accusing you of anything, just trying to understand what happened. If you forgot, that explains how the thieves got in. But if not, then someone else must have unlocked it later."

Grant gave that a moment's consideration. "I don't know," he final-ly said. "It isn't keyed. It only unlocks from the inside. Someone would have to get into the back without myself or Mr. Ferring knowing, and one of us is always on duty. We'd know."

Peller hadn't been thinking of intruders. "What about your other employees?"

"We have four, three guys and a girl."

"They have unrestricted access to the back, I assume."

"Oh." Grant sounded embarrassed that he hadn't considered the obvious. "Yeah, I guess."

"Could one of them have unlocked the door?"

"They aren't supposed to, but yeah, I guess so."

"Can you get me their names and numbers?"

"I'll have to check with Mr. Ferring on that."

Peller didn't argue. Grant was probably in enough hot water as it was. "Please do. Ask him to text or email me the list." He gave Grant his email address and signed off.

So the others weren't supposed to unlock the door. If any had, Geri Franklin might have lifted their prints from the lock. The ID would be easy, since she would have fingerprinted the whole crew for elimination.

Peller pulled up the forensics report on his computer. There it was: three distinct sets of prints. One matched to Chuck Ferring, one to Bobby Grant. The other belonged to an employee named Andrew Hunt.

The lab reported on the bones late Thursday. The skeleton was male, approximately twenty years old. It had been buried in the ground for some fifty to sixty years. Its owner hadn't perished in the flood, but he was neither Colonial settler nor ancient Native American. Not even a slave. The skull, although intact, showed signs of trauma to the lower right parietal bone. The skeleton revealed no definitive injury. A humerus and a few ribs showed cracks, but it wasn't clear whether those were injuries during life or damage that occurred in the ground. The specimen was sixty-three percent complete, making Geri Franklin's estimate spot-on. She was right about an-other thing, too. There were no duplicate bones, suggesting they all came from the same individual. DNA tests had been submitted to make a final determination, but those would take a couple of weeks, minimum.

Holly Ross came to Theresa Swan's cubicle so they could review the reports together. She pulled the guest chair around and was leaning on the desktop, arms folded together. "Here's the good part," she said. "Soil embedded in small cracks in the bones matches samples taken from the basement of the Colonial Bakery. That's definitely where Napoleon was buried."

Swan raised an eyebrow. "Napoleon?"

"Bone-apart." Ross snickered. "Get it?"

Swan groaned. "That's terrible."

"Glad you appreciate it, but don't tell the bosses. I don't want them to think I don't take the case seriously."

"Why would they? Eric pulls coins out of people's ears." Swan nodded at the computer. "So, what happened? In the nineteen forties or fifties, somebody klonked his head and was buried in the cellar. Maybe he fell down the stairs."

"Really, Theresa? Was it too much trouble to carry him out for a proper funeral?"

Probably not, but they had so little evidence. If Montufar had drummed anything into her head, it was patience. Collect the data first.

Ross plowed ahead. "It's clearly manslaughter or murder, and it's not that hard to guess who did it. James Ferring told me his grandfather moved there in 1928. Napoleon died ten or twenty years later. It happened on his family's watch, so one of them has to be the undertaker. I say we go for it."

She would. Ross was a bit younger than Swan, a bit less experienced, and way too eager to prove herself. She needed an injection of caution. "We're talking fifty, sixty years ago. If it was homicide, the killer might be dead. Besides, it certainly could have been an accident, and if it was a killing, someone else certainly could have been the killer."

Ross wanted none of that. "You don't bury an accident victim in the cellar. Also, two Ferrings refuse to talk about what's going on. This is definitely a Ferring family homicide."

"Definitely?"

"Okay, maybe not definitely, but isn't it worth a look? What about the bakery's history? What did you find there?"

Nothing, that's what. Swan's research had been a waste of several long hours. "The alarm was triggered two years ago, probably due to a system fault. The investigating officers found nothing amiss. Aside from that, zilch. No thefts, no vandalism, not even a suspicious-looking kid loitering outside. Whoever's persecuting Chuck Ferring isn't after James, but so what? They're distant cousins and barely know each other."

"According to Chucky," Ross said. "But you heard Rick. He gives that zero credence."

Swan had to give Ross that one. She wasn't about to second-guess Peller. "Fine, but this is a history project. We'll start with the family's background. News archives, maybe?"

She might as well have handed Ross a moldy peach. "Archives, hell. Let's interview the family."

"Captain Morris doesn't like fishing expeditions. Besides, if the rest of the family is as tight-lipped as Chuck and James, we won't get far."

Ross threw herself back in the chair and crossed her arms. "I can't do nothing. This is my first big case."

"Holly."

"What?"

"Is that really what's important?"

"It is to me."

Clearly, she needed a babysitter. "All right," Swan said. "But let's start simple, okay?"

"Fine." Ross muttered. "But I'll bet there's more than one skeleton in that closet."

On a gently sloping lot west of Columbia Town Center, an aging two-story building reposed beneath a canopy of tall oaks. White with angled glass curtain walls that shone like copper, it might have been a small Mayan temple hidden in the jungle. Now thirty years old, the building had been designed for the *Columbia Flier* and served it well over the decades. To reporter Jack Collins, it once doubled as a second home.

In those days, he arrived early and worked late and sometimes slept on a cot a photographer had stashed in the studio. He loved his work that much, besides having no other life. His relations lived in Philadelphia and D.C., and his attachments outside work were practically nil.

Until he met Ella Montufar one rainy night when her car stalled in front of the *Flier*'s office. She limped into the parking lot on the little momentum remaining to the vehicle and, seeing lights inside, banged on the door. It was nearing ten o'clock, and Collins was the only one still there. Knowing little of mechanics, he couldn't get her vehicle running, so he offered to drive her home. She insisted on buying him dinner the following evening to thank him. She was too pretty to refuse. After that, they saw each other with increasing frequency. Upon the death of Ella's father four months ago, Collins found himself drawn into the Montufar clan, and he could see in their eyes that everyone expected him to propose, the sooner the better. He meant to, but Eric Dumas had proposed to Corina first. Collins thought it prudent to wait until he knew their wedding date. He wouldn't want to step on any toes.

Then again, maybe he was just stalling.

That, however, was an internal struggle for another time. He had a story to research, and until James Ferring IV recovered sufficiently from the shock of the flood, Collins would have to do it the hard way.

At his desk in his home away from home, Collins got to work. Public records and news archives gave him the basics. In 1890, James Ferring opened a small bakery on Main Street a quarter mile west of Mt. Misery Road. (*Cool name,* he thought.) The business perched on the edge of Ellicott City in those days, a bit distant but accessible to travelers entering or leaving the city and convenient enough to the Patapsco Flouring Mills just across the river. James unimaginatively named the establishment Ferring's Bakery and built a steady clientele from families and businesses in the area, including the Patapsco Female Institute, a girls' boarding school atop a hill north of the city.

The world had changed since then. Ferring's son James Junior inherited the bakery. In 1928, he moved it to its present location in the Historic District and renamed it Colonial Bakery. Mt. Misery Road acquired the less colorful name Hill Road. The Patapsco Female Institute closed, morphed into the Patapsco Heights Hotel, was shuttered again, and was reborn as a partially restored historic site.

Fascinating stuff. Collins nearly lost himself in historic maps, name changes, the intrusion of new roads, and the disappearance of old ones. He could spin a thousand and one stories from the footprints history had left in this little city.

The Ferrings left footprints of their own. James Junior's descendants in the firstborn male line—James III and current owner James IV— kept the Colonial Bakery alive and well. James III's younger brother Andrew sold farm equipment and supplies, a business still run by his descendants, although the company eventually moved west to Frederick County. The brothers had a couple of sisters, but they faded from the record, shadows vanishing in the sunset.

Still, anonymity could be a good thing. At least the women hadn't left bloodstains on the books. Collins found those, too, metaphorical and real. James Junior's brothers William and Roger struck out on their own. William tried his hand at the restaurant business, where he failed three times before leaving the kitchen for a hardware store. That business stayed afloat until the waters dried up with the rise of national chains. His descendants slipped without remark into the world of common labor.

Roger's path was more tragic still. He rose to the defense of his country when World War I beckoned only to be sent home with a dishonorable discharge. According to news reports, he later became embroiled in a deadly altercation with his nephew George Ferring and was arrested but died before the trial when an outraged mob attacked him as he was being brought into court. The year was 1937. He was only thirty-nine.

Still, it wasn't all darkness. Roger had left a son and a daughter. His son William vanished not long after his twenty-first birthday and was presumed dead, but his daughter Ruth was still alive at age 82. According to a news article from two years before, she had been honored by a small local charity for her support of single mothers. She lived with her husband Terrence Vickeridge in Dayton, Maryland, west of Columbia. They had two grown children and five grandchildren.

Collins read that article a second time. Ruth's story felt like a great introduction to the history of a family who had, through good times and bad, left a mark on the local landscape. He dug up Ruth's phone number and placed the call.

A thin, quivering voice answered. "Vickeridge residence."

Collins was pretty sure it was a man. "Could I speak with Ruth Vickeridge, please?"

"Who's calling?"

"My name is Jack Collins. I'm a reporter with the *Columbia Flier*."

"Another damn reporter, Ruth!"

The phone changed hands, and a woman's voice, less frail than the man's, said, "It's not like they call every day, Terry."

Collins suppressed a laugh.

"This is Ruth."

Collins introduced himself again. "I'm doing a story on the Ferring family and thought you'd be a good place to start, since you're a local celebrity."

"I got a small award once, that's all."

"For important work," Collins assured her.

She neither agreed nor disagreed. "Why the Ferrings? What's so important about them?"

"Partly because of the flood in Ellicott City. They've run several businesses in the area since the late 1800's, some of which are still thriving today. People like to read about families who've been around that long, the ups and downs, the failures and successes. It gives them a sense of history and hope for the future."

"I doubt you'll find much hope in the Ferring family." She might have been laughing or crying as she said it. "I suppose you'll want to visit."

"If you wouldn't mind."

"Tell him no!" her husband called in the background.

The line crackled as she covered the receiver with her palm, although Collins heard her well enough. "Why don't you go trim the bushes, Terry, and let me deal with this."

"They don't need trimming."

"Sorry," Ruth said into the phone. "My husband doesn't like strangers in the house."

"We could meet somewhere else," Collins suggested. "A restaurant, a park."

"No, you're welcome to drop by tomorrow afternoon. I'm sure Terry can find someplace to hide. At least he won't be following me around like a lost puppy."

Terrence made a comment Collins couldn't decipher, which was probably for the best.

"All right. How does one o'clock sound?"

"That will be fine."

He thanked her. After they hung up, he researched her husband. Terrence Vickeridge, it turned out, had been a Howard County police detective before his retirement nineteen years before.

"Great," Collins muttered. "Why couldn't I have found that out first?"

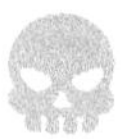

Chuck Ferring phoned moments before Peller left his desk to go home. "I've called a staff meeting for tomorrow morning," he said. "If you want to talk to my employees, they'll all be here."

"Thank you," Peller replied. "I'll need to interview them individually. Can that be arranged?"

"Sure, I have a small office in the back. You can use that."

"What time?"

"We'll be starting at eight, should be done by eight thirty. The store opens at nine. Tara Saunders is on duty. Talk to her first and we'll be good."

"Sounds like a plan, Mr. Ferring. I'll see you at eight thirty." No sooner had that call ended than his cell phone went off. This time, it was Joan Churchill.

"Got any plans tonight?" she asked.

"Nothing in particular." Peller continued for the door, silently chastising himself. He'd planned on a quiet evening at home. He needed it. Only two days had passed since he'd been battered by the flood. But Churchill had a talent for ambushing him, plus he found it hard to disappoint her, especially since she so readily rode to his rescue when he was stranded in the hospital.

"One of the movie channels is running a John Wayne marathon tonight. I know you like westerns, so I thought we could get together for pizza and shootouts."

"I suppose that would make a change of pace. What time?"

"I'm about to leave work. Give me an hour, anyway. What do you like on your pizza?"

"Nothing crazy. Pepperoni, sausage, onions, green peppers, tomatoes, and black olives are safe, in whatever combination you want."

"I can work with that. See you soon, Sherlock!"

Peller shook his head as he pocketed his phone. He really wished she'd stop with the Holmes thing. Sooner or later it was going to get out, and then he'd never hear the end of it.

He drove home. Jerry Souter was sitting on his front porch, basking in the warm evening, watching birds flit through the trees and the occasional car pass by. When Peller waved, Souter motioned him over.

"Take a load off," Souter insisted.

"Just for a moment." Peller sat.

A short silence ensued. Souter broke it. "Guess what tomorrow is."

Peller didn't have to guess. "Your ninety-fifth birthday. Throwing a wild party, are you?"

Souter cracked a slight smile, but otherwise his military bearing didn't slip. He'd fought with the ninety-second infantry in the Italian campaign during World War II and always looked ready for the next battle. "Just a day like any other."

"Don't tell me you're tired of birthdays?"

"When you get to be my age, you wish they'd stop ambushing you. I wouldn't mind being ninety-four for a few more years."

Peller thought he probably would be. Mounting age hadn't seemed to affect Souter over the past five years.

"Besides," Souter continued, "they're all the same. The kids call, I get cards in the mail. Already got a few." He paused to pick up a couple of envelopes from a table at his side and pass them to Peller. "But you can't put ninety-five candles on a cake without burning the house down, and there's no challenge in blowing out two of those number candles."

"In a few more years," Peller said with a mischievous smile, "you'll get to blow out three of them." He looked at the cards, all garden-variety, sappy verses wishing a father or grandfather or friend a happy day. One card from a granddaughter named Hannah bore a lengthy note catching Jerry up on the progress of his great-grandson Marcus, who was now walking and talking up a storm. "Do you see the family often?" Peller asked. He'd occasionally seen visitors at Souter's house, but he was never sure who was family.

"Nah. The distance is too far and travel too expensive. Anyway, I'm too settled to go gallivanting around."

Peller noticed Souter didn't say "old." In Jerry's mind, the aging of the world hadn't touched him. "How about I buy you dinner tomorrow," he suggested, "and you can tell me war stories?"

Souter shook his head. "You've heard them all. All the ones fit to tell, anyway."

Peller rose. "I'll pretend to be interested. Six o'clock?"

"I don't need your charity, young man."

"Not even for that new steakhouse out route forty?"

Souter glanced at Peller, his eyes not conceding anything. "Better make it five thirty."

"Deal," Peller agreed. "I have to run. I got roped into pizza and movies tonight."

Souter watched a flock of starlings swoop over the neighborhood. "Bless Joan's heart."

Peller wasn't sure if he meant it or was being sarcastic. Souter didn't much care about anyone's personal business, but he was good at reading Peller—and most other people. Sometimes talking to Jerry was like having a brutally honest conversation with yourself. Though Peller had told Souter little about Joan beyond her existence, he inferred a lot.

They exchanged goodbyes and Peller returned home, changed into jeans and a blue button-down shirt, and hit the road. He arrived at Joan's third-floor apartment almost exactly an hour after she called. The building, called Orchard Meadows, sat neither by an orchard nor in a meadow. Route 29 traffic rushed behind it, screened by a narrow strip of woods.

Churchill met him at the door wearing a white blouse dotted with tiny red roses and a black skirt. "Come on in," she said. "I ordered the pizza. It should be here in half an hour tops. The movie's about to start."

She padded barefoot across the light gray carpet and motioned him to the sofa. She kept a feminine place, but not overwhelmingly so. The colors were muted, the furnishings soft and pillow-laden, the artwork bright with flowers and forests. She had a modest flat-panel TV on the wall but no family photos anywhere. Peller never asked much about her relations. She once told him she came from a small family. She had been married and divorced twice but never mentioned any children.

They settled in, maintaining a respectful distance, and she flipped through the channel guide to her destination. *The Man Who Shot Liberty Valance* was up first. They watched with little conversation until the pizza arrived thirty-five minutes into the film. Churchill had loaded it up with Peller's full list of ingredients and added a side of root beer, since he didn't drink alcohol. *The Sons of Katie Elder* followed. *Rio Bravo* was slated for the finale, but by then it was ten o'clock, and Peller reminded Churchill they both had to work in the morning.

"One late night won't kill us," she said. "You could sleep on the couch if you're too tired to drive."

"Better not," Peller replied. "People might get the wrong idea."

Her expression was hard to read. He had either disappointed her or irritated her. "Nobody's watching, Rick. I can't even tell you what my neighbors look like."

Peller pointed to the wall on their left. "The couple over there are in their seventies, staunch Baptists, and inveterate gossips."

That got a laugh. "Oh, really. And how do you know that?"

"The last time I was here, I met them. They were bringing in groceries when I arrived. I offered to help, and the husband pointedly informed me he was quite capable of managing, thank you very much. They definitely looked to be in their seventies."

"And the rest of it?"

"I added it for flavor."

"Sure you don't want to stay and watch *Rio Bravo*?" She patted the sofa invitingly.

Peller felt torn between an almost irrational need to escape and not wanting to disappoint her. She could probably see it in his face. "It's been fun, but I think I'd better go."

She didn't object further. On the drive home, he wondered if he could have handled that better.

No, he thought he heard Sandra laugh. *Not you.*

Chapter 7

On Friday morning, another bright day with high wisps of cloud, Peller drove straight to the Lodge and arrived at eight fifteen, square in the middle of the staff meeting. He'd planned the intrusion, hoping it might throw someone off balance.

The door was locked when he arrived, so he knocked and peered through the glass. Chuck Ferring stood behind the counter, tapping on the case with his index finger to make a point. The other five employees were seated on folding chairs arrayed in a slight arc before the boss. Jeans and plaid shirts seemed to be the dress code. The one female in the group, a slight, dark-haired woman who would be Tara Saunders, jumped up and skittered to the door to let Peller in. Borderline terrified, she said nothing but a timid, "Hi," as she admitted him. Her plaid shirt was green and blue with sleeves rolled to her elbows.

"Good morning, Tara," Peller murmured. His knowledge of her name further disconcerted her. She fumbled with the door lock before trotting back to her chair, giving him a worried glance over her shoulder.

"Hi, Lieutenant," Ferring said with a half-hearted wave. He didn't look pleased by the intrusion, even though he'd been expecting it.

"Don't let me interrupt," Peller said. "I'll wait over here. He sauntered to the far side of the store and looked over the archery equipment hanging on the wall: straight bows, recurves, compounds fitted with pulleys and lines. He supposed all that hardware made bow hunting easier, but he wondered if it didn't take some of the sport out of the sport. The bow possessed a romance the gun never could: clean, elegant, older than history.

"Nothing to be afraid of," Ferring was telling his crew. "Just routine, but make sure you cooperate. Questions? No? Okay, about the schedule…"

Peller noticed he hadn't actually given time for questions. Ferring ran on about summer hours and vacations and whatnot, a one-man show neither expecting nor accepting questions, comments, or complaints. Was this his modus operandi, or was he just unnerved by Peller's presence?

Ferring moved on to pending shipments, followed by a problem customer perpetually trying to exchange half-used boxes of ammunition for new ones. "If I'm not here when he walks in," Ferring said, "get me on the horn. No exchanges. He just wants something for nothing. Understood?"

After a murmur of assent, Ferring straightened. "Anyone have anything to bring up?" The silence affirmed that nobody dared. "Okay. Lieutenant Peller will talk with Tara first, so we can get the place open. The rest of you stick around and wait your turns." He motioned Peller over. "Anything you want to say?"

Peller crossed the store and stood by the display case so everyone could see him without craning their necks. "Not really. I'll just introduce myself. I'm Detective Lieutenant Rick Peller, and I'm investigating the break-in. I'll be speaking with each of you one on one. It shouldn't take long." He turned to Ferring. "You mentioned an office in the back."

"Right," Ferring acknowledged. "Tara, show Lieutenant Peller where it is."

Saunders slid forward and pushed herself up, hands trembling. "This way," she nearly squeaked. She led Peller into the storeroom, turned left, and led him to a small office tucked into the corner. White walls enclosed the makeshift room, which contained a cheap wooden desk and a rather more expensive black chair. A couple of metal folding chairs faced the desk. A two-drawer filing cabinet that had seen better days occupied the back corner. The lack of space reminded Peller of the conference room scene in *Attack of the Killer Tomatoes*.

He squeezed behind the desk to sit in the comfortable chair and motioned Tara to one of the metal seats. She folded her hands in her lap and tried without success to keep them still. She couldn't look Peller in the eyes. "How long have you worked for Mr. Ferring?" he asked.

"Um." Peller waited while she found the courage to answer. "Two years, about."

"How old are you?"

"Nineteen."

"Going to college?"

Saunders shook her head slightly.

"Graduated high school?"

"Yeah."

Peller leaned forward, crossed his arms on the desk, and studied Saunders, who still refused to look at him. She had a thin, angular face and dark eyes that might have been alluring if they weren't so distant. "Do you like working here?"

"Yeah." Her mouth twitched. "Pay sucks."

Peller smiled. "That, unfortunately, is all too common. What are your duties?"

"Helping customers. Ringing up sales. Sweeping the floors at the end of the day." She looked up, suddenly defiant. "Not 'cause I'm a girl. We all do when we're on duty. Sweeping up, I mean."

"Of course," Peller said. He wasn't sure why she felt the need to explain, but a bit of fire had been kindled within her, at least.

"Customers always think it's 'cause I'm a girl, like that's the only reason I could possibly be here. They don't like talking to me about the product. They must think I'm stupid. But I know everything about everything, as much as Uncle, I mean, Mr. Ferring does." Her gaze slipped to the side again.

Peller wondered why she felt a need to hide the relationship. Lots of people worked in their family's businesses. Pretending he hadn't noticed, he said, "If it's any consolation, I don't think you're stupid. In a small operation like this, everyone has to know everything."

Saunders nodded and relaxed a bit.

"Do your duties include receiving deliveries?"

"We put them away." Her mouth twitched in irritation. "Mr. Ferring doesn't let anyone but Bobby and himself open the receiving door and sign the papers. He doesn't trust us."

"Or he just wants to be careful. Somebody seems to have a grudge against him."

"Just nut jobs. Gun shops always attract anti-gun freaks." She stole a glance at Peller to gauge his reaction. He didn't give her one. "That's what Mr. Ferring says, anyway."

"Tara." He stared at her until she felt compelled to look back. "Is something wrong?"

She swallowed. "Like what?"

"You've been a nervous wreck since I arrived."

"Um. No." She tried to laugh but that only betrayed her further. "Maybe a little," she admitted.

"Why?"

"You're a cop." As if that explained everything.

Peller waited, but she volunteered nothing. "Were you on duty the day of the robbery?"

She shook her head.

"Do you know who robbed the store?"

"How would I know that?" Her eyes flitted over everything but him.

Peller gave her a quick once-over, noting that her forearms were pale and unblemished. No obvious sign of a drug habit, anyway. "That's a good question."

"I'm not a thief," she protested.

"And aside from the pay, your uncle treats you well?"

She frowned, realizing she hadn't gotten away with the slip of the tongue, but she didn't answer. She couldn't without admitting the relationship.

Peller leaned back. "All right," he said. "I'll let you get to work."

Saunders tangled her fingers together and untangled them again before rising. "Should I send someone else in?"

Peller stood, too. "No, I'll get them myself. Thank you." He motioned her to the door and followed her out. When they returned to the sales floor, Ferring was doing some paperwork in the back while the others were clustered near the door, talking quietly. The young men all looked up when Peller and Saunders walked in, eyes wide with curiosity.

Peller motioned to them. "Over here, gentlemen. Mr. Ferring, I'm going to take these fellows in back so they won't interfere with your work. I'd appreciate it if you let them wait there while I talk to each in turn."

Ferring nodded. "Be my guest." He returned to his paperwork as though unconcerned. The others followed Peller into the back, unhappy at being cut off from all possibility of gossip. "Let's have introductions," Peller said. "Bobby Grant?"

The oldest and tallest raised his hand. He wore his thinning brown hair long and had a pair of wire-rim glasses.

"Andrew Hunt?"

Hunt looked to be the youngest, probably not much more than twenty. He was a thinner version of Chuck Ferring except for his sloping forehead. Tara Saunders wasn't the only family member in the store.

"I haven't heard your names yet," he said to the other two, a pair of stocky young men with dark, wavy hair and round faces. They might have been twins except the taller looked older.

"Peter Mitchell," that one said. "This is my brother Mark."

Peller nodded. "Find a place to sit, gentlemen. I'll start with you, Mark."

Once seated in the office with the door closed, Peller asked Mitchell how long he had worked for Ferring.

"Seven years next month, sir. Peter and I started at the same time."

Peller didn't think he looked that old. "You're, what, twenty-five?"

"Twenty-four, sir."

"So you were seventeen when you came to work here?"

"It's not illegal, sir, if you have your parents' written permission."

"You don't have to call me 'sir' all the time."

Mitchell's expression didn't change. "My dad says always call the police 'sir.' Sir."

Peller declined to fight a losing battle. "Did you go to college?"

"Community college, sir. I got a certificate."

"And you're still here?"

Mitchell shrugged. "It's a job, sir. I like working with the product and our customers. I know everything there is to know."

"As much as Tara?"

Bristling, Mitchell leaned forward and lowered his voice. "I know twice as much as that slut."

The animosity surprised Peller. "That's pretty harsh, isn't it?"

"That's what she is, sir. And stuck up. She thinks she's Mr. Ferring's favorite."

"Is she?"

Mitchell bit off whatever he was about to say. Crossing his arms over his chest, he looked away. "You tricked me into saying that. Forget it."

Peller wasn't about to do that. "How are you related to Tara?"

"We aren't related." The sirs had vanished without a trace. Apparently, following daddy's advice proved harder when Mitchell was angry.

"Isn't this a family business?"

Shifting in the metal chair, Mitchell looked at his hands. "No."

"But you are jealous of her."

"I am not!"

"You said she's Mr. Ferring's favorite."

"I said she *thinks* she is. He can see right through her."

"Hmm." Peller folded his hands on the desk and stared at Mitchell. "You also called her a slut. Why?"

Mitchell shrugged. "Nothing. Forget it."

"That's a hard thing to forget." When Mitchell didn't respond, Peller changed the subject. "Do you receive deliveries?"

Mitchell drew a breath as though he'd narrowly escaped injury. "No, sir. Only Mr. Ferring and Bobby do that. We just put product onto the shelves."

"Were you working here the day of the robbery?"

"No, sir. Andrew was on that day, and Mr. Ferring."

"Were you dating Tara?"

Mitchell looked up sharply. "How ... damn it, I said forget it!"

"You don't give me orders," Peller snapped back. "Answer the question."

Folding his arms over his chest, Mitchell shook his head. "I got rights. I don't have to answer without a lawyer present."

Peller laughed. "Yeah, you were. So what, Tara jilted you? Or did she cheat on you? Is that why you're so angry Mr. Ferring dotes on his niece? Is that why you helped rob the store?"

Mitchell's face morphed from anger to terror. "I didn't! It wasn't me!"

"But it would be so easy to unlock the back door and let the thieves in."

"I never touch that door! Mr. Ferring doesn't allow it!"

"Somebody touched it, Mark. We know that much from our lab results."

Mitchell looked about as though the real culprit might be standing in the shadows waiting to be fingered. His voice dropped to a whisper. "I know who it was."

Peller leaned forward and whispered back, "Who?"

"Andrew."

Which matched the fingerprints. "You saw him?"

Nodding frenetically, Mitchell leaned forward, too. "I saw him go out for a smoke once. I told him later he shouldn't go out that way. I told him Mr. Ferring wouldn't like it. He told me to go to hell."

"Going out for a smoke doesn't equal taking part in a burglary."

"Like I said, Andrew was on duty that day. Sir." Mitchell looked hopeful Peller would see the connection and agree with his conclusion.

Peller stared at Mitchell long enough to call that hope into doubt, then straightened. "You can go home now." He rose and motioned toward the door.

"I have to wait for my brother, sir."

"Then I'll talk to him next. You wait out front with Mr. Ferring." Peller followed him out and called Peter Mitchell over, making sure the two had no chance to talk.

Peter proved thriftier with the sirs than Mark had been and was nowhere near as flappable. He answered Peller's basic questions clearly and efficiently. He had worked at The Lodge for seven years next month. He had persuaded Ferring to hire Mark a few days after he started work. He wasn't on duty the day of the robbery and had no idea who might have been responsible. Aside from Ferring, only Bobby was allowed to open the back door and complete the receiving paperwork. He didn't even blink when Peller threw him a curveball.

"Did your brother date Tara Saunders?"

"I wouldn't call it dating," Mitchell said. "They saw each other outside work for maybe two months, but not often."

"When was this?"

"February, March. Around then."

"Why did they break up?"

Mitchell cocked his head as though he didn't get the question. "I wouldn't call it a breakup."

"True," Peller agreed. "More like World War three, the way Mark carried on."

"Oh." Mitchell waved that away. "He gets wound up, sir. He's not as even-tempered as me."

"Wound up enough to plot revenge?"

"No, he just beats his chest and roars until it blows over."

"So why did they break up?"

"I wouldn't—" Seeing the hard set of Peller's eyes, Mitchell thought better of reiterating the denial. "He caught her sleeping with someone else. I mean literally, caught them in bed together."

"That would do it," Peller agreed. "But why be mad at Mr. Ferring? It's natural enough he'd favor his niece, especially when you're not his relatives."

A slight crack opened in Mitchell's calm. For a moment, he looked panicked, but then he steadied himself. "How do you figure she's his niece?"

"Isn't she?"

Mitchell gave Peller a bland smile. *We're men of the world*, he seemed to be saying. *We don't need to play this game.*

Peller played it anyway. "Figuring things out is my job."

Not questioning the explanation, Mitchell returned to the subject of his brother. "Mark doesn't take rejection well. He wants to see her fired."

"Failing that, would he want Mr. Ferring punished?"

Mitchell laughed until he saw Peller was serious. He took a moment to work out the implications, then objected, "No, sir. Absolutely not. He wouldn't do that."

"And if he did, you'd be there to protect him." Which Peller knew was an unfair statement. Mitchell could neither answer yes without potentially incriminating himself nor no without lying.

He said the only thing he could. "I grew up with Mark, sir. I know him. He just wouldn't do that."

Peller dismissed Peter Mitchell to retrieve his brother and take him home, then called in Bobby Grant, leaving Andrew Hunt to stew a bit longer. When Grant was seated, Peller said, "The man who last opened the door. I'm sure you've been wracking your brains since we spoke on the phone. Any new insights?"

Grant shook his head miserably. "I just can't remember, Lieutenant. I've never forgotten to lock the door before, but it was unlocked, so I guess I must have. I just don't remember either doing it or not doing it."

"How long have you worked for Mr. Ferring?"

"Eleven years."

"Making you his most senior employee as well as assistant manager."

Grant nodded.

"So you know about the various attacks on the store, I suppose. The vandalism and prior break-ins."

"Pretty much."

"What do you make of them?"

Grant looked puzzled. "What do you mean?"

"Both Mr. Ferring and Tara Saunders tell me they're the work of anti-gun protesters. Would you agree with that?"

Squirming uncomfortably in the chair, Grant took his time answering. "I don't really know, Lieutenant. I guess it makes sense."

"Not to me," Peller said. "It looks to me like someone holds a grudge against Mr. Ferring, particularly given the note the burglars left this time. I assume you've heard about that."

Grant nodded.

"So?"

"Mr. Ferring is the nicest guy I know. I can't imagine anyone having a grudge against him, not unless they *were* anti-gun."

"That's the story, and you're all sticking to it. Is that it?"

Again, the puzzled look. He was rather good at it, Peller thought, but not quite good enough. Grant's eyes were looking for something, some sign that he'd fooled Peller, perhaps.

"How many of the employees are relatives of Mr. Ferring?"

"None."

Peller raised a skeptical eyebrow.

"He used to employ a few relatives, but none of them are here anymore."

"What about Tara Saunders? Isn't she Mr. Ferring's niece?"

"Who said that?"

"I said that. Is it true?"

Grant ran his finger over the desktop and inspected it for dust.

"Answer the question, Mr. Grant."

With a heavy sigh, Grant relented. "He didn't want anyone to know."

"Why not? It's a family business. Why shouldn't there be family members working here?"

"You'll have to ask him that."

"I'm asking you."

"I don't know."

Peller let that one go. It might be true. "Who else is a Ferring relative?"

"Just Tara."

"What about Andrew?"

Grant looked weary, as though admitting Saunders' relationship to the boss had doomed his employment prospects forever. "No."

"He looks like a Ferring. Haven't you noticed?"

With a small shake of his head, Grant denied it.

"That will be all, then. You can go home." Peller and Grant rose, and once the assistant manager was gone, Peller called Andrew Hunt in. He went quickly through the preliminaries. Hunt was the newest employee, with only two years on the job. He was working the day of the robbery, but nobody had opened the door that day. He never opened the door himself; only Mr. Ferring and Bobby were allowed.

"We have a problem with that," Peller told him. "Your fingerprints were found on the door and the lock."

With an unconvincing shrug, Hunt mumbled something.

"I didn't catch that," Peller said.

"I said, we've probably all touched it in passing."

"Apparently not. Yours are the only unauthorized prints we found."

"Doesn't prove I opened the door."

Peller stared at Hunt.

"You think I did?" Hunt asked.

"I know you did."

With a definitive shake of his head, Hunt stared right back, unblinking.

"The question," Peller said, "is why." When Hunt offered no explanation, he added, "If you'd rather, we can discuss this back at my office."

Hunt transformed from obstinate to panicked. "You can't arrest me!"

Peller dug his cell phone out of his pocket and checked his messages. There weren't any.

Leaning on the desk, Hunt pleaded, "Mr. Ferring would fire me!"

"Why? You didn't do anything wrong. Or so you say."

"But it would look like you think I did!"

Nodding, Peller agreed. "It probably would."

Hunt's voice dropped to a whisper as he furtively checked that the door was closed. "I go out back for a smoke sometimes. Mr. Ferring doesn't like me smoking in front of the store. It's a lot shorter to go out the back door, especially when it's cold."

"When did you last go out that way?"

"The day of the robbery." He hung his head and feigned shame. "I'm pretty sure I locked it when I came in."

He would say that either way. "How are you related to Mr. Ferring?" Peller asked.

That change of subject gave Hunt mental whiplash. He looked up suddenly, terrified. "Who said I was?"

"Nobody said it. I can see the resemblance."

It took Hunt a moment to come up with the obvious denial. "Just a coincidence. I'm not—"

"Stop lying," Peller snapped. "I already know Tara Saunders is his niece, and I can see you're related. What are you, his son?"

"No! I'm …" The way his eyes shifted about, Peller wondered if Hunt was tracing a family tree. "I'm not related," he finally decided.

"I could waste taxpayer dollars proving otherwise. It would be more efficient if you just told me. Either way, I'll have the answer." But Hunt was done and wouldn't be budged on the question. Peller tried to wait him out to no avail, so he returned to the matter of the door. "I'll tell you my working hypothesis, Mr. Hunt. You used the back door not only to get outside for a smoke. You unlocked it for a gang of thieves. They either paid you up front or promised to pay after the haul was sold. I hope for your sake it wasn't the latter, because if it was, you'll probably never see them again. You'll take the fall and won't receive one penny in compensation. I don't know why you and Ms. Saunders won't admit your relationship to Mr. Ferring, but I can always ask him about that. I imagine he's behind those denials anyway. Have anything to add?"

Hunt was quivering with fear. "I'm not," he mumbled. "I'm not. I didn't."

Peller rose. "You did something," he said. "You can rest assured I'll find out what it was. You'd save yourself a lot of trouble by admitting it."

Hunt wouldn't or couldn't reply, so Peller left him there and returned to the showroom.

Chapter 8

The young men had left. Chuck Ferring was outside the front door, talking with a short fellow who might have been a refugee from the sixties, except he wasn't near old enough. His stringy blonde hair fluttered in the breeze. His beard looked scraggly, as though it had never entirely grown in. The man was talking with his hands as much as with his mouth, enthused by whatever the subject.

Ferring shoved his hands in his pockets and nodded without speaking.

Tara Saunders, meanwhile, leaned on a counter, paging slowly through a catalogue of weaponry, so focused she might have been cramming for a final exam. Peller stopped across from her and nodded to Ferring. "Who's he talking to?"

Without looking up, Saunders said, "Customer. Mr. Williamson. He's one of the regulars."

"Why are they talking outside?"

She snapped a page over. "It's a nice day, I guess."

"You dated Mark for a time."

Pushing herself upright, Saunders glowered at Peller. "That your business?"

"Depends. He seems to think your uncle is biased in your favor."

She went back to her catalogue and snapped another page.

"It must be tough working with your ex." Peller turned to watch Ferring and his customer, who was still going full throttle. *Must be a fascinating topic*, he thought.

"I don't work with him. We don't have the same shifts."

"But your uncle does favor you."

"Because I'm good. I sold the most three months in a row, and I'll beat them all again this month."

"Why doesn't he want me to know you're related to him?"

She slapped the catalogue shut and stuffed it somewhere behind the counter, then pretended to straighten some boxes on the shelf along the wall.

"Okay," Peller said. "That'll be the first thing I ask him." He left her to her work, such as it was, and pushed through the door.

His arrival signaled the end of the conversation. Ferring's customer said a hasty goodbye, got into a battered blue Chevy pickup, and drove off. Ferring watched him go. "That man talks way too much."

"But he's a good customer," Peller said, "so you have to put up with it."

"Basically. All finished, then?"

"With your employees, yes."

"Then I'd better get back to work." Ferring turned to go inside.

"Not quite with you."

Although he didn't look happy, Ferring stopped and waited for whatever would come next.

"How many of your employees are family members?"

Surprised, Ferring took a moment to answer. Peller allowed him the space to decide whether to be honest or make up something. When the reply came, it was more creative than Peller expected. "How many do you think, Lieutenant?"

"Two, at least. "

Ferring peered into the distance and thought about that. "Just one. Tara's my niece."

"Not Andrew Hunt?"

"Nope."

"The resemblance is pretty obvious."

Ferring shook his head. "Is this important, Lieutenant?"

"Probably, or you wouldn't hide it."

"I'm not …" Seeing Peller's look, Ferring threw up his hands. "I used to hire family members, but it caused problems with other employees. They thought I was playing favorites. So I stopped doing it. I probably shouldn't have hired Tara, but her father was a hunter and taught her everything he knows. She's a natural." He glanced through the window at her and couldn't help a quick smile.

"Mark has it in for her," Peller observed.

"She's not as smart in her personal relationships as she is with customers," Ferring grumbled.

"And Andrew?"

"Any resemblance is coincidence. He's no relative of mine."

Peller doubted that. He didn't forget faces. But he also knew he could waste all day talking to Ferring and get nowhere, so it looked like a public records search was in the offing. He made one last ditch effort, any-way. "Don't think I won't find out, Mr. Ferring."

"I'm not hiding anything, Lieutenant. I'd just rather not broadcast that Tara's my niece. I don't need the others thinking I show her favoritism."

Too late, Peller thought.

On his return to Northern District Headquarters, Peller found the video footage from the Lodge awaiting his review. Geri Franklin had ex-tracted the relevant portions, a few minutes of disjointed snippets from the day of the robbery.

The sequence began with Andrew Hunt slipping out at ten fifteen. The back door eased open a crack. After a pause in which a shadow could be seen peering out, it swung open just enough for Hunt to slide through. He shut it carefully, keeping a hand on it the whole way, then lit up a cigarette. After a few puffs, the footage jumped to the next event: Hunt just as carefully opened the door, vanished within, and closed it with an abundance of caution.

The one-man play reprised a few minutes after noon, again just be-fore two o'clock, and once more at four.

At seven minutes after five, a new show premiered. Three figures, bundled in black pants, black jackets, and black hoods drooped over their faces emerged from the trees behind the building and sauntered across the asphalt. Their manner suggested teenagers taking a forbidden shortcut, but their target was clear. Without deviating, they approached the door. The tallest extended a gloved hand, gently pulled the door open a crack, and peeked in. With a nod, the intruder motioned the others, and they vanished inside. Six minutes later, they emerged with less caution, each carrying a box, and slipped back into the woods.

They'd been smart and efficient, hiding their identities, preventing fingerprints, probably knowing exactly what they wanted and wasting no time in procuring it. They couldn't be ID'd from the footage alone, although analysis of the video would provide approximate heights and weights. He could tell by their gait as they left that two were male and one female. Not much, but better than nothing.

Another snippet followed, this one from inside the store. Chuck Ferring, more enthusiastic than Peller had yet seen him, was demonstrating the features of several handguns to a man with wire rim glasses and a neatly trimmed beard. The customer looked to be in his mid-thirties. Every so often, while the guy picked up a weapon to examine it, Ferring's eyes shifted to something off-picture on the far side of the store. Peller wondered what had attracted his attention. A few minutes into the clip, Ferring turned with a frown to the storeroom, said something, and left to investigate. Once he was gone, the customer turned and extended a hand. A woman with long blonde hair, a skimpy tank top, and an artfully exposed cleavage came into view. She took her partner's hand and, with a wink, led him out of the store.

The times were just right: Ferring went into the back seconds after the thieves left.

At least Peller had a couple of faces now. He forwarded the last clip to ATF Special Agent Zee Mirlo to release with his reward posting, then he called Geri Franklin to arrange another trip to The Lodge.

But he didn't like it. Why, when the thieves had been so careful to conceal their faces, had their diversion made no effort to hide? Certainly, they couldn't march into the store hooded or masked, but hadn't they done their homework? Hadn't they known the positions of the cameras in advance? Stupid criminals Peller understood. Smart criminals, too. But he never liked it when crimes displayed elements of both. It generally meant he wasn't understanding something. Often, it presaged an explosion of violence.

Time for a second opinion, maybe a third. Peller called Montufar and Dumas over and replayed the footage for them, withholding comment so they could form their own opinions.

"Is that the designated smoking area?" Dumas asked as he watched Andrew Hunt's third egress.

"Unofficially," Peller replied. "He's not supposed to use the back door, but he's also not supposed to smoke in front of the store."

"So did he let the thieves in intentionally or accidentally?"

"Intentionally," Montufar said. "The thieves might have noted his routine, but how would they know the door would be unlocked just then? If he left it unlocked all the time, the boss would have noticed."

Peller agreed. "Chuck Ferring would have blown a gasket."

They watched the remainder in silence.

"Ah," Dumas said as the woman appeared on screen and exited with her partner. "The classic misdirection technique."

"Never saw you use *that* in your magic tricks," Montufar said, deadpan.

"I wouldn't dare." He winked at her, pulled a half dollar from his right pocket, and performed a vanish.

Peller had seen the trick about a thousand times. "Part of the plot, you figure?"

"Absolutely," his companions both said at once. They glanced at each other, momentarily taken aback, then Dumas laughed. "The proverbial great minds, thinking alike."

Looking a bit sheepish, Montufar quickly changed the subject. "The smoker, what's his name?"

"Andrew Hunt," Peller said.

"He'll know the names of the others. Get him to talk, and you'll have it wrapped up."

Dumas shook his head. "You'll have the story they want you to have. You might nab Hunt and that last pair, but the thieves themselves?"

"The DA would likely give Hunt a slap on the wrist in exchange for the others," Montufar said. "I don't see the problem."

Peller noted the misgiving in Dumas's eyes. "You think they've threatened him to keep him quiet?"

"I'm not sure he knows the whole story."

"Why not?"

"He's an idiot. He's on camera every time he opens that door, risking his job to save a few steps. The thieves, though, they came prepared. So why pin success on an idiot, and why put such an obvious couple on camera?"

"Good questions," Montufar said. "Got any good answers?"

"One," Dumas replied. "Maybe Hunt and that other pair are *supposed* to get caught."

The Vickeridge home was a comfortable, older house with blue trim and rounded shrubs in front of the windows. It sat off Linthicum Road flanked by newer, larger homes that probably topped half a million in sales value. Driving by, Jack Collins wondered how much it cost to heat, furnish, and landscape them. Probably more than he could make in thirty years. He could see Ella Montufar and himself living in Ruth and Terrence's house, though, out here in the country, surrounded by green, distanced from the rush of traffic.

Ruth admitted him with a quiet smile and sat with him at a round oak table in her living room. Light filtered through the lace curtains and gave a soft, sepia glow to the woods and fabrics in the rooms. Collins couldn't help but be wide-eyed as he settled his tape recorder on the table. "This furniture has been around a long time," he said, "yet it looks brand new."

"It's old," Ruth agreed, "but they made good stuff back then, and I take good care of it. That couch belonged to my grandmother. She bought it two months before she died sleeping on it."

Collins stared at the beige fabric. He could almost see the old woman, the very image of Ruth, lying there gray and wrinkled, that same smile on her lips, her eyelids drawing down like a curtain at the end of a play.

Ruth studied him with some amusement. "It's not contagious, you know."

"No. It's just …" He thought of Ella's father, who had passed away four months ago. "Death's come too close recently. I don't want to be reminded that it's coming for me. I'm not ready to face it yet."

"We all must, sooner or later."

Collins could wait. Ruth Vickeridge, being on the high side of ninety, didn't have that luxury, even though the sparkle in her eyes and the strength of her voice said she'd outlast a century. "I hope you don't mind if I record our conversation."

"Not at all. Would you like something to drink? I have iced tea, or I can make coffee."

"No thank you," Collins said. "I don't want to be a bother."

She laughed. "Terrence thinks you've been an infernal nuisance already."

"Where is he?"

"At the barber shop, he said. Not that he needs a haircut. He's barely got any hair left."

"I'm sorry if I inconvenienced him."

Ruth waved off the apology as though it had been a gnat. "He needs to get out more anyway. What do you want to ask?"

Collins clicked the recorder on. The couch, its morbid fascination aside, gave him an opening. "You mentioned your grandmother. Was that James Ferring Senior's wife?"

"Yes, Amanda was her name."

"What was she like?"

"She was a vibrant woman, strong and opinionated. That didn't sit well with everyone, so I hear, but the family wouldn't have been the same without her."

"How so?"

Settling back in her chair, Ruth twined her fingers in her lap. "Why are you really here, Mr. Collins?"

"Local history. Human interest. The Ferring family is—"

"The Ferring men, you mean. Entrepreneurs, movers and shakers, local celebrities. Is that right?"

Collins squirmed a bit. "I suppose." He knew the broad strokes of the family's history, most of which did indeed focus on the men. In news clippings, the women were mentioned only in passing.

"The lot of them would have faded into obscurity without Amanda." Ruth's eyes gleamed with pride, as though her grandmother's victory had been her own.

Willing to atone for his *faux pas*, he said, "I'm all ears."

"Pop-pop owned the bakery, but she was an equal partner in its operation. Good thing too. He would have squeezed the life out of it, obsessing over expenses and profits. Mom-mom was more liberal with the funds. She said if they put customers first, money would follow."

Collins imagined James and Amanda Ferring butting heads at every turn until one or the other relented. "Did they argue a lot?"

"Not in public or in front of the rest of the family. But once or twice I saw steam coming out of Pop-pop's ears, and I knew whenever I saw Mom-mom's narrowed eyes and pinched lips that he'd done something stupid. I was just a little girl, but I could tell."

"How old were you?"

"Not very. Pop-pop died when I was ten. Mom-mom outlived him by eight years."

"Did she keep her hand in the business her whole life?"

"Oh, yes. By then, Uncle Jim was running the bakery, but she was the elder stateswoman, so to speak, and not just for the bakery. She kept her fingers in all the family businesses right up to the end."

Collins asked about those other businesses, and Ruth enumerated them, corroborating the research he'd already done: farm equipment and supplies, restaurants, hardware stores. She added a clothing store owned by James Senior's daughter Sarah and her husband Anthony, a venture that lasted a little over a decade before failing in the Great Depression.

"After James Junior took over the bakery, he moved it down to the historic district," Collins said when she had finished. "That was before your grandparents passed away, right?

"It was. Pop-pop was still the legal owner of the business, but he no longer cared to manage it, and Uncle Jim was going to inherit it anyway."

"What did James and Amanda think of the move?"

"That was the only time I heard them openly argue. Pop-pop thought it was a stupid move because of the risk of flooding. Mom-mom said floods be damned. They needed to be where the people were, in the thick of things." Ruth laughed. "You couldn't drown her spirit, even if the store washed clean away."

"But the floods did come," Collins said, feeling as though he had to defend the old man.

"Yes. Just in Pop-pop's lifetime, he'd seen enough of them: 1901, 1917, 1923. He knew people who lost a lot and some who lost everything. When the 1938 flood hit, it was a good thing he wasn't there to say 'I told you so.' But the bakery survived it, and all those since then." That look of triumph returned.

"I understand this flood was pretty bad for them, though."

She didn't give any quarter. "I haven't paid much attention. I'm sure they'll pull through."

Odd that she hadn't followed the news. It was her family, after all. "Don't you keep in touch?"

"No. I live out here in my quiet little world, where I can happily pretend the Ferrings don't exist." She looked out the window.

Now that was interesting. Collins invited her to explain: "They've certainly had more than their share of trouble, according to old news reports."

But no explanation was forthcoming. Ruth stubbornly soaked up the greenery, the blue sky, the puffs of cloud, her calm outwardly undisturbed.

"What do you remember about your father?" Collins had already done the math and knew she hadn't been quite thirteen when Roger Ferring was killed by the mob. Even had he lived, Ruth's life would have been shattered. Her father was headed for prison.

"I gather you know what happened," she said.

"In broad outline."

"I remember that he loved me and I loved him. He promised we'd be together in eternity, so I shouldn't worry if I didn't see him for a while."

She delicately wiped at her eyes with her fingers as though removing a speck of dust.

"Did you know what was happening?"

"Only later. Much later."

Collins wondered what it would be like, being so young, knowing your father was being taken from you, not knowing why.

Ruth turned from the window and smiled, old, tired, resigned. "It was a long time ago. Nothing can be changed. I just want him to be proud of me."

Before Collins could dig deeper, the front door opened and Terrence stomped in. He barged into the living room wearing an impressive frown above his blue polo and dark khaki pants. Collins about evaporated under his hot glare.

Ruth raised an eyebrow at her husband. "I thought you'd be longer, with all that hair on your head."

Patting his bald scalp, Terrence looked momentarily confused. "Oh, that's right. It all fell out. That's what being a cop does do you." He narrowed his eyes at Collins. "You ever report on *that*? The high incidence of hair loss among detectives?"

Collins tried to smile through the sickly feeling that had overtaken him.

"No, of course not. You hang out with female detectives. They don't go bald like us guys."

"Terry," Ruth said. "Why don't you get yourself some iced tea? I'll be along soon." She waved him toward the kitchen.

Ignoring the suggestion or command, Terrence faced down his nemesis. "I talked with some of the guys. This little pest is dating the sister of a hotshot lady detective."

Ruth's eyebrows arched at Collins as though she'd uncovered a traitor.

Terrence pointed at the door. "The only dirt you'll find here is in the garden. Get out. Now."

Collins rose slowly. "I ..." He looked to Ruth as though she might be able to overrule the command.

She stood, too, and went to her husband's side. "There's no need to be rude," she said, although not with much conviction. "Mr. Collins is just doing a human-interest story on the Ferrings."

"Then talk to *them*, Collins. My wife ..." He put an arm around her shoulder and pointed at her as though Collins didn't know who he was talking about. "... has nothing to do with those people. Leave her alone, or you'll be dealing with me."

Collins wanted to apologize, but his voice failed him, so he snapped off his recorder, shoved it under his arm, and slipped out. Twenty minutes later, sitting in the parking lot of the Columbia Flier, tremors of fear a thing of the past, Collins began to wonder at Terrence's outburst. Even if he didn't like intrusions or reporters, why mention dirt? And why had Ruth given him that betrayed look?

His recorder nestled in the passenger seat. He pushed the record button.

"Did Terrence Vickeridge ever investigate the Ferrings?" he asked the device. He clicked it off and thought some more, then turned the key and made for Northern District Headquarters.

Chapter 9

By the time he got there, clouds had filled the sky, light and wispy in the east, dark and damp in the west. An afternoon storm was brewing, and Collins hadn't brought his umbrella.

Once admitted to the detectives' offices on the second floor, he made for Corina Montufar's desk and found her mulling over notes scribbled on a notepad.

The sight of her presumed future brother-in-law surprised and pleased her. "Jack! What are you doing here?"

Unsure how to start, he opted for small talk. He nodded at her notes and asked, "Another big case in the works?"

Montufar eyed him like he'd asked to borrow five hundred dollars. "Why do you ask?"

"Just making conversation."

"Not fishing for a story?"

"Of course not."

She tossed her pen onto the notepad. "This one's just a nuisance. One of our more prominent citizens insists he's being stalked. The evidence is slim to none."

"So why not drop it?"

"I would, quicker than Ella can bat an eyelash. But he has Chief Jeffries' ear, and worse, Eric has one of his feelings. Those are hard to brush off."

"Why?"

"Because he's so often right. Let's change the subject. You're here because..." She motioned him to finish the sentence.

Collins sat in the guest chair. "I need information."

"That's what public relations is for."

"This isn't about a current investigation."

"Uh-huh."

She was almost family. Shouldn't she trust him farther than that? "I'm doing a human-interest piece on a local family affected by the flood. I was interviewing a family member when her husband showed up and threw me out."

Montufar laughed. "What did you say to her?"

"Come on, Corina."

"Sorry, you're ever the gentleman, aren't you? If you want to know your rights, you don't have any with respect to another man's house. He can throw you out if he wants."

"It's not that. He's a retired Howard County detective. His name is Terrence Vickeridge. He said he talked to 'some of the guys' and learned I'm dating your sister."

"Snoop. You just can't trust a detective." She winked at him.

"I'm serious, Corina. He thought I was spying for you guys."

"What do you expect me to do about it?"

Now that it came to it, Collins wasn't sure he could make it sound reasonable. Montufar probably couldn't help him even if she wanted to. "Terrance warned me about digging up dirt. Which got me thinking—"

"Ah," Montufar interrupted. "You figure there must be dirt. Why?"

"Because of the family background. Ruth is related to James Ferring IV, who owns the Colonial Bakery. I thought—"

Montufar rocked forward, suddenly engrossed. "You're interviewing the Ferring family?"

"You know them?"

She didn't answer, but she didn't need to. He could tell. She motioned him to continue.

"Terrance was furious. I don't know why. He wasn't even there during the interview. But then I thought, maybe there are a few skeletons in the Ferrings' closets."

Montufar covered her mouth to stifle a laugh.

"Now what?

"Nothing, Jack, nothing. Go on."

Something, he was sure. "In fact, there is something. In 1937, Ruth's father killed one of his nephews and was in turn killed by a mob on the way to court. Ruth now lives in Dayton and says she wants nothing to do with her family. I think there's more to the story. Maybe Terrance Vickeridge investigated a more recent crime connected with the Ferrings. Maybe he found something that implicated his wife and covered it up."

"That's a serious charge, Jack. Do us all a favor and keep it to yourself unless you have evidence. Do you?"

"That," Collins huffed, "is why I'm here."

She turned pensive. "I don't know Terrence Vickeridge. When did he retire?"

"Nineteen years ago."

"Yeah, that was before my time. Rick and Captain Morris would have been here." She picked up her phone. "Let's not get ahead of ourselves. First, we need to hear your whole story." She pushed buttons, then said, "Hey, Rick. Can we get the gang together? Jack Collins stopped by with some interesting information on the Ferrings. He's doing a story on them. No, just background, but there's a strange twist. Thanks." She hung up and rose. "Conference room, Jack."

Following Montufar through the cubicle farm, Collins felt like he was training for the Olympic walking team. Montufar didn't know the meaning of "leisurely." They arrived at the same time as Peller and Dumas. Holly Ross and Theresa Swan had beaten them and were seated on the window side of the room. Montufar introduced him to the younger detectives, ending with, "Rumor has it, Jack will be my brother-in-law someday." She turned an inquisitive look on him.

He smiled, embarrassed at having been put on the spot. "Yeah," he mumbled, "that will happen."

Once they were seated, Montufar said, "Tell us what you know, Jack."

"We've been doing research," Ross chirped before Collins could start. "We probably already know as much as Mr. Collins." She had a notepad in front of her, its front page filled with her scrawl.

Swan didn't look all that confident. She might have been mortified by Ross's interruption.

"Okay," Dumas said. "Let's compare notes, then."

Ross rattled off names, dates, and events, dwelling on the deadly altercation between Roger and George Ferring and Roger's death at the hands of a mob. When she finished, she looked at Collins as though daring him to provide anything further.

He couldn't. They'd obviously read the same sources. "That's pretty much it," he admitted.

"Except," Montufar said, "for the matter of Terrence Vickeridge."

"Who?" Dumas asked while Ross frowned.

Simultaneously, Peller asked, "Terry? What's he got to do with anything?"

"His wife is a Ferring," Montufar explained. "Do you know him?"

Peller shook his head. "Only by reputation. He was here when I arrived, but I didn't work with him. Whitney did."

Collins related his interview with Ruth Vickeridge and its untimely death at the hands of her husband. In the silence that followed, he wondered why they were interested in the Ferrings and what, if anything, his story could add. Montufar wouldn't have brought them together for nothing.

Theresa Swan broke the silence. "What's your next move?" All eyes swiveled to Collins.

"I'll try to interview James again. I'll approach a few other family members, too." He took in their reactions: Montufar approving, Dumas skeptical, Swan waiting for her superiors to weigh in, and Ross keen to confiscate his tape recorder and do the job herself.

And then there was Rick Peller. Peller had noted everyone's reactions and leaned forward. "News stories are Jack's purview. Crime is ours."

Ross started to say something. Dumas waved her to silence, but he couldn't keep Montufar from taking the reins. "His news stories could be helpful. So far, two Ferrings are giving us the silent treatment. Now Vickeridge, a former detective married to a Ferring, is stonewalling."

"Stonewalling Jack," Peller corrected, "not us. You know better than to fish for connections, Corina. There may not be any."

"But there might be," she insisted.

Peller raised an eyebrow at Dumas, who shrugged. Then he turned to Collins, as though the reporter had raised the objection. "If there are, they'll surface in due course. Don't speculate. Stick to facts. We all see dragons in the clouds, but they're never real." Peller tapped his fingers on the table for a moment, then rose and left.

Swan pointed after him. "Did he just…"

Montufar grinned. "Yep."

Collins didn't know Peller well, but he hadn't expected an invitation to collaborate, especially given he had no clue about their interest in the Ferrings. What the hell was going on?

Dumas broke the silence. "Okay, Jack. Bring us what you find, but get it right. The boss doesn't like shoddy research."

"Uh," Collins said. "Sure."

Montufar rose and motioned Collins to follow. "Come on," she said. "Let's see what the Captain remembers about this Vickeridge guy."

He followed, once again straining to keep up until they came to Captain Whitney Morris' corner office. Montufar knocked on the open door and motioned Collins to follow her in.

Morris turned from her computer monitor and raised an eyebrow at the reporter's presence. "What are you doing here, Jack?"

Montufar sat in one of the guest chairs and all but pulled Collins into the other. He had only met the Captain once, a brief encounter while shadowing Eric Dumas a few months back, and he'd never been in her office. It looked a curiously relaxing place to work: windows on two walls overlooking the tree-lined street and parking lot below; bookcases filled with law and police procedure; the clean desktop adorned with nothing but a computer, a notepad and pen, and photos of Morris's husband and three children. The photos must have been outdated. Surely her kids were older than that by now?

Montufar explained for him. "He's doing a story on the Ferrings. Turns out one of the clan is married to a retired Howard County detective named Terrence Vickeridge. Rick says you knew him."

Morris picked up her pen and clicked it a few times, which Collins read as irritation. They probably shouldn't have bothered her with this. "I knew Terry. Sharp guy, more of a grouch than Bill Trengove."

Montufar smiled in amusement. Collins didn't know who Morris meant.

"Is there a chance," Montufar asked, "that he investigated the Ferrings?"

"There's always a chance. Why?"

Collins shifted uncomfortably. "He chased me off, said I shouldn't try to dig up dirt on his wife's family."

Morris clicked her pen again. "I don't like that insinuation."

"I'm not insinuating anything. Mr. Vickeridge has a right to protect his family. But Corina's interested in the Ferrings, so it feels odd."

Morris scooted up to her computer. "The potential homicide from ancient history."

"With a potentially living perp," Montufar reminded her.

Collins made a mental note of that. He'd have to find out what the case was about without looking like he was digging for it.

The Captain tapped on her keyboard and studied the results. "Yeah, there's something."

Collins realized he was holding his breath in anticipation. He forced himself to relax while Morris frowned at the monitor, eyes darting back and forth.

"On December eighth, 1992, Terry investigated an incident at the home of Art Ferring, owner of Ferring Agricultural Supply in Lisbon. A horse belonging to Ferring was shot and killed. No suspects were identified." Morris leaned back and gave Collins an apologetic look, as though she wished she could deliver darker news. "It was deer season. Probably a hunting accident."

"Just another unlucky day in the life of the Ferrings," Montufar said, not bothering to disguise the sarcasm.

Both Collins and Morris raised an eyebrow.

"If you'd seen the files," she started to explain, but Morris stopped her.

"There's a reporter sitting beside you. Watch what you say."

"He won't print anything without our approval." She turned to Collins. "Right?"

"Right," he replied. He wondered if that constituted a binding oath.

Morris waved her on.

"Chuck Ferring's gun shop," Montufar continued, "has a target painted on it. A skeleton washed out of James Ferring's bakery. A literal skeleton. A skull that may be related showed up down the river with signs of trauma to the lower right parietal bone. Ruth Vickeridge's father killed his nephew and was in turn killed by a mob, and Chuck Ferring's grandfather vanished without a trace. Now we learn about this horse. Ask any of them about this stuff, and they lose their voices. What would you call it?"

Morris didn't blink. "PTSD. Sometimes bad things happen over and over to the same good people. It takes a toll."

"Or they're afraid to finger their persecutors."

Morris leaned back and clicked her pen a few more times. With a nod at Collins, Morris asked Montufar, "He does know, doesn't he, that he's a Howard County reporter, not a Baltimore reporter?"

Irritated, Collins snapped "Yeah, he knows. What did Vickeridge say about the horse killing?"

"Just what I said. Hunting accident. There's nothing in the report that would suggest anything else."

"Hunting accidents, skeletons accidentally buried in the cellar. Yeah, I can see that." Collins sprang to his feet and stalked to the door.

"Where are you going?" Montufar asked.

"Libertytown."

"Where?"

"Frederick County. That's where Art Ferring moved his business. Maybe so he wouldn't lose another horse to blind hunters."

He left in an angry rush, not realizing how wound up he was until he stepped into a downpour and remembered he'd forgotten his umbrella. He rushed to his car, a string of curses falling behind him with the rain.

"A reporter, Corina?" Morris shook her head.

Montufar gave her an impish smile. "My future brother-in-law."

The Captain stared, incredulous.

"He's dating Ella. He hasn't proposed yet, but it's only a matter of time."

"Great. Nepotism."

"Admit it, you think he's got a point."

"Points do not make a case. What does Rick think of all this?"

"He thinks Chuck Ferring has an enemy who means him harm, but he can't get the guy to talk. Ferring insists he's being targeted by anonymous gun opponents."

Morris shrugged. "Maybe he is."

"Come on, Whitney, you don't honestly believe—"

"I believe in evidence. And so do you, Corina."

Montufar felt like Morris had slapped her face. Of course she believed in evidence, but that's why she wanted Collins to keep digging. Maybe a reporter could get the Ferrings to open up where the police couldn't.

"Don't turn this into a circus," Morris continued. "Terry Vickeridge isn't an idiot. He and Chief Jeffries were good friends back in the day. If he had a mind to, he could cause all kinds of blunt trauma to this department."

"I'm sure Jack didn't know an ex-detective was hiding in the woodpile." She meant it neither as justification nor apology, but somehow it felt a bit of both.

Morris looked out the window. "What about Eric?"

The Captain was probing the terrain, Montufar knew. She had even more faith in the Peller-Montufar-Dumas collaboration than in evidence. "He hasn't weighed in yet."

"That's totally backwards. Rick has a feeling, Eric doesn't, and you're engaging outside consultants."

Montufar's frustration vented in a small laugh. "Jack came to me."

"If you're trying to force me into retirement so one of you can get my job, it won't work. I'll recommend Bill for promotion, and then you'll all be sorry."

As luck would have it, Trengove was passing by and heard the comment. He stuck his head through the door and flashed a Jack Nicholson smile. "Today the Captaincy, tomorrow the White House. I'm sure I can count on your vote. If not, you're fired." He vanished before they could reply.

"I rescind that threat," Morris groused. "One other thing. The press is all over us about the skeleton. I've told them we're waiting for lab results, but it won't be long before they figure out we already have them. What can we release?"

Montufar explained the details, then added, "Most of it's safe to release, but let's keep the bakery connection to ourselves. Somebody out there might know about it."

Morris jotted a note. "Keep Jack on a leash, Corina."

Montufar smiled.

Morris didn't.

Geri Franklin brought her own umbrella. Peller was ready to share his, but he should have known there would be no need. She was always prepared, no matter the eventuality. The rain fell in heavy spatters as they pulled into the gun shop's empty parking lot and walked to the door, Franklin carrying her equipment bag and Peller a manila folder. "You picked great weather for this," she said with no hint of amusement.

"Not my fault," Peller objected. "There's a permanent cloud hanging over the place."

"Probably serves somebody right. I hope it's not me."

Peller laughed, half at the joke and half in surprise that she'd made one. Closing their umbrellas and shaking them off, they went inside. A bell rang as they opened the door.

Tara Saunders was arranging a display of hunting knives in one of the glass cases on the left side of the store. She looked up with a friendly smile that faded when she realized the bell hadn't heralded a paying customer. "Oh," she said. "Back so soon?"

"Apparently," Peller told her. "Is Mr. Ferring about?"

"In the back. I'll—" She turned to get him, but Ferring appeared in the storeroom doorway at that moment, so she silently resumed work.

Peller crossed the room with Franklin at his side. "Mr. Ferring. I need a favor."

Ferring's irritated frown gave way to worry. "What now, Lieutenant? I've given you everything you asked for."

"Not everything. And since that's not likely to change, I'm doing it the hard way. Have a look at these." He dropped the folder on the display case and opened it. Within were printouts of three stills he'd lifted from the security videos showing the alleged customer handling the weapons Ferring had been trying to sell him.

"What about them?" Ferring asked.

"My tech..." Peller motioned to Franklin. "...will check for prints on those weapons. I need you to get them out."

Ferring made a show of studying the photos, as though he wasn't sure which guns were involved. When he glanced up at Saunders, Peller noticed her watching, bright-eyed, aching for a chance to prove she could identify them faster. "Do you have a warrant?" Ferring finally asked.

Peller wasn't surprised, but he feigned it. "Don't you want the thieves caught, Mr. Ferring?"

Ferring's delayed answer suggested not. "Of course. But the interruption to my business..." He motioned vaguely around the store.

Peller did a three sixty examination, taking his time. "I don't see any customers at the moment. Anyway, this won't take long."

With a resigned nod, Ferring collected three handguns and placed them before Franklin. She slid a consent form at him, which he signed, then the men watched while she gloved herself, transferred the weapons to a white cloth, photographed them, and lifted fingerprints. She worked with practiced efficiency, no movement wasted, and completed the job in short order.

"He was just a customer," Ferring said while she packed up her gear. "Why is this important?"

Peller pulled a folded paper from his left pants pocked, unfolded it, and smoothed it on the display case in front of Ferring. The customer's companion winked at him from the page. He licked his lips and looked away.

"Call me cynical, but I don't trust that woman." Peller refolded the paper and tucked it back in his pocket. "All set?" he asked Franklin.

"All set."

"Thank you, Mr. Ferring."

Ferring nodded and waved them out.

Peller and Franklin popped open their umbrellas and returned to his car. Once they were on the road, he asked, "How did it look?"

"Rather smudged," she said, "but I got a couple good prints. Question is, will they be anybody you know?"

It was a longshot, certainly, but they might get lucky. "Those two looked like pros," he said, as much to assure himself as Franklin. "If they aren't in the database, they probably should be."

"You did your job for the week, anyway. You can spend a relaxing weekend with your girlfriend. Maybe take her out to dinner."

Peller glanced at Franklin. "Girlfriend?"

"The one who calls you Sherlock." She smiled at the rain, her teeth flashing as white and brief as lightning.

"Who told you that?"

Now she looked completely innocent. "You're the detective. You figure it out."

Don't worry, he fumed. *I will.*

Chapter 10

The rain fell heavier the farther west Jack Collins drove until, nearly blind, he pulled off the road five miles east of Frederick to wait it out. He wasn't the only one. Other drivers, lights on and wipers whipping furiously, slowed to a crawl or parked on the shoulder, hazard lights flaring red while rain hammered their roofs. Twenty minutes later, the line of storms passed and the lowering sun broke through, igniting a brilliant double rainbow in the east.

Collins saw it in his rearview mirror as he readied to get back on the road. Instead of moving on, he got out of his car long enough to snap a few photos with his cell phone and sent them to Ella Montufar. He had a momentary urge to ask her to marry him, but proposing by text seemed tacky, even if accompanied by rainbows.

Not long after, he arrived in Libertytown and the home of Ferring Agricultural Supply, a sprawling place dominated by an enormous metal shed—the warehouse—with a brick storefront on one end. A smattering of cars and pickup trucks were parked in the oversized lot, most near the store. A couple of drenched tractors sat along one side, and a semi was parked at a loading dock on the far end of the warehouse. To the west, the Appalachians rolled north and south, sparkling wet after the storm.

Collins parked and splashed to the storefront door. Within, the place smelled of fertilizer and herbicide. He wondered how anyone could stand to work all day in that environment. The storefront's shelves were filled with seed packets, gardening implements and supplies, and bags of potting soil. A few customers browsed the merchandise for their next home garden project. In the back, behind a counter stacked high with farm catalogues and equipment brochures, a pair of towheaded young men were busy, one writing up an order for a customer, the other on the phone talking heavy equipment.

Collins approached the counter and waited. The man on the phone, identified as Tom by his nametag, finished first. "What can we do for you, sir?"

"I'd like to talk to Art Ferring, if he's in."

Tom glanced over his shoulder toward the warehouse. "Sure, can I ask your name?"

"Jack Collins. I'm a reporter with the *Columbia Flier*. I'm doing a human-interest piece on the Ferring family. Local history, that sort of thing."

Reporters might have visited all the time, given Tom's lack of reaction. "Give me a few minutes. I'll see if I can find him. He could be anywhere."

Collins stepped aside so he wouldn't be in anyone's way. Five minutes later, Art Ferring came out to greet him. "Free publicity, eh?" he said with a grin. "I'm on board with that. Jack, right?"

They shook hands. About sixty with a full head of gray hair, Ferring had a strong grip,

Collins nodded. "Pleased to meet you, Mr. Ferring."

"Call me Art. Let's go in back where we can talk. I have an office here somewhere."

Ferring ushered Collins into the warehouse, through racks and stacks of merchandise, and finally to a walled-off area staffed by a team of four middle-aged women who were busy typing on computers and talking on telephone headsets.

"Quite an operation," Collins remarked as he followed Ferring into a separate office that looked like it belonged in a much fancier building. The walls were paneled in faux wood, the desk broad and deep, the filing cabinets practically shining. The space was windowless but well lit.

"We've done well for ourselves," Ferring agreed. He motioned Collins to a comfortable leather chair and sat behind the desk in his own more comfortable one. "Especially since we moved to this location. We're a bit more in the thick of things here. Howard County isn't what it used to be."

"It's growing," Collins agreed. "How long have you been in this location?"

"Since 1993. Business was flat, then. I didn't see any hope of improvement unless we reached a new market. We toyed with opening stores in other counties, but it turned out more economical to pull up stakes and come here. We irritated a few customers back in Howard County, but most of our big clients never set foot in the store anyway. We do a good catalogue and online business."

"Entrepreneurship runs in the family," Collins said.

"Back to my great-grandfather, anyway." Ferring flashed a lopsided grin. "I like to think I've outdone them all, though."

"Which is something, since you weren't in the line of succession for the bakery, so to speak."

"Done your homework." Ferring nodded approval. "My Uncle James was the oldest. My father, he was the second son. His name was Andrew. You probably already know that. He had to strike out on his own, so he started this business and did well by it, but I'm the one built it into what it is today. I won't say we're a household name, but we have customers in seven states, which is more than any of my relatives, including Dad, could say."

Collins thought Ferring was skirting the line between justified pride and boastfulness, a good time to stick a pin in the balloon and see what happened. "You've had your tough times, too, though. There was an incident just before you moved."

Ferring examined his fingernails. "I guess that would be in your archives."

The reporter nodded.

"Ancient history."

"Did they ever find the shooter?"

"Nope. It was a horse, not a person. Legally it was just property damage. The police did what they could, but they wouldn't spend much time and money on it." Ferring shook his head and rearranged the papers on his desk. "Being a businessman, I can't blame them, I guess."

Collins found that an odd statement. "What do you think happened?"

"A careless hunter. It was deer season. Hunters shoot all kinds of things you wouldn't expect." Ferring brightened suddenly and laughed. "I once knew a guy who got paid by a farmer to paint the word 'cow' in bright white on his cows at the start of deer season. The poor guy still lost a few to the hunters every year."

"Was it a racehorse?" Collins thought that might make a difference. With the Preakness just next door, central Maryland was racehorse country. Most racehorses were money pits, cheap neither to acquire nor to maintain, with little chance of a payoff. Still, someone might have a motive to keep a promising horse off the track.

"His name was Benjamin, and no, he wasn't a racehorse. I like to ride. Liked to. I don't anymore."

"Why not?"

Ferring shrugged at the papers. "No time, I guess." He picked up a pen and rolled it between his fingers. "Horses live up to thirty years. They become a part of your life. Dad gave me Benjamin for my twenty-fifth birthday. He was killed on my forty-fifth. A rotten twist of fate."

"Was that in your mind when you decided to move out here?"

The other looked up sharply. "I moved for business reasons."

"But you also got away from where it happened."

Collins couldn't read Ferring after that. The businessman's face became stone, his voice flat and devoid of emotion. "Tragedies happen wherever you are. You run away, they follow you."

Which wasn't an answer, but Collins let it go. "True enough. Your family has certainly had its share."

Ferring neither confirmed nor denied

"Your uncle George, for example. I know you're too young to have known him, but did you hear stories?"

"Same ones you've heard. My great uncle Roger killed George and then was killed by a mob. George was an innocent, only sixteen years old. He was cheerful and hard-working. He worked in the bakery, so everybody knew him. Everyone liked him. That's why the town went mad and took matters into their own hands. Such is the oral history."

"Nobody ever talked about how it happened? Why it happened?"

Ferring rose from his chair like an old man who'd lost his cane. "Human interest. I should have known. People are far more interested in salacious gossip than in honest, hardworking folk. They'd rather watch others crawl disgraced through the mud than read success stories. I have to get back to work. I'll have someone show you out."

He left without giving Collins a chance to reply. A moment later, one of the women from the office appeared in the doorway. "Art asked me to take you up front," she said with a pleasant smile.

Collins followed in silence until they were back in the storefront. Before she returned, he asked, "Have you been with the company long?"

"Twelve years."

"You didn't work at the Howard County store, then."

"No, that was a little before my time. Why?"

"I was just wondering why Mr. Ferring moved out here."

"You should have asked him that when you had the chance."

"Slipped my mind," Collins said with an apologetic shrug.

The woman leaned forward and said in a conspiratorial whisper, "I don't know for sure, but I suspect he wanted to escape his family. He's not too keen on them." She slipped away without allowing him any follow-up questions.

But a theme was developing. Ruth Vickeridge had expressed the same sentiment.

Peller excavated Andrew Hunt's ancestry. He was born in 1987 to Franklin and Cassandra Hunt, Franklin being the son of Stephen Hunt, son of Brian Hunt, husband of Clara Hunt nee Clara Ferring, daughter of James Ferring, Jr. So that answered that.

But did Chuck Ferring know? Did Andrew Hunt? Maybe not. It wasn't a close relationship. James Jr. was Andrew Hunt's great-great grandfather, while James' younger brother Roger was Chuck Ferring's great grandfather. That made Chuck and Andrew third cousins once removed.

Sensing that the family tree had bearing on several matters, Peller charted it on a piece of paper and invited Dumas to have a look. Dumas rubbed his eyes in mock bewilderment. "How does anyone keep all this straight? I could never be a genealogist."

"Fortunately, we don't have to be. We only care that the relationship exists, and then only if they know it and are lying about it. If they don't?" Peller shrugged.

Dumas picked up the paper and studied it. "If they don't, it's a hell of a coincidence."

"Why?"

"Because I say so." Dumas laughed. He handed the paper to Peller. "You don't accidentally steal from a relative. If you do it, you do it with malice aforethought. I'd lay money on it, if I had any."

"Too bad you don't," Peller quipped. "One of us could get rich."

"Rich? How many quarters have you set aside for discretionary spending? Mine always vanish."

"Stop practicing magic and they won't. Speaking of which…" Peller's gaze turned to stone. "Geri Franklin conjured up that nickname Joan gave me. How do you suppose she did that?"

Dumas put up a hand. "Hey, *I* didn't tell her."

"I don't imagine you did. Problem is, I don't remember mentioning it to anyone but you."

Montufar slipped into Peller's cubicle, picked up the family tree, and scrutinized it. "She probably overheard."

Peller inwardly groaned. He hoped she wouldn't ask for an explanation. One too many people already knew the story.

"Impossible," Dumas said. "Rick and I weren't even in the office when it came up."

"But you and I were when you told *me*." She put a hand to her mouth. "Oops. I wasn't supposed to say that." She winked at Peller.

"Damn it, Eric," Peller groused.

Dumas looked away, embarrassed. "Of course I told Corina. She's my fiancée."

Before Peller could reply, Montufar tapped the paper and offered her assessment. "You should talk to Jack Collins about this."

"I already talked to him once today. Why's he nosing around in police business, anyway? Shouldn't he be practicing for proposing to your sister?"

"You gave him permission."

"Only because he was already hip deep in it."

She smiled at the paper, unfazed. "He's on a journalistic mission. It just happens to cross paths with ours. He thinks the Ferrings are hiding something."

That was hardly news. So did the rest of them. "Where is he?" Peller asked.

"Frederick. One Art Ferring owns a business out there. He moved it from Howard County fifteen years ago after somebody shot his horse. A hunter, the report says, but Jack didn't buy that."

Peller didn't either, given what he knew of the Ferrings. "I'll catch up with him on Monday, then."

"I'll tell him to come see you first thing." Montufar set the paper on the desk and stood, then hooked her arm through Dumas'. "Come on," she said. "It's almost closing time, and we have a lot to discuss."

Peller watched her pull Dumas through the rows of cubicles at her breakneck pace. He was happy for them, but he wished Dumas had kept his mouth shut. Regardless, it was time for him to go, too. He'd promised Jerry Souter a ninety-fifth birthday dinner.

Chapter 11

On Saturday, a cool wind pushed ragged cumulus clouds over the land. Dumas opened his apartment windows to the breeze while he vacuumed carpets and waited for Montufar to arrive. Today was launch day for wedding planning, she had decreed, and her to-do list rivaled the Appalachian Trail in length. Dumas preferred simplicity, himself. He'd have been happy to sign the legal papers and be done with it. But he knew she needed to do it up right, so for her sake he would consent to complexity.

Montufar, having chores of her own to dispatch, promised to be there by ten o'clock, lists and catalogues and planner in tow. Waiting and vacuuming, Dumas mulled over the mundane details of life that would follow the honeymoon. Which apartment should they keep? Or should they buy a house? Which side of the bed would be whose? Which side of the closet? Joint or separate bank accounts?

And most perplexing, what would they do about Ozzie White?

The thought surfaced when Ozzie's unmistakable rapping—a series of six knocks—sounded at the door. Unmistakable, yes, but not what it had been. No longer a burst of rapid-fire hammering, these knocks mimicked Frankenstein's monster clomping down the hall. Gone was Ozzie's irrepressible enthusiasm and overwhelming energy. Sunk in grief for four months, he emerged from his darkened apartment only for work, necessities, and the occasional visit with Dumas, usually when Montufar was present. He still possessed that uncanny ability to sense when one of them walked by his door, but he didn't pop out to greet them nearly as often, and when he did, it was in desperation rather than joy.

Dumas supposed this was Ozzie's unique take on the grieving process. Defying the experts, Ozzie had crafted his own innovations on the theme. His path wandered through desperation, bewilderment, a protracted depression, and in the past few days, total apathy. The latter change was subtle. It might have represented progress, but Dumas doubted it. It worried him.

Dumas silenced the vacuum, opened the door, and motioned Ozzie in. Neither man offered a greeting. Ozzie shuffled by, short, dressed in jeans and a black t-shirt, his mop of light hair more disorganized than usual. He made for the forest green couch and flopped on the end, his eyes distant, his mouth a thin line. Dumas settled on his right and gazed out the sliding glass door at the apartment building across the way.

A good ten minutes passed before Ozzie broke the silence. "Where's Corina?"

"She'll be here soon."

"Okay."

Dumas waited, but Ozzie said no more, so he asked, "Anything I can help with?"

"No. I just…" He shrugged.

Dumas knew. Ozzie wanted to see Montufar, wanted to hear her voice. Four months ago, he fell hard for a woman wearing a mask of affection that concealed a killer's heart. She hadn't loved Ozzie; she merely used him to get at Dumas. In the aftermath, Montufar protected Ozzie and nursed him through the trauma. Dumas and even Rick Peller lent support, but Montufar became Ozzie's surrogate mother. Dumas only now realized he had never once heard Ozzie speak of his parents. Where had his real mother been through all of this? Had he no family to turn to?

The thought was a shock. Maybe he and Ozzie were more alike than he realized. Dumas, too, had no close family, or didn't before Montufar came into his life.

"You're welcome to stay," he told Ozzie. "You don't mind if I finish cleaning?"

Receiving neither objection nor consent, Dumas resumed vacuuming. Ozzie remained on the couch, unmoving and silent. He might have been a decoration, except every now and again the breeze blowing through the open windows rustled his hair.

Montufar arrived five minutes early wearing jeans and a floral blouse with a thick blue backpack slung over her right shoulder. Dumas, having just finished his chores, met her at the door, and she paused in the foyer on seeing Ozzie. Dumas shrugged, kissed her on the lips, and put an arm around her. "I suspect," he whispered, "today won't go quite as planned."

She nodded, disentangled herself, and sat by Ozzie. "Hey," she said. "How's it going?"

Ozzie shrugged.

"Meaning?"

"You know."

"Tell me anyway." She smiled and nudged his shoulder.

He didn't smile back. He didn't even look at her. "When's the wedding?"

Dumas hadn't expected that question. Ozzie couldn't have much stomach for romance yet.

Montufar unslung her backpack and set it on the couch. "That's what this is for. We're doing intensive planning today."

Ozzie stared out the patio door, blank, unmoving.

Dumas wandered to the door and watched the clouds blow by. "You want to be a groomsman? I've reserved a spot for you." When that didn't prompt a response, he shot Ozzie a mischievous grin. "Or would you rather buy an Internet ordination and perform the ceremony?"

Montufar shook her head. "Eric."

"It might simplify matters."

"You're not getting off that easy, Sergeant."

"Yes, Sergeant." Dumas gave Ozzie a long-suffering look. "We never win, do we?"

Nowhere near amused, Ozzie stood. "I don't think I'll be there."

Montufar caught his hand. "Come on, Ozzie, we'll be disappointed if you aren't."

He gently pulled his hand from hers and shuffled to the door.

Irritated, Dumas snapped, "So why did you ask?"

Ozzie shrugged again and left.

"Next time," Dumas muttered, "I'll keep my mouth shut." He joined Montufar on the sofa. "That kid needs help."

"I've tried to talk him into counselling, but he refuses."

"Maybe that's not the kind of help he needs."

Montufar leaned into Dumas. He wrapped his arm about her shoulders. "What've you got in mind, a blind date?"

"Not blind per se. Someone safe. Properly vetted and briefed."

"Vetted and briefed?" She laughed. "How romantic."

"I just mean—"

"I know what you mean." Montufar picked up her backpack. Unzipping the main compartment, she began extracting wedding planning materials and placing them on the coffee table: magazines, catalogues, brochures, web printouts. "He won't talk to a woman until he's ready. He barely talks to me."

"But that's the problem, Corina. It could be months or years before he's ready. And if we leave before he's gotten through this ..." He couldn't finish. In spite of the aggravation Ozzie had caused Dumas during the time they'd been neighbors, they'd become honorary brothers. Dumas couldn't abandon him.

"So I'll move in with you," Montufar said reasonably, "and we'll have a built-in problem child to raise." She spread her hands. "Just like you always wanted."

"Whoa, we haven't even discussed children yet."

"So we'd better."

Foul treachery, turning the discussion that direction. "All right. What number do you have in mind? Ten? Fifteen?"

Montufar's eyes widened. "Look, Sergeant, just because I'm Catholic doesn't mean I intend to breed like a rabbit."

Dumas wiped non-existent perspiration from his brow. "Thank God for that. Ozzie will be a handful all by his lonesome. So what's your ideal family size?"

"I haven't given it much thought. I think I'd like to be surprised. Within reason, anyway. How about you?"

He didn't have a number in mind, either. Not a real number. "You know my experience of family. My gut instinct is to not go there." He watched Montufar's reaction, expecting anger, sadness, something, but she didn't blink. Because she did know. His disappearing parents, his drug dealing cousin, his uncle who took him in only to throw him out. He'd told her everything. "Your experience trumps mine," he decided. "I trust your judgment."

She caressed his cheek. "We'll change your experience," she promised. "And if you need a number, let's say one for starters and see what happens after that. I'm sure we'll run out of energy before we reach eight."

Dumas smirked. "I would hope so. Does that settle the question of issue?"

"So ..." Montufar rummaged through the printouts. "There is one other bit."

"That being?"

"Religion."

They had danced around that subject for some time without much discussing it. Montufar was Catholic and Dumas a semi-lapsed Protestant. She, too, had lapsed while struggling to prove herself in her chosen career. As a woman and an immigrant, she'd had an uphill battle in law enforcement. But recent events—the loss of her father not the least of them—had drawn her back into the fold. "Specifically?" he asked.

"I'm obligated to do what I can to raise our children Catholic."

"Ah." Dumas preferred a more free-ranging approach. His religious views had never been structured, and he was still uncertain where he would land. To his mind, that had its advantages. He'd sampled a variety of faiths and found something in all of them. He would naturally encourage his children to do the same. Still, being raised in one faith didn't preclude learning about others, and in the end, children grew into autonomous adults. No point in making a big deal of it. "I don't see a problem with that," he said.

Montufar stopped messing with the papers. "One hurdle cleared," she said with a relieved smile.

"Are there more?"

"Hundreds. The date, the guest list, food, clothing, flowers, the honeymoon, getting out of my lease, and on and on and on. Oh, and one more weird religious thing."

"Every religious thing is weird. So is life itself, for that matter. God has a bizarre sense of humor if you ask me. What is it?"

"Don't take this the wrong way, but I have to inform you that I have an obligation to make sure my faith isn't undermined."

Dumas laughed. "Oh, I am *so* going to pressure you to convert to Rastafarianism."

Montufar gave him a twisted smile. "I'm surprised you even know the word."

"I glommed onto it in case you confiscated my word-a-day calendar. Come on, Corina, I don't force my beliefs on anyone. You know that. I barely know what they are myself."

"I didn't say you would. I only said I have to inform you."

"Wonderful, I've been informed. Now how about we talk about something normal, like food?"

With a long-suffering sigh, Montufar rummaged through her pile of stuff one more time and found the caterers' brochures. "Typical male. Here, have a look at these and tell me what makes your mouth water."

"You," he said, taking the materials without looking at them.

"Down, boy."

"Fine. Plan now, play later."

Montufar opened her planner and settled it on her lap, pen in hand.

Peller rolled out the lawn mower immediately after breakfast Saturday morning and spent forty-five minutes pushing it around his yard.

The breeze was cool and the sun warm, a fine morning for yard work. As he passed by the rose bushes along the front of the house, he noted weeds popping up among them. The roses weren't yet in bloom, but in his mind he saw them in their summer colors: a deep red at the corner of the house, a pale yellow beside it, then a stunning black, then a pure white. Sandra had picked them out, and they had planted them together shortly after moving to Ellicott City from Lockport, New York twenty-six years before. Five years had passed since her death, and he still maintained them for her. He maintained everything exactly as she wanted it.

For the first time in all those years, he wondered if he wasn't a bit obsessed.

Obsessed? he heard Sandra say. *You?*

More than usual, I mean, he replied.

After the mowing was done and the machine stowed in the garage, he donned a pair of gardening gloves, got a trowel, and dug the weeds.

That finished, he stood and stretched. His spine wasn't happy with so much activity. He pressed a fist into the small of his back before noticing Jerry Souter standing on his porch, watching, shaking his head.

"We can't all be as young as you," Peller called.

"Ain't that the truth," Souter replied. He slowly descended and joined Peller in front of the roses. "I guess I'll have to give you my lawn service's number."

"I'm a public servant. I can't afford your lawn service." Peller nodded toward the garage. The duo sauntered toward it.

"You could afford that steak dinner last night."

Peller stashed his gloves and trowel. "That was my one wild indulgence for the year. But it was a friend's birthday, so what the hell."

Souter gave Peller a lopsided smile. "You should have spent it on Joan."

"Don't start. I have four women in my life right now, each one trouble in her own way."

"Sounds about right."

They left the garage. Peller closed up and Souter suggested they sit a while on his porch. Once they were comfortably settled in a pair of rocking chairs, he picked up the thread. "I only count two, Joan and that genius lady detective you work with. What's she done lately?"

"Not that I can comment on ongoing investigations, but she's encouraging her almost-brother-in-law to meddle in police business."

"Ah, nepotism. Gotta love it. And the two mystery ladies?"

"Sandra isn't a mystery. Not in that sense, anyway."

Souter eyed the homes across the street as though calculating the cost of repainting them. "What's she done lately? Haunted the house?"

"Just my head."

"That's normal, if you ask me."

"Amanda does the same for you?"

"Not as much these days as the first eight years, but yeah, on and off."

It probably wasn't the same. Peller's experience of Sandra was terribly immediate. Sometimes he swore she was standing right behind him while they talked. But it was too intimate to discuss even with Souter, so he changed the subject.

"The other's a young woman I encountered in the course of an investigation a few months back. There wasn't much left of her. I try to help, but..." He shook his head.

"Drugs." It wasn't a question.

"Among other things."

"And you're all she's got now."

Peller nodded. He watched a blue pickup zip by, going twenty over the speed limit.

"No, you're not," Souter said.

"Everyone who was ever important to her is dead."

"People, maybe. But rumors to the contrary, the Almighty still lives."

Peller didn't think Shania North was much into religion.

Displaying his uncanny ability to read minds, Souter said, "You don't have to bind and gag her and haul her into church slung over your shoulder, son. Just pray for her and keep on doing what you're doing."

"What *am* I doing? It's just talk."

"You're being a friend."

"An uncle, she suggested."

Souter nodded. "There you go, then. She still has family."

Irritated without knowing why, Peller rocked a bit harder.

Souter smiled a crooked smile and matched his pace.

Only hours later, as afternoon slipped into evening and Peller was broiling a t-bone for himself did it occur to him that Shania did have one tenuous religious connection. While working as a stripper before her slide into drugs and near death, she became involved with a young man named Jayvon Fletcher. On a spiritual quest, Fletcher had been learning about the Bahá'í Faith when he crossed paths with Shania and tried to rescue her from her lifestyle. It was a classic case of white knight syndrome, but his friendship had touched Shania and might have done her some good had Jayvon not been murdered.

The young man was gone, but his contacts in the Columbia Bahá'í community remembered him. Should he put Shania in touch with them? Not that she'd be interested in the religion, but maybe through them she could reconnect with Jayvon in some way. That might give her strength to keep fighting.

Peller let the idea swirl through his mind as he ate, and by the time dinner and cleanup was done, he knew he had to try. He looked up his contact in the Bahá'í community—Winston Marley—and placed the call. Marley answered just before voicemail kicked in.

"Lieutenant Peller! How've you been? I didn't expect to hear from you again." His voice projected the same curious mix of friendliness and authority that Peller remembered from before.

"I didn't expect to be calling. I need a favor."

"Something to do with Jayvon?"

"Peripherally. You recall he had a girlfriend he was concerned about."

Marley started to laugh, then coughed in a feeble effort to cover it up. "Yeah, I remember."

Peller didn't blame him. One of Jayvon's friends called Shania "possessed." Peller never did learn if the suggestion was serious or facetious, but Jayvon had taken it seriously and grilled Marley on the subject. "Well," he said, "she's in a bit of trouble. She could use some help."

"What sort of trouble?"

"Opioid addiction. She's bouncing in and out of rehab and is pretty low right now."

The dead air suggested Marley wasn't thrilled about jumping into that mess, but eventually he asked the logical question. "What can I do for her? Rehab isn't my specialty."

Marley didn't even know Shania's name, only that she existed. This would be a lot for him to digest. "When Jayvon disappeared, she had no idea what became of him. She thought he'd abandoned her. After that, she fell in with a bad crowd, the very people mixed up in his death. You were one of the last people to know Jayvon. I think she might respond to that. It might help her keep going."

"That sounds like more than a bit of trouble."

Peller didn't bother agreeing with the obvious.

"I can talk to her, I guess, but I'm neither a doctor nor a therapist."

"You don't have to be. A connection to Jayvon and a sympathetic ear could be enough at this point."

Marley gave it a moment before asking, "What's her name?"

"Shania North."

"She have any family?"

"She doesn't have anyone but me at the moment, and that's not much."

"What's your connection, aside from the fact that you caught Jayvon's killer?"

"Nothing at all, Winston. I just don't want her to end up dead, too."

One final moment of silence later, Marley capitulated. "Then I can hardly refuse. How do we do this?"

Peller hadn't thought that far ahead. "I'll talk to Shania, see if she's interested in meeting you. If so, we can get together somewhere of her choosing. I'll let you know when and where."

"All right, then. I'll wait for your call."

"Thank you, Winston. This means a lot to me."

"I guess it must. No problem."

After he hung up, Peller wondered what was going through Marley's head now. That must have been the strangest request he'd ever received. Peller hoped the deal wouldn't blow up in his face. Shania might be angry with him for telling Marley about her. Or their meeting might make matters worse. Not for the first time, he wondered why he was meddling in Shania's life.

But how could he not when she needed help and he alone could give it?

Peller could tell he wasn't going to sleep well that night.

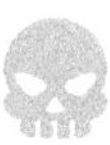

When on Sunday afternoon the deal did blow up in his face, the explosion erupted in an unexpected quarter. It began when Joan Churchill called for a favor.

"I bought a new dresser," she explained. "I didn't realize until I got home that I can't get it into the apartment alone. It's one of those assembly required units packed in three heavy boxes."

"It could stay in your SUV," Peller quipped. "Might come in handy there."

She laughed. "Oh, stop. Could you come over this afternoon?"

"Yeah, I can schlep heavy stuff. What time?"

"Whenever you're free. I'll be here."

He told her three o'clock and got there with two minutes to spare. He parked next to her vehicle and called her. She came down, and they jointly hauled the first box into the building, rode the elevator up, and wrestled the load through her door. He detected without identifying or even quite noticing it the smells of something good simmering on the stove. A short trip down a narrow hall followed, then a left turn into her bedroom. She had already removed whatever the new dresser was meant to replace, and her clothes were stacked in neat piles on the double bed. Peller didn't mean to snoop, but his detective's eye took the garments in with a glance. His key takeaway, embarrassingly enough, was that she wore utilitarian underwear.

Two more trips, and the delivery was complete, but then she needed help assembling the unit, so Peller assisted with that, and by the time they were done it was after four o'clock. Churchill suggested he might as well stay for dinner. "I'm trying out a Bolognese recipe I got online. I made plenty."

So that's what smelled so good. A trap nicely sprung. Peller consented to stay, grudgingly on the inside and with a smile on the outside. He comforted himself with the knowledge that she was a good cook. "I have to make a phone call, though," he told her.

"Don't tell me you're working on Sunday again."

"Not exactly. It's a volunteer activity."

"You're just trying to get out of helping me. Never mind, I'm just going to cut up a few veggies for a salad." She set to work, pulling a chef's knife from a block on the counter and a red onion, a green pepper, and a tomato from plastic bags nearby.

Matters were getting a bit too domestic for Peller's taste, but he didn't comment. He placed the call. When he said, "Hi, Shania," Joan's mouth twitched.

"Hi, Rick. Didn't think you'd be checking on me again so soon."

"I think I found some help for you."

Shania didn't answer at once. She'd probably had her fill of people trying to help. "What kind?"

"Call it emotional support. There's someone I'd like you to meet. He knew Jayvon. He was one of the last people to see him."

More silence, then she whispered, "Jay."

Peller waited. Joan sliced with a bit more force.

"What's his name?" Shania asked.

"Winston Marley."

"Was he Jay's friend?"

"More of an acquaintance." Peller didn't think it would help to mention the religious nature of the connection.

"Why?"

"I just think you should talk to him. It might help you work through some things."

"He's not a counsellor, is he?"

"No. Just—" Peller wasn't sure how to put it. He wasn't even sure it made sense, now that he'd asked her. "Jayvon had questions. Winston tried to help him find answers. I think he could help you, too."

Shania drew a long breath. "I don't know what good it will do."

"I don't, either, Shania, but maybe it's worth a shot."

"Okay."

The trust implicit in the single word rattled Peller. He almost wanted to tell her to forget it, but he couldn't betray her faith. "When and where is up to you. Whatever you're comfortable with."

"I'll be here for another week. You can bring him when you visit Wednesday, if you want."

"All right. I'll see if he's available."

After they said their goodbyes, Peller leaned back and watched Churchill. Pointedly ignoring his attention, she wielded her knife a bit too hard, pushed the vegetable slices around with a tad too much force. He didn't need to ask why.

She slammed a drawer shut for emphasis.

Might as well get it over with. "Just say it," he prompted.

"I don't know why you waste your time on that girl."

"She needs help."

"You're not in that business. You catch criminals. You don't rehabilitate addicts." Almost inaudibly, she added, "Or sluts."

"Joan—"

"She's a stripper, Rick. How does it look, you hanging around with her?"

Peller stood. "I'm not hanging around with her. I'm—"

"What would you call it? You visit her, you call her, you—"

"Don't accuse me of cheating, Joan. I'm not one of your ex-husbands. I'm trying to help someone who's been through hell. Why is that a problem?"

She slammed the knife flat side down on the cutting board. "I don't understand your obsession with her."

"Sandra would have."

Joan leaned heavily on the counter, shaking. He could imagine her squeezing her eyes to keep back tears. He shouldn't have said that, but she was way out of bounds, too.

Head down, she didn't move. Neither did he. The silence all but suffocated him.

"I'll let myself out," he said. He paused at the door, but she neither moved nor spoke, so he left. Only once he was in his car pulling out of the parking lot did he wonder if he had left too precipitously. He should have apologized, should have given her a chance to apologize, should have tried harder to explain. It wasn't anybody's fault, really. Joan had been wronged, too. She wasn't so much reacting to Peller's need to help Shania North as to ghosts of her own past.

Sandra might have told him to go back, but she wasn't talking to him, either.

He stopped for a drive-through cheeseburger on the way home.

Chapter 12

On Monday, June fifth, storms rolled in before sunrise, darkening the world from rush hour to late morning. Rain fell in waves, heavy, light, heavy, light, but what little thunder there was remained distant.

Peller found it hard to concentrate on much of anything beyond the previous evening. He kept replaying his argument with Churchill as though he could turn back the clock and make it right. Fortunately, Jack Collins showed up to distract him. The reporter nearly bounded in at nine thirty, two manila folders jammed with papers tucked under his arm. Peller wondered why he didn't keep his notes on his cell phone like every other kid in the world these days.

Settling in beside the desk, Collins slid one of the folders to Peller and said, "Copies for you." Then he opened the other and spread out a few papers. Some were printouts of old newspaper articles, some hand-drawn snippets of family trees. Others were transcripts of the interviews he had conducted. He started with the latter, pushing a paper at Peller but giving him no time to read before launching into an explanation.

"Ruth Vickeridge," he told Peller, "idolizes her grandmother, Amanda Ferring. According to Ruth, Amanda was the driving force behind the family's success. Her uncle, James Ferring, Jr., moved the bakery from its original location west of town into the historic district in 1928 over his father's wishes. He got away with it because Amanda approved the move."

Collins pulled the paper back and shoved some news clippings at Peller. "Enter George Ferring, James Jr.'s son. He worked in the bakery and according to Art Ferring was a popular figure about town. Cheerful, hard-working, well-liked. When Ruth's father, Roger Ferring, killed him during an altercation, a mob exacted revenge before Roger got to trial."

"In 1937," Peller recalled.

"Right. George was only sixteen, Roger thirty-nine, and Ruth thirteen. She only learned later why her father had been killed."

Peller scanned the news reports. "Rough, but she survived it. She's in her nineties now."

"She hates her family, though. She has nothing to do with them anymore." Collins tapped one of the news reports. "I first thought her disaffection grew from that seed, but there's more. Roger Ferring fought in World War I. He received a dishonorable discharge."

"Yeah, we knew that, too. Did you find out why?"

Collins shrugged. "Ruth didn't say. I'm not sure she knows. But he was a black mark on the family's good name. A couple of his relatives, including James Jr., said so on the record."

"You think that's what alienated her?"

"It sure would have alienated me."

Peller picked up one of the family trees Collins had drawn and leaned back. "Chuck Ferring is Roger's great-grandson."

Collins arched his eyebrows, but not in surprise, given his smug grin.

Peller could guess what he was thinking. An entire branch of the family ostracized, an old homicide possibly stemming from that, descendants perpetuating the fight. It made for an interestingly dark tale, but it was mere speculation. "Even Eric wouldn't go out on that limb without some evidence," he said drily.

"Oh, there's plenty of evidence."

Peller put down the paper and waited.

Collins held up his hand and ticked off his reasoning on his fingers. "A body buried under the bakery. The history of vandalism and theft targeting the gun shop. Art Ferring's horse, which was a birthday present from his father, killed by an alleged hunter on Ferring's birthday twenty years later. The fact that none of the family will talk about any of it."

"The horse was killed on Art Ferring's birthday?"

"It was."

"That's interesting," Peller said, "but it's all circumstantial. A family feud might be suggestive if it wasn't seventy years ago. But after that much time?" Peller shook his head. "Even the Hatfields and McCoys weren't at each other's throats for that long."

Collins wouldn't be deterred. "We know Roger was a family pariah, that he killed George, and that he paid for it with his life. The Ferrings owned several businesses over the years, but the only three remaining are the bakery, the farm supply company, and the gun shop. Two of those have been targets, and a skeleton washed out of the third."

Peller pushed all the papers back to Collins. "I'd be lying if I said I wasn't intrigued. But I'm afraid it's not enough."

Collins grinned and removed another paper from the folder, placing it on the table like the final card of a royal flush. "Roger's son William disappeared and was presumed dead in 1947. He was twenty-one when he vanished, leaving a young wife and a son barely a year old." He leaned back. "Do the math."

Peller didn't need to calculate. Had William's remains washed out in the flood? It would be easy to check, assuming Chuck Ferring was willing to part with a DNA sample. His stonewalling over the robbery notwithstanding, he might care to know what became of his grandfather. Picking up the paper and scanning the old news story, Peller nodded. "That," he said, "is something we can use. Why did you bury the lead, Mr. Journalist?"

"Because," Collins said, "you wouldn't have listened to anything that followed."

Peller wasn't sure if he wanted to laugh or punch him. He settled for a tight-lipped smile. "What's next on your agenda?"

"I'm going back to James Ferring. If nothing else, he's the flood victim. I can't very well do the story without him."

"Good luck with that. Not that I'm counting on it, but feel free to drop by if you learn anything of interest to us."

After Collins left, Peller assembled an email recapping Collins' information. He directed Theresa Swan to visit Chuck Ferring. Ferring was sick of Peller's face and would see more of it before this was done, so prudence demanded someone else ask for the DNA sample. He assigned Holly Ross to follow up on the horse shooting. It would be good experience for her.

That done, he opened the folder Collins had left him and used the material to update the family tree he had started.

Leaning back, he picked up the paper and studied it. This investigation rather resembled the tree, branches spread far and wide. How long until Captain Morris told them to file it away unresolved? If murder lurked here, it was sixty years past and the culprit likely old and bent if not dead and buried. The vandalism and killing of the horse were but property damage with three-year statutes of limitations. Only the gun theft was clearly actionable. Yet that sense of unease remained with him. He couldn't explain it, but he knew.

Something worse was coming.

The rain continued, lighter now, as Detective Swan maneuvered her emerald green Toyota Corolla into The Lodge's parking lot. She'd picked up the five-year-old car for a song eighteen months ago and hadn't regretted it. It got her there and back again without trouble and fit her public servant budget. That's all she asked of a vehicle at this stage in her life.

Parking beside a huge black Dodge Ram with oversized tires, she spent a few minutes examining the building. She liked to get the lay of the land before talking to people, on the theory that places could tell you things just as surely as people. If the weather had been better, she would have taken a walk around the parking lot and checked it out front and back, but she didn't feel like splashing through puddles. Anyway, The Lodge didn't look like much. A freestanding building, its storefront could have been any small shop: big glass windows, a glass door with the hours posted on it, a bit dingy with age. If anything stood out, it was the bars on the windows. The store gave no indication of the excess hostility it had attracted over the years.

Had the other detectives missed something? If so, she was missing it, too.

Stepping out of her car, she trotted through the rain into the store, where she recognized Chuck Ferring from Peller's description. He had a careless look to him. Maybe it was his untucked button-down shirt or the way its stripes undulated over his stocky frame or his beard, bushy and tangled. He leaned on the glass display case at the back of the store, a stack of papers before him, his face taught with concentration. He didn't look up when the bell jangled at Swan's entry.

The sound did get the attention of the other two men present. Discussing a weapon inside the display case, they paused to stare at her. Behind the counter, a young worker who must be Andrew Hunt had a startled look about him. Swan could see why Peller pegged him for a Ferring. Although thin and clean shaven, the shape of his face mimicked Chuck Ferring's, save his sharper nose.

Hunt's customer towered over him, a good six and a half feet tall with wiry gray hair. Dressed in gray slacks and a pale blue shirt, he might have been a business leader. His eyes narrowed as he studied her, then he muttered and turned his back on her. Hunt resumed his sales pitch.

A wave of unease coursed through Swan's body, but it passed quickly. This would be a simple job. No need to be jumpy. "Mr. Ferring?"

Ferring looked up. "Yes, ma'am?"

"I have an unusual request."

"I have a request, too," the customer grumbled.

Ferring glared at him. "Don't start, Brandon."

"I'll start whenever I damn well want," Brandon replied without turning.

Ferring shook his head. "Sorry, ma'am. Go on."

"I'm Detective Theresa Swan, Howard County Police." She showed her warrant card. "We—"

Ferring crossed his arms over his chest. "Come on! I already told Lieutenant Peller everything I know!"

Andrew Hunt's head snapped up in alarm. Brandon turned, jaw clenched, anger flashing in his eyes. That sense of unease overtook Swan again. Fighting the urge to walk away, she lowered her voice. "This is a different matter, sir, not about the robbery. Maybe we could talk in private?"

Brandon started toward them with measured steps, his eyes locked on Swan's face. "Don't do it, Chuck. Don't let her get you alone."

Ferring pointed a finger at him. "Can it, Brandon. I'll handle this."

Brandon snorted. "You? You don't know what the hell you're doing. You never did." He had halved the distance between himself and Swan. "And you, girl, get in your Matchbox™ car and go back to your mama in Alabama."

Swan's heart hammered in her chest. The rest of her body froze in place.

Brandon spat at her but wasn't close enough to score a hit. His saliva splashed on the floor two feet in front of her. He followed with a racial epithet that hit Swan like a gut punch.

"Brandon!" Ferring roared. "Get out *now* or I'll call the cops!"

"I'm not the one's leaving. This bitch is."

Trembling uncontrollably, Swan backed up until she ran into the counter while Brandon closed the gap in seeming slow motion. Thought abandoned her. She knew the fear of a mouse cornered by a cat. Brandon loomed over her. He could pick her up and throw her through the window one-handed if he wanted.

A noise echoed in her ears, someone shouting across a great distance, pleading, "No, no, no!" and Brandon backed off, eyes wide, hands high in the air, mouth blubbering, "I'm kidding, just kidding, okay? C'mon, it was just a *joke!*"

At first, Swan didn't know what was happening. Then she realized her arms were stretched before her, her trembling hands training her gun on Brandon's chest. If he came at her again, she'd kill him. She wouldn't be able to stop herself. She might do it anyway. He deserved it.

She *wanted* to kill him.

"Ma'am," Ferring whispered.

She swallowed. Her hands trembled but didn't lower.

"Ma'am?"

Swan took a deep breath. *Steady*, she told herself. *Steady*. "Maybe you guys missed it," she said with more conviction than she felt, "but I *am* the cops."

Brandon nodded far too emphatically. "Yeah, yeah, I got it."

She looked at the gun. She looked at the fear and hatred in his eyes. He deserved it. But she didn't fire. If she did, he would win.

"Get the hell out of here before somebody gets hurt." She shifted her aim to the ground without lowering her guard. Brandon scuttled to the door, dove into his truck, and roared off. A full minute passed in dead silence. Neither Swan nor Ferring nor Hunt moved. They might not have breathed.

"God." Swan tucked the gun away and turned on Ferring. "You sell firearms to that scumbag?"

Ferring and Hunt leaned on their respective counters. They both looked like they might pass out. "He's harmless," Ferring said. "He wouldn't—"

"It sure looked like he would. I almost killed him."

Ferring's jaw clenched. He looked away.

"God. 'Black female cop kills white man.' I'd be hanged, drawn, and quartered." She leaned on the counter, too.

"You need to sit down?" Ferring might have needed a chair more than her. He still couldn't look her in the eye, but his concern felt genuine.

"No." She wasn't about to show further weakness. "No, I'm good."

He nodded without much conviction. "You said—you said you needed my help."

Probably any chance of gaining his cooperation had been blown, but she had to try. "We think we've found the remains of your grandfather, William Ferring."

Ferring gaped at her. Hunt, more frightened than ever, scuttled into the back as though he'd remembered an urgent chore.

"Where?" Ferring said. "How?"

Her hands, still pressed to the countertop, trembled. "The flood washed some bones out of the ground. They belonged to a man of about twenty and date to the time of William's disappearance."

"The bakery?"

How had he known? "Yes." She waited for him to say something, anything, but he seemed to be staring across the decades and no longer registered her presence. "Does that mean something to you?"

Ferring blinked himself back to the present. "No. My dad always said granddad went west, to the Rockies. Said he'd talked about it for a couple of years. Then one day, he was gone."

"Leaving a wife and small child?"

Ferring, rediscovering his irritation, shuffled his papers. "It happens. What's it to do with me?"

"To identify the remains, we need a DNA sample from a close relative."

"Talk to my father or my great aunt Ruth."

"We didn't want to bother Ruth." Not after Jack Collins had done such a great job of bothering her. "And we don't have contact with your father right now. I have the kit with me. I can get the sample and we'll let you know as soon as we have the results."

"I tried to be helpful and look where it got me. You cops are a damned nuisance, you know that?" He sure had changed his tune in a hurry. Moments ago, he would have done anything to make her forget Brandon.

She withdrew the sample kit from an inside pocket in her jacket and set it on the counter. "It's easy, just a cheek swab, the same as those ancestry DNA tests everyone is into."

Ferring made a face like a kid confronted with steamed spinach. "I'm not into it. I've had enough of my family."

"Don't you want to know—"

"No. I never knew my grandfather. I grew up believing he'd abandoned his family. Now you're saying he was lying dead under that damned bakery all these years with dear cousin Jim keeping watch over him. That'd be far worse. If that's what happened, I'd rather not know. Unless you plan on buying something, leave me the hell alone."

Swan pocketed the test kit and left, consoling herself that the trip hadn't been a total waste. Peller would be disappointed, although not surprised, that Ferring hadn't cooperated, but he'd be pleased to learn that Andrew Hunt definitely knew he was a Ferring.

Not to mention that Chuck Ferring knew where his grandfather had surfaced.

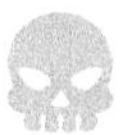

Detective Holly Ross threw herself into her assignment. First order of business was a review of the case file on the shooting of Art Ferring's horse on December eighth, 1992. She got a mug of coffee, pulled the file up on her computer, and read it in detail, twice. There wasn't much. Ferring owned a large home and a modest stable of four horses west of Glenelg off Triadelphia Road where he lived with his wife Cassie, their son Doug, who was a senior in high school, and when she wasn't away at college, their daughter Carol. Ferring's favorite horse, a bay named Benjamin, had been a gift from his father on his twenty-fifth birthday. Ferring had been at work and the kids at their respective schools when Cassie heard gunshots and called the police. She gave a minimalist statement and left her husband to do most of the talking even though he hadn't been there at the time of the incident. That seemed curious. Ross jotted it down on a legal pad.

Peller had passed along a new tidbit from Jack Collins: the horse had been killed on Ferring's forty-fifth birthday. The file contained no mention of that detail. Probably Ferring hadn't volunteered it, which Ross thought odd. Surely the man would have found it significant and said something? She made a note of that, too.

Benjamin had been out to pasture on the north side of the property near a stand of woods where a hunter might have been prowling, but Ross didn't like it. Consulting a map, she found those woods long and narrow with a cluster of homes on the far side. Nobody should have been hunting there. It was part of Ferring's property and posted no hunting. Another note on the legal pad.

The manner of the killing also bothered Ross. Benjamin had been shot by a thirty-caliber rifle, a popular weapon for deer hunting. He had been struck three times, not with incredible precision but enough to do him in. A hunter would have tried to kill with one shot and dispatched the animal with a second if the first wasn't clean. Ross wrote it down.

Then-detective Terrence Vickeridge had recorded the facts but didn't go out on a limb. It was easy to conclude the shooting had been an accident, and anyway the victim was only a horse. The only possible crimes were trespassing and property damage, and Ferring hadn't pressed for any other conclusion. He suggested neither suspects nor motives. A search of the woods turned up nothing by way of footprints, torn clothing, or spent casings. At the end of the day, Vickeridge probably had no choice but to call it accidental. So, one final note on the legal pad.

The anomalies suggested somebody wasn't being entirely truthful, but who? Art Ferring? Terrence Vickeridge? Ross couldn't go to Vickeridge; Sergeant Montufar had warned her off that route. Collins had recently visited Art Ferring, so she didn't think it prudent to approach him immediately. Given the circumstances, the best person to interview was the all but forgotten woman, Cassie Ferring.

Ross dug up her address and phone number, then placed a call to a detective on the Frederick City police force, Sam Kohler. Ross and Kohler had dated briefly in high school. Although they hadn't quite clicked, they remained friends ever since. Living in different counties now, they maintained occasional, semi-professional contact.

"I need a favor," she told him.

"So long as it doesn't cost me anything,"

"We're investigating a family situation, and part of the family lives in your jurisdiction."

"Making an arrest?"

"Just talking."

"About what?"

"It's an old case," Ross said. "Fourteen years old. A horse belonging to the family was shot and killed. It was probably an accident, but something doesn't add up. I want to double-check a few details."

She could almost see the sparkle in Kohler's eyes when he said, "This must be an excuse to visit me, right?"

"If I needed an excuse, I'd think up a better one than that, Sam."

Kohler laughed. "I hope so. Which I guess means the horse thing is real."

"Very real."

"Okay, no problem. I'll clear it for you. You want an escort, for old times' sake?"

"That would be great. If it's not too soon, I can be there in an hour."

"Perfect. And after, I'll buy you lunch."

"That'll cost you," she reminded him

"Damn," Kohler quipped. "Stuck with the bill again."

Art and Cassie Ferring owned a three-quarters of a million-dollar home northeast of Frederick, where civilization abutted the Blue Ridge of the Appalachians and the surrounding forest absorbed the noise. Sam

Kohler called ahead to let Mrs. Ferring know they were coming and verified that her husband would be at work.

"He's the last person I want to talk to," Holly Ross explained as they drove north on U.S. 15. "A reporter of our acquaintance already visited him. It didn't go well."

"A reporter." Kohler kept his eyes on the road but couldn't disguise his disbelief.

"Not my fault. He came to us. Plus, he's dating my Sergeant's sister."

Kohler shook his head. "If you want a transfer, one of our guys is retiring in six months. I can put in a good word for you." Clear of the city, he exited the highway and took a country road westward.

Ross watched the green and golden pastures and fields passing by. Probably Kohler was joking, but it didn't sound like it. He only had two voices, one all business and one lighthearted. This time, he straddled the line. "I'll let you know once the case is put to bed. These people are practically living legends in our department. I suppose they know what they're doing."

"They say it's a fine line between genius and madness. So what's the story on the horse?"

Ross gave him the twenty-thousand-foot overview of the Ferrings and what she'd picked out of the investigation report on the shooting. "The timing is the weirdest thing," she said. "Ferring's reticence is second. And it's not just him, it's the whole family. A skeleton washes out of a basement, and they shrug their shoulders. Their gun shop is vandalized over and over, and they act like it's no big deal. How can anyone have that big a target painted on them and not know it?"

"I gather denial isn't the going theory."

"They're hiding something for sure."

They passed horse and crop farms, produce stands and woods, all dotted by clusters of houses. The line of the Blue Ridge lurked behind everything.

"You think Cassie Ferring knows?" Kohler asked.

"I think she knows something. Maybe not everything, but something."

"Why?"

"Because her husband didn't let her talk."

Kohler flashed a lopsided grin. "According to most wives, most husbands don't."

"Is that what Mary says about you?" Kohler and his wife Mary had celebrated their first anniversary three months before. Ross had met the lady only once and found her pleasant enough, although she had to admit to a surprising twinge of jealousy.

He smiled at the road. "Not yet, but guys more experienced than I say it's only a matter of time."

They arrived at the Ferring home and drove up a long, sloping driveway that led to a four-car garage to the left, at the south end of the house. White with black faux shutters flanking every window, it had a strangely unpretentious look, its size notwithstanding. The mountains loomed behind, no more than half a mile distant. Parking, they approached the door to find Cassie Ferring waiting for them in black jeans and a dark green blouse, her thin, gray hair hanging loose just above her shoulders. She might have been a country grandmother but for the incongruity of the almost-mansion.

After introductions, she led them inside to a sitting room where wingback chairs and a floral sofa huddled around a cherry coffee table. A vase of white and yellow roses sat on the table, and family pictures hung on the walls.

"Coffee, tea, anything?" she asked.

"No thank you," Ross replied. Kohler put up a hand to signal he was good.

Cassie settled herself in her chair and cocked her head. She might have been waiting for a child to explain a broken china plate.

"Detective Kohler mentioned I'm from Howard County?" Ross asked.

"He did. Which means it must be about Benjamin, although I can't understand why you'd want to talk about that all these years later. In fact, I don't remember you at all."

"I wasn't involved in the investigation. It was a little before my time."

Cassie arched her eyebrows.

"We junior detectives get to clean up old files," Ross said.

"What's to clean up? It was an accident."

"A few questions never got answered, or even asked. Mostly routine stuff."

"Then you should talk to my husband. It was his horse."

Ross leaned forward, her face expressionless. "You reported the incident."

After a moment of silence, Cassie nodded. "I did, but I only heard the gunshots and saw Benjamin on the ground. I don't know anything else."

"You didn't go out?"

"I know a gunshot when I hear it. I didn't see anybody, but they could have been back in the woods, waiting. I wasn't about to go out there."

"Benjamin was a birthday present, wasn't he?"

"That's right. Art's father gave him the horse on his twenty-fifth birthday." Cassie smiled to herself. "He was so surprised. We were dating at the time. We went straight out and spent the rest of the day riding."

Ross waited, but Cassie didn't volunteer the rest of it. "Strange, wasn't it, that Benjamin was killed on your husband's birthday?"

Cassie clasped her hands in her lap and frowned but didn't answer.

"Stranger still that nobody, not even your husband, mentioned the fact."

"He was in shock. He was very fond of Benjamin. It was like losing a family member."

"But you might have mentioned it. Why didn't Mr. Ferring want you talking to the police?"

Cassie looked out the window. "What does that mean?"

"The investigator spoke with you once, according to the report. After that, he only spoke with your husband, even when reviewing your statement."

"Art knew everything I told the police. There was no need to talk to me again."

Which was deflection, but Ross let it go. "What do you think happened, Mrs. Ferring?"

"It was ruled an accident."

"I didn't ask what it was ruled. I asked what you think."

"I don't like what you're insinuating."

Ross raised her eyebrows. "I don't care whether you like it or not. I want your answer."

"I have nothing to say," Cassie snapped. "So you can leave now."

Kohler put up a hand. "Let's take a breath here. Ma'am, Detective Ross is only trying to tie up a few loose ends. She's not accusing you or your husband of anything. You have to admit, it's one crazy coincidence, a horse given to your husband as a birthday present also being killed on his birthday. Wouldn't you say?"

Cassie flexed her fingers and refolded her hands in her lap. "I suppose. But so what?"

"If the original investigator had known about it, he might not have been so quick to call the shooting an accident. He might have dug a little further. But as it is, it could look like somebody didn't want him digging. You see?"

She didn't answer, so Ross retook control "Why didn't Mr. Ferring want it mentioned?"

"It's nothing," Cassie all but whispered. "Family business, nothing to do with the law. I probably shouldn't even have called, but I heard the gunshots and saw Benjamin on the ground, and I was afraid ..." She put a hand to her forehead and closed her eyes.

"Afraid of what?" Kohler asked gently. "That someone meant to hurt you or your husband?"

"Of course not." Recomposing herself, Cassie met Ross' eyes. "Whatever you're fishing for, it doesn't exist. Benjamin was shot by a stupid hunter who couldn't tell the difference between a deer and a horse." She rose. "I'm sorry you wasted your time coming all the way out here, but I have nothing else to say. And I have things that need doing."

Ross wanted to press further, but Kohler stood and with a subtle waggle of his fingers motioned her to follow suit. "All right," she said. "Thank you for your time, Mrs. Ferring." She handed the other woman a business card. "If you happen to change your mind about telling the truth, here's my card."

Seething, Cassie escorted them to the front door and slammed it behind them. Once they were back in his car, Kohler laughed. "That wasn't your smartest parting shot, Holly."

"Maybe not, but she's on notice now. Something might come of it."

"Like a complaint to your superiors?" He started the car and backed down the drive.

"This is my first real chance to prove myself," Ross said. "I'm going for the win."

"It could be your last, if you're not careful."

She grinned at him. "Nah. I know a guy who'll put in a good word for me with another department."

Forty-five minutes after the cops left, Cassie hadn't calmed down. She retreated to the kitchen for a splash of red wine and tapped a contact on her cell phone. When the other party answered, she said, "I screwed up."

"You sound horrible," Denise Ferring told her. "What happened?"

"The Howard County cops sent some young lady detective out here to ask about Benjamin."

"What? Why?"

"I don't know. But I got rattled and…" She leaned on the counter and choked back a sob. "Art's going to kill me."

"Does he know they were there?"

"No."

"So don't tell him."

"Why did they come here, Denise? After all this time!"

Denise didn't answer at once. Cassie gulped down another swallow and tried to think, but her mind only had room for fear.

"It's nothing to do with you. We had a little trouble here after the flood, and now the cops are grasping at straws, trying to make something of it."

"What kind of trouble?"

"Nothing important, and certainly nothing you need to worry about. You and Art have a good thing going out there. A great business, a beautiful home, peace and quiet. Focus on that. Forget everything else. It was never your problem, anyway."

Cassie took a few deep breaths. "You're sure it's okay?"

"Absolutely. Nothing's going to come of it, and if something does, Jim will take care of it. You and Art will be fine."

They would be fine. She set down her glass and told herself that three times. "Thank you, Denise."

"No problem. We should get together sometime soon. It's been too long."

"Maybe you and Jim could come out for a weekend sometime."

They agreed that would be wonderful and promised each other it would happen without setting a date, and after they hung up, Cassie's calm gradually returned and she put detectives from her mind.

Chapter 13

Theresa Swan called Peller's cell phone just after noon. "Bad news and good news," she said.

He was just out the door in search of lunch and didn't break stride. "No DNA sample," he guessed. "What's the good news?"

"Andrew Hunt knows he's family. He about jumped out of his skin when I mentioned Chuck's grandfather. Better yet, Chuck guessed the bones washed out from under the bakery before I said so."

That brought Peller up short. "Really."

"Yep."

"Did he say how he knew?"

"No. He claims his father told him granddad ran off to the Rockies. He suggested we ask his father or Ruth Vickeridge for the DNA sample."

"Ruth's out of bounds for now." Peller mentally reviewed the family tree. "Chuck's father is Andrew Ferring."

"Another Andrew," Swan said.

"Yeah. I think he's in his sixties. See if you can find him."

"I'll get on it. Anything else?"

"No, just fill in Corina when you get back." He pondered for a moment. Ferring wouldn't admit to anything, but Andrew Hunt might be another story, if pressed. Peller already knew he was a Ferring and they had him on video opening the door. "I'll pay The Lodge one last visit and make myself even more unpopular," he decided.

Swan said nothing, not even to wish him luck.

"Something else?" Peller prompted.

"So...no, nothing. I'll let you know about Andrew Ferring."

Something, clearly. Peller didn't push, but he could guess. Swan and Ross both had a lot invested in this case. It was their first real chance to show the powers that be what they could do. "Don't worry about the DNA test," he said. "We can do without Chuck. There are other options."

Swan replied with a muted, "Yes, sir."

Peller drove to a nearby deli and got a foot-long roast beef sub, fully loaded. He ate in his car with the radio tuned to the local classical station, which was playing some baroque piece he didn't recognize. That was fine.

He wasn't listening anyway. He pondered how Chuck Ferring knew about his grandfather's remains. Not from the news. Information on the source of the bones had been withheld. Ergo, Ferring had prior knowledge, or at least suspicions. Were the attacks on his business reminders to keep his mouth shut? Punishments for failing to do so?

Peller recalled the note left by the thieves: *Your life will be destroyed. Your means will be taken from you. Your weapons will turn against you. Those you wronged will be avenged. The end has begun.*

The end of what?

Setting course for The Lodge, Peller plotted his approach. His main objective was Andrew Hunt. Confront him with the evidence against him, push until he caved. Hunt was the weak link, a poor liar and nervous as hell. He knew he was sinking with a rock tied to him. After he broke Hunt, Peller would try to strike a deal with Ferring. Try. He had about zero hope of success, but accumulating evidence might spark in Ferring a conversion experience.

Predictably, Peller's arrival precipitated Ferring's anger and Hunt's fear. So far, so good. The more off-balance they were, the better his chances of getting somewhere. "I need to speak with Mr. Hunt," he told Ferring.

Ferring about bit Peller's arm off. "I'm sick of all these disruptions! Nobody died, damn it, it was just a *robbery*!"

"You sure?" Peller snapped back. "Who has your guns? How're they being used? I need to talk to Mr. Hunt."

Ferring showed no contrition. He maintained his angry act. "You know where the damn office is."

Peller motioned Hunt to lead on. Hunt skittered ahead of him, eyes darting as though seeking escape. Peller sensed Ferring's eyes on his back, heard him mutter curses. As they passed through the door, Ferring called, "I'm calling my lawyer!"

Peller shunted Hunt into the office and closed the door. "You may want to talk to your lawyer, too, Andrew."

Hunt's hands shook. He clasped them in a vain effort to still them. "Why?"

"We have the whole thing on video. You going out for a smoke, the thieves coming in shortly thereafter. The timing is too convenient. Also..." Peller pulled the folded family tree from his pocket, opened it, and pushed it across the desk for Hunt to examine. Hunt no more than glanced at it before looking away. "Turns out, you *are* related to the boss. It's hardly a close relation, but you knew, didn't you?"

Hunt shook his head.

"One of our detectives was here earlier today. When she mentioned finding the remains of Mr. Ferring's grandfather, it spooked you."

The young man's jaw worked for a moment before he said, "It surprised me, that's all. I didn't know Mr. Ferring's grandfather had been killed."

Peller leaned back and crossed his arms. "Who said he was killed?"

"You said—"

"I said we found his remains. I didn't say how he died."

Hunt squeezed his hands tighter. His fingers turned white.

"Let's do this the easy way, Andrew. Tell me everything you know, and I'll put in a good word for you with the DA's office. You were just an accessory. Help us convict the real criminals, and the judge will probably just wag a finger at you." He leaned forward and tapped the paper. "I'll find out with or without your help. This is a one-shot deal. I won't offer it again."

Running a hand over his face, Hunt straightened and really looked at the family tree for the first time. He spoke with a tremor. "I wasn't entirely lying. I didn't know we were related when Mr. Ferring hired me. I only found out later."

"When?"

"Just before Christmas. I was at a family party and met a distant cousin. We figured out our relationship."

"Who was this cousin?"

"Her name's Alice Crandall. She's James Ferring's daughter."

"James IV?"

"James V."

Peller extracted a pen from his pocket and amended the diagram. "Like that?"

Hunt nodded.

"And then you knew. Why does it matter?"

"It doesn't."

"So why the denials and deceptions?"

Hunt shrugged.

Leaning back again, Peller drummed his fingers on the desk. The hammering sounded unnaturally loud in the enclosed space. "One-shot deal, Andrew."

"I don't know much. Honest."

"Tell me what you do know."

Hunt licked his lips. "It was better Mr. Ferring didn't know. His side of the family doesn't get along with mine. He might have fired me."

Peller nodded and waited for more.

In a suddenly cooperative mood, Hunt leaned forward and lowered his voice. "He still doesn't know. She told me to keep quiet about it, so I did. And she asked for a favor."

"Alice?"

"Yeah. She already knew I slipped out back for a smoke sometimes. I don't know how. She asked me to leave the door unlocked just one time. I didn't know what they were going to do."

Peller could believe Hunt was that stupid. He waited for more, but Hunt shook his head and squeezed his eyes shut. "That's all," he said.

"I'm about to walk, Andrew. If I do, you have zero protection."

He hung his head. "If I tell you, they'll come after me."

"Not if I get them first."

That didn't comfort Hunt, but he complied. "Alice and her friends wanted to play a practical joke on Mr. Ferring."

"Some joke. Who are these friends?"

"I don't know. I never met them. I only ever talked to her."

"Got her address or phone number?"

With a sigh, Hunt pulled out his cell phone. He flipped through his address book, then picked up Peller's pen and jotted a phone number on the family tree. "Don't tell her you got this from me," he said. "Please."

Peller offered no assurances. "That's everything?"

"It is."

"If it's not, I'll find out."

"It is," Hunt repeated.

Peller rose and motioned him to the door. "Tell Mr. Ferring I'll see him now."

"Please don't tell him."

"That you're his relative, or that you helped rob him?"

"Either."

Peller waved him on.

After Hunt left, Peller packed up the family tree and resumed his seat. He allowed himself a moment of elation. He didn't doubt Hunt had told the truth about Alice Crandall. From the surveillance footage, one of the gang had been female. With one fingered, the others wouldn't be long in surfacing.

Ferring showed up in less than a minute. He took a seat and met Peller's eyes with a hard glare. "What?"

"You'll be happy to know we've ID'd one of the thieves."

But no, Ferring wasn't happy. Alarm flitted across his face before he got himself under control. "That's good," he mumbled.

"That depends on what we learn from the suspect, doesn't it?"

"Meaning?"

Peller leaned on the desk and spoke more quietly. "You're in some kind of trouble, Mr. Ferring. I'd like to help, but so far you've thrown up roadblock after roadblock."

"I've cooperated every step of the way," Ferring objected.

Peller shook his head.

Suddenly angry, Ferring pounded on the desk. "Damn it, what more do you want from me?"

Peller didn't react to the outburst. "How did you know your grandfather's remains were buried under the Colonial Bakery?"

Ferring pushed himself to his feet. "Time for you to leave, Lieutenant."

"What're you afraid of? What does that note mean?"

"I said, leave."

"Cooperated every step of the way." Peller rose and marched without a backward glance through the storefront to the exit. Ferring followed as though not trusting Peller actually would go. He might have been ready to lock the door behind the detective.

Pushing the door open, Peller paused. "You've got your wish, Mr. Ferring. I doubt I'll return, but you have my number. When things get ugly, which I predict they will, feel free to call."

Montufar received the fingerprint report on the gun handled during the robbery diversion. No matches had been found. So much for that. Maybe the ATF's reward posting would do better. Montufar was about to move on to the next thing when Theresa Swan slipped into her cubicle and sat. "Can I talk to you, Corina?"

"Sure." Montufar pushed back from her computer. "How did it go at The Lodge?"

"I gave Lieutenant Peller my report, but ..." She studied her hands, which had begun to tremble. "I left something out."

Montufar leaned close and lowered her voice. "Should we go to a conference room?"

Swan shook her head. "It's okay. I just …"

Montufar waited.

"There was a customer. He threatened me and I …" She looked up, fear flooding her eyes. "I drew. I think I had to, but…"

Montufar took Swan's shaking hands in her own. "Did you fire?"

She shook her head. "He backed off. I told him to leave, and he did."

Thank God for that. "What else?"

"That's it, but…Corina, I *wanted* to shoot the bastard. I *wanted* to kill him."

"Why?"

"Big tough white guy trying to intimidate a black woman. More than trying. He threatened me and called me…things."

Montufar didn't need details. She'd been on the receiving end herself and knew the fear, the anger, the gun so conveniently to hand. "You think he'll file a complaint?"

"I don't know. I don't care. Mr. Ferring would probably back me up, if it came to that. But it's not that. Corina, I'm not afraid of him. I'm afraid of *me*."

"You acted in self-defense, Theresa. You did what you had to do, nothing more. You deescalated and everyone walked away unharmed. That's a good thing." But she knew better. Unharmed? Hardly.

Swan pulled her hands from Montufar's and folded them in her lap. "Maybe next time I won't. Maybe next time I'll pull that trigger. How can I know?"

Montufar understood the feeling, but she'd never been that close to the line. She'd never pointed a gun at anyone in such a situation. She'd never felt the urge to kill. How could she possibly answer? She only knew one person who might have the right words. "You should talk to Rick."

"Lieutenant Peller?" She shook her head. "I can't. He'll—"

"No, he won't."

"I…I don't think I can."

"Don't be afraid of him. He's got more scars than the rest of us combined. He'll understand better than anyone."

Swan fidgeted with her fingers, then rose. "Thank you." She slipped away in silence. Montufar stared at the empty chair. How did anyone with a conscience survive this line of work?

Holly Ross looked triumphant when she presented herself before Dumas, smug smile and all. "Moderately good news?" Dumas chided.

"Cassie Ferring is a terrible liar." Ross sat in Dumas's guest chair and leaned an elbow on his desk.

"Who's Cassie Ferring?"

"Art Ferring's wife. I took a little trip to Frederick County to talk with her."

"And?"

"Guess why nobody mentioned Art Ferring's horse was killed on his birthday?"

"Stress," Dumas guessed. "Anger, fear, confusion." If he had been Art Ferring, those would have been his reasons.

"Family business." Ross beamed at him.

"Family business?"

She nodded.

"What the hell does that mean?"

"It means it's none of *our* business, which I figure means it very much ought to be our business. Try this on for size. Some family member shot the horse to teach Art Ferring a lesson. Cassie called the cops because she was afraid, but Art didn't want the truth getting out. The family deals with its problems its way. Art told Cassie to shut up while he conned the investigator into blaming a brainless hunter. Same basic story as Chuck Ferring blaming his troubles on anti-gun nuts."

Dumas squeezed his eyes shut. "God. Corina will never let me hear the end of this. She'll accuse me of teaching you to think crazy thoughts."

"It makes sense, doesn't it?"

"There are indications along those lines," Dumas conceded. "Ruth Vickeridge told Jack she wanted nothing more to do with the Ferrings, and Art Ferring might have moved to Frederick for that same reason. Tell me everything Cassie said."

Ross related the entire interview.

After the recitation, Dumas had to admit there weren't too many reasonable interpretations. Cassie Ferring had slipped up and tried her best to backpedal, but by then it was too late. Clearly, she was hiding something, most probably her own error in calling the police. Yet it seemed strange that in a family so vindictive—the intentional slaughter of a horse was hardly a small slight—nothing had come of it. Even most of the attacks on the Lodge had been petty by comparison. Nobody had been hurt, so far as police records could show. If the Ferrings were waging an internal war, it was mostly being fought with pop guns, not pistols.

When Dumas mentioned that to Ross, she reminded him of the one known exception: George Ferring, who had been killed by his uncle Roger in 1937.

"Ancient history," Dumas said.

"And William Ferring, Roger's son," Ross said. "Disappeared in 1947 and buried under the bakery."

"*Possibly* buried under the bakery." Dumas shook his head. "Then nothing until 1992 when the horse is shot? Then nothing again until the sporadic attacks on The Lodge, which started six years later? What kind of family feud are we talking about, Holly? Blood in the streets I could understand, but this makes no sense."

She grinned. "We'll crack it. We just have to keep pushing."

Dumas wondered if her enthusiasm was running away with her. "I'd recommend caution. Let's remember what we have here. At most, it's a very old homicide. The killer might not even be alive anymore. Even factoring in the gun theft, it's not entirely horrible as crimes go. And you can't tar and feather an entire family, even if some are guilty."

"But solving it will make us all look good." She hopped out of her chair, raring to go. "And I have some ideas about that."

Jack Collins accepted a cup of tea from Denise Ferring while her husband James waited quietly, hands folded over his abdomen. They were seated in the Ferring's richly-appointed living room over the bakery. From outside, sounds of power tools and hammers testified to the rebuilding underway up and down Main Street.

Once the refreshment had been served, Denise seated herself beside her husband, her alert eyes studying the reporter as though checking him for weapons while gently stirring her tea. She made little figure-eights in the liquid.

"I understand your grandfather started the Colonial Bakery," Collins said, and the interview commenced with a long recitation of the history of the establishment. Without embellishment, Ferring offered the same details Ruth Vickeridge had. Denise added nothing. Her eyes never left Collins, not even when taking dainty sips from her cup. Collins let his tape recorder gather Ferring's recitation.

"You've suffered losses from flooding before," the reporter prompted, and Ferring rattled off that history, too, missing no dates but offering few details.

That done, Collins brought up the interesting bit: "This one had a weird twist, didn't it?"

Ferring shifted uncomfortably. "That's one way of putting it."

"Any idea who it could have been?"

Ferring looked at his wife, who shrugged and stirred her tea again, this time counterclockwise.

Evasion. Totally expected. Collins leaned forward. "The remains have been dated to around the time you were born. The bakery was already here when the deceased was buried in the cellar. Are there any family stories about it?"

Ferring looked out the window again. Denise carefully shook a few drops of liquid from her spoon and set it on her saucer. "How do you figure that?" she asked as though making small talk.

Collins had the feeling she was testing him, but it was an easy question. "That's what the police said."

"Oh, yes," Denise agreed, "Now I remember. I heard that on the news."

Something in her tone suggested Collins had made a mistake, and he immediately realized what it was. While the police had released most details about the bones, they hadn't pinpointed their origin. They only stated the remains were strewn up and down Main Street, with the bulk of them coming to rest in the HorseSpirit Arts Gallery. Collins shouldn't have known they had washed out of the bakery's cellar.

It was too late to pretend, so deflection seemed the best course. He dropped the subject and moved on.

"How long will repairs take?"

Back on *terra firma*, James Ferring rattled off a list of damages and the work to be done. "It's going to take a full month to complete," he said, "but we'll open in about two weeks."

Collins ended the interview there and thanked the Ferrings for their time. Denise escorted him to the door while her husband vanished into the recesses of their home. "He's taken it pretty hard," the reporter observed.

"That water didn't just rip into the building, Mr. Collins. It ripped into Jim's heart and soul. This bakery is more than a business. It's his family. His life. You don't take a hit like this without feeling it. But we'll pull through. We always do."

Thanking her again, Collins descended to street level, walked a block to his car, and sat behind the wheel, kicking himself for being so clumsy. Maybe the Ferrings wouldn't have let slip anything anyway, but now he'd never know. He didn't dare talk to any of them again.

Not that it was a total loss. At least he had enough to spin his story for the *Flier*.

Chapter 14

"Got some good news for you, Rick." ATF Special Agent Zee Mirlo sounded more awake than Peller ever got. Maybe he'd had three cups of coffee already.

It was Tuesday morning, June sixth. Peller had just arrived at his desk to start the day and hadn't even sat down before the phone rang. He lowered himself into his chair, cradling the receiver between his ear and shoulder. "Fire when ready."

"Somebody hit the five-thousand-dollar jackpot, if this pans out. We got a tip late last night on your video clip. A caller ID'd the male suspect as Troy Nye, a guy he knows from a local gaming store. Customers play *Dungeons and Dragons™* there on Friday nights. The name of the store is Troll's Den. Appropriate, no? The store is in Elkridge, and Carter Pearce is the name of the owner. Nye is allegedly a friend of Pearce from way back in high school. I love it when these young bucks think high school is way back, don't you?"

Peller laughed. "No comment, Zee. You have addresses and phone numbers?"

"For both informant and store. I'll shoot you an email with the latter. Let me know how it goes. I have a government handout dying to be awarded."

"You got it," Peller said as he logged into his computer to check email. Mirlo's notes weren't long in arriving. Peller printed them out, stuffed the sheet in his pocket, and was out the door. He passed Montufar and Dumas in the stairwell. "Got a tip on the diversion from the Lodge theft," he said as he flew by. If his colleagues remarked on it, he didn't hear.

Twenty minutes later, Peller pulled into the parking lot of a small strip mall along U.S. Route 1 and found Troll's Den Gaming sandwiched between a deli and a Mexican grocery store. The storefront was jammed with a hodgepodge of board and video games, more the disorganized piles one might expect from a messy teenager than a shop owner, but then maybe that was part of the ambiance. Trolls live here.

Peller pushed open the glass door and found himself in a long, narrow space enclosed by wooden floor-to-ceiling shelves of games. Folding tables piled high with more games cluttered the place. On the left, a young man was doing paperwork behind a similarly messy checkout counter. A handful of customers, mostly young men but two accompanied by their lady companions, browsed and talked in subdued tones. Approaching the register, Peller asked, "Is Carter Pearce in?"

Without looking up from his papers, the clerk pointed to the rear. "He's in the game room, straight back."

Peller took his time going back. Looking through the piles and shelves, he tried to make sense of the organization and could only conclude there wasn't any. Titles weren't alphabetized, games from varying companies were mixed, and even game themes had been stirred together in a nearly homogenous stew. Spaceships, werewolves, comic animals, railroads, evolutionary biology, word games...how could anyone find what they wanted?

At least he found the door to the game room. That was plain enough: an opening in the middle of the rear wall with a dark red curtain hung over it, now pushed aside. The room behind was big enough to hold four large tables and plenty of chairs. At the moment, it was occupied only by two men, one a moderately overweight fellow with wire rim glasses and brown hair starting to thin, the other a rather younger man, rail thin and tall, with wide eyes and a loud voice. The latter was rendering his opinion on the latest superhero movies and what was likely to happen in their sequels.

Peller waited patiently in the doorway until the older man put up a hand to stop his companion. "What can I do for you?" he asked.

"You're Mr. Pearce, the owner?"

"That's right."

"I need some information about one of your customers." Peller produced his ID. "Detective Lieutenant Rick Peller, Howard County Police."

The younger man cleared his throat. "Gotta get back to the office," he muttered. "See you Friday."

Peller didn't forget faces. This guy wasn't the one they were looking for, so he stepped aside to let the man exit.

Pearce came around the table to check Peller's ID. "Some kind of trouble?"

"I understand Troy Nye is a friend of yours."

Suddenly wary, Pearce motioned Peller to a chair and pulled one out for himself. They sat facing each other. Pearce folded his hands on the table before him. Looking Peller in the eye, he said, "That's right."

"Old high school buddy, I hear."

"Yes."

"Tell me about him."

Pearce cocked his head. "Why?"

"Because I asked nicely."

"And if I don't, you'll get out the rubber hoses."

Peller's mouth smiled, but his eyes didn't. "Only metaphorically."

"Hmm." Pearce leaned back and crossed his arms over his chest. "Troy's a smart guy. He's a help desk consultant. Computers. He's also a sharp gamer. We met at a local convention when we were sophomores at Long Reach High School, became friends, and kept in touch ever since. He plays here when he can, which isn't every week but a lot. He's got a steady girlfriend, a townhouse in Dorsey's Search, and is a decent human being. Again, why do you ask?"

Peller ignored the question a second time. "Not a trouble-maker then?"

"Absolutely not, unless you count the occasional traffic ticket, which we all get. Except maybe you cops. You're such good drivers."

Peller laughed. "Not always. I caused an accident once, in my patrol car no less."

"Did you get slapped with a fine?"

"A marriage license."

Pearce stifled a smile.

"Can you give me Troy's address or phone number?" Peller hoped he had Pearce on his side now.

Alas, he didn't. "Not unless you tell me why."

Best, then, to keep it simple and non-threatening. "He may have been present at a burglary."

"Troy's no thief."

"I didn't say he was. I said he may have been present."

Pearce stared hard at Peller, as though that might make the detective open up. When it didn't he said, "You mean he's a witness."

"He may be able to shed some light on what happened. I know you don't want to get your friend in trouble, Mr. Pearce, but a business was robbed and we'd like to find out who did it. I'd think a merchant would appreciate that."

Maybe, maybe not, but Pearce dug his cell phone from his pocket, leaned forward with a sigh, and flipped through it. "Here you go," he said, and rattled off an address and a phone number.

"Thank you." Peller rose, pulled out his own phone, entered the data, and pocketed the device again.

Pearce raised an eyebrow. "You don't want to double-check that?"

Peller smiled a thin smile. "I'll let you get back to work."

Another twenty-minute drive brought Peller to Troy Nye's townhouse near the intersection of Little Patuxent Parkway and U.S. 29 on a loop of a road tucked into the edge of a golf course. The three-story units looked well-maintained, with tan vinyl siding and neat if unimaginative landscaping consisting of young trees and low shrubs surrounded by circles of brown mulch. A respectable-looking neighborhood with but one downside: the traffic noise from the nearby highways.

Peller knocked on the door three times without getting an answer, then he called Nye's phone number and got voice mail. Probably the guy was at work. Peller didn't leave a message. He preferred to surprise Nye, given the circumstances. He would come back later, around dinner time, and catch him then.

On patrol at eight thirty that morning, Officer Kevin Graham was looking forward to a quiet day interrupted by little more than a few traffic citations. The temperature was slowly climbing from an overnight low in the upper sixties to an expected high in the mid-seventies, the cloudless sky was brilliant, and the trees rustled in a light breeze.

Everything was beautiful.

He was northbound on Old Frederick Road just west of the sprawling grounds of the Howard County Conservancy when the day took a sudden turn to the dark side.

As he came upon Dorchester Way, a jogger ran into the intersection. Graham hit the brakes and was about to cuss out the young fool, but this guy wasn't oblivious. He was hysterical. Dressed in blue running shorts and a white t-shirt, he was wearing headphones around his neck instead of over his ears. Frantically waving his arms over his head, he screamed out words Graham couldn't understand.

Graham lowered the window and waited.

"Please help!" the man cried as he approached. "There's a, there's …" He pointed down Dorchester Way . "At the pumping station. They're dead!"

As the jogger reached the squad car, Graham asked, "Who?"

Pointing again, the other said, "Two people. I don't know them. I was running by and ..." He pressed a hand over his forehead.

"Did you see anyone else hanging around or passing by?"

"No, just the ... just them."

"I'll have a look. Get a grip and don't go anywhere."

Graham eased onto Dorchester. A large pond nestled in an open space just off the intersection. A small white shed sat beyond it, and a little further down he came upon a sewage pumping station, a brick structure surrounded by trees and an eight-foot chain link fence. A short drive led to the fence. Graham pulled in and stopped before the closed and locked gate. Getting out, he studied the area inside the compound but saw nothing.

Almost breathless, the jogger trotted up the drive and halted beside Graham. He doubled over, hands on knees, sucking lungfuls of air.

"Where are they?" Graham asked.

Straightening, the man pointed left. "Over there, in the trees just outside the fence. They're easier to see from the road."

Graham picked his way to the corner of the fence, watching for signs that anyone had passed by. There weren't any. When he reached the corner, he saw them: two bodies, male and female, face down in a tangle of arms and legs with the man's body slantwise on top. Both wore jeans, the man in a green t-shirt, the woman a yellow blouse. Both garments were stained with blood. A pair of wire-rim glasses hung off the man's left ear.

Graham returned to his patrol and opened the rear door. "Why don't you take a load off," he suggested to the jogger. "We'll need to talk in a minute."

The other man clapped his hands to his temples and mumbled something unintelligible but slipped into the car without coherent complaint.

Graham got in front and called in. "Ten-eighteen, Waverly Sewage Pump Station, corner of state route ninety-nine and north end of Dorchester Way. Two victims, one witness, zero suspects."

The dispatcher responded, and Graham turned sideways, legs out of the vehicle, so he could look at the man in the back seat. "Let's start from the beginning," he suggested.

The jogger looked up, half scared, half put out.

So much for a quiet day.

"Must be an exciting tip," Dumas said. He took Montufar's hand and they ascended the stairs to the second floor side-by-side. "Rick hasn't run that fast since I met him."

Montufar knew he was joking, but her thoughts were elsewhere. "He did say it was the diversion from The Lodge. If he catches that pair, he could wrap up the case."

"And do what? Get back to his staff reports? A good case like this must be savored, like a perfect dish of—"

"General Tso's?" Montufar quipped. "I didn't know you were a gourmet."

"If you're going to marry me, Sergeant, you'd better know it."

He pushed open the door to the office and motioned her in. They made their way through the cubicles to his workspace, where he sat in his chair and she perched on the edge of the desk, as usual. And as usual when nobody was around, he admired her legs.

She didn't notice. Her mind was on work. "It's a bit of a long shot, isn't it? They might refuse to talk, and it's not like we can charge them with anything."

"You think they know that?"

"Probably. Andrew Hunt might be clueless, but not those two. They had to know they'd be on camera, and they didn't care. Maybe because they'd never been on the police radar before."

"Then they're just overconfident."

"Sure, but that just means we won't break them."

Dumas shrugged. "I'll bet Kevin Graham and I could."

She'd seen Dumas and Officer Graham at work a couple of times. Graham, a veteran patrol officer who had come from Jamaica in the long ago, would have made a great detective, if only he had the interest. Better still, he was a big guy who unnerved suspects. He and Dumas had known each other for nearly as long as they'd been with the department. They possessed a chemistry that rattled even composed subjects. But the reticence displayed by nearly everyone involved in this case went beyond composure. Whatever the Ferring family secret, they seemed determined to keep it buried.

He noticed her misgivings. "We could," he insisted. "If Rick brings them in, I'll get Kevin over here and we'll deal with them straightaway."

He was so adamant that she couldn't help but laugh. "You're on," she said. "Loser buys the General Tso's."

Before Dumas could think of a comeback, the phone rang. He groaned and reached for the receiver. Montufar smiled at him. "Duty calls again."

He lifted the phone to his ear. "Dumas. No, Rick's out." He grabbed a pen and a pad of sticky notes and jotted an address. "Talk about coincidences. Nothing, forget it. I'll be there in fifteen." He hung up and stood. "Want to work a double murder with me?"

Montufar sighed and slid off the desk. "Is this what happens when two detectives get hitched?"

"Probably. You'll never guess who called it in."

She arched her eyebrows.

"Okay, you did. Come on. It's not far."

A drive of less than fifteen minutes brought them to the Waverly Sewage Pump Station, Kevin Graham, and his dejected witness who was still in the back seat of the squad, looking like he'd rather be on a jogging path in Barbados.

"We were just talking about you," Dumas said to Graham. "Who's that?"

Graham motioned the detectives toward the fence. "That is poor Chris Hammacher, who just wants to keep in shape and not find dead bodies. Which are over here." He pointed.

Dumas and Montufar looked. From this distance, they could only tell what they already knew: two victims, a man and a woman, both shot. Behind them, tires crunched as a third vehicle crowded into the pumping station's drive. Photographer Scott Sahin climbed out from behind the wheel, while Geri Franklin exited the passenger side. "Whoa, whoa, whoa," Franklin called. "Stay out of my crime scene."

Montufar pointed a finger at Dumas. "His fault," she said.

Dumas pointed at Graham and said nothing.

Graham's face creased in mock irritation. "Don't tell me how to do my job, young lady. I've trained kids younger than you."

Franklin grabbed her bag from the back seat and joined them, with Sahin and his camera right behind. He was smiling and shaking his head. "I have nothing but respect for *you*, Kev," Franklin said. She gave his arm a light punch in passing.

Montufar laughed. Dumas pointed to the squad. "While the experts work, let's see what Mr. Hammacher has to say."

Hammacher watched their approach with less than enthusiastic eyes. Dumas figured he felt cornered with three cops converging on him. Montufar must have had the same thought. She quick-stepped ahead of Dumas to start the conversation while the men hung back.

"I'm Detective Sergeant Corina Montufar," she said. "I hear you reported the trouble."

Hammacher nodded. "I really need to get going. Do I have to stay?"

"I'm sorry, but we just have a few questions. Do you mind?" Before he could answer, she motioned Dumas forward. "This is my colleague, Detective Sergeant Eric Dumas. Could you tell us what happened?"

"I already told officer Graham," Hammacher complained. "I should be at work by now." He lifted his cell phone and frowned at the time.

"We'll be as quick as we can," Montufar promised.

Dropping the phone on the seat beside him, Hammacher sighed. "I run every morning. This is my usual route. I happened to look over and saw the …" He swallowed. "The bodies. At first I thought somebody had dumped garbage back there, then I realized it was people, but they weren't moving. I figured they were in trouble, so I went to see if I could help. I got about to the fence and realized they were dead. The blood…" He shivered. "I didn't know what to do. Then I saw the police car coming up the road, so I ran and flagged him down. That's all. That's the whole story."

"What time was this?" Dumas asked.

"It was … I don't know. I guess twenty, thirty minutes ago?"

"Do you live back here on Dorchester?"

"Farther west, on Star Chaser Circle. Officer Graham took my info."

Montufar glanced back at Graham, who gave her a thumbs up. She bent down so she could see Hammacher better. "Did you go any closer than the fence?"

He shook his head harder than necessary.

"So you couldn't see the victims' faces."

"No. And I didn't want to."

"No idea who they are? Neighbors, maybe? Did their clothing look familiar?"

"No. I don't know anything about them. Can I please go now?"

She nodded. "I think so. Eric?"

Dumas stepped back and motioned Hammacher out of the car. "We can always call if we need anything else."

He swallowed, nodded, and stood. "Thank you," he said. They watched him walk to the road, where he did some stretches before taking off westward at a run.

"I'll bet he changes his route after this," Dumas said.

"Must've been a shock," Montufar agreed.

They both turned at the sound of Franklin's voice: "You lovebirds will want to see this."

Dumas winced. "Is she getting cheekier?"

"Maybe she's discovered there's more to life than forensics."

They walked back to the bodies, checking the ground. They saw nothing, but if anything had been there, Sahin or Franklin would have found and documented it.

Once they got close enough, they could see the dead couple had been shot from behind. The wounds in their backs were entrance wounds. They had been dumped haphazardly, the woman on the ground face-down and the man on top of her, with their limbs falling as they would. There was no sign of blood on the ground, so they had been killed elsewhere. There were, however, footprints in the soft earth around the bodies, and a few more to the north, away from the road.

"The perps probably came in from the back," Franklin said, pointing. "We found footprints pointing both directions. They go around the back side to a track by the pond. The ground is more solid there, so no prints or tracks, but they could have driven up there, unloaded the bodies, and carried them here to dump."

"Why carry them all that way?" Montufar asked. "Why not dump them in the pond?"

Dumas shrugged. "Maybe they're environmentalists and didn't want to pollute the water. Any ID on the victims?"

Franklin shook her head. "We'll be turning them over for mugshots once you're done looking around."

"I'll take a walk around back in a minute, but otherwise I'm good. Corina?"

"Likewise."

Sahin helped Franklin do the work, laying the bodies out next to each other. Once they were face up, Dumas sucked in a breath. "Damn it!"

Montufar winced. "It's them, all right."

Lining up his first mugshot, Sahin paused. "Who?"

"Rick's looking for this pair," Dumas said. "They provided misdirection for a robbery."

Sahin resumed his work. Franklin packed up her bag and stood. "Bummer," she said. "But at least he found them."

Chapter 15

The fresh bodies changed everything. No longer was it about burglaries, disappearances, or old bones. At his desk, Peller received the news from Montufar with tight-lipped silence. There was little he could say aside from cursing Chuck Ferring, at least until the photos and lab reports came in. Yet this wasn't what he'd expected. He figured Ferring himself would come under attack. Why were members of the gang showing up dead instead?

Dumas joined them a moment later, setting his hand on top of the cubicle wall as though he needed its support. "Any thoughts?" he asked.

Peller leaned back and stared at Dumas while he mentally replayed his interviews with the employees of The Lodge. Nothing came to mind.

Dumas misread Peller's look. "*I didn't kill them.*"

Peller raised an eyebrow.

"He totally suspects you," Montufar said, deadpan.

Peller sighed. "You're as likely as anyone. Ferring's been trying to brush off the burglary. I can't see him drawing further attention by killing Nye and his girlfriend when we already know they were part of it. Bobby Grant is Ferring's loyal right-hand man. He'd keep his head down, too. Peter Mitchell is just looking out for his younger brother Mark. Mark Mitchell—the betrayed lover—has it in for Tara Saunders with good reason, but she isn't the one who got killed. And Tara? She's just a young woman trying to make it in a man's world, for which she blames every perceived inequity. But she isn't likely to kill over it."

"Inequity?" Montufar laughed. "You've been borrowing Eric's thesaurus, haven't you?"

Peller finally cracked a smile. "No, I went to a decent school. Point is, none of them were thieves and all of them make unlikely murderers, with the possible exception of Mark, who at worst would only murder Tara or her lovers. That leaves Andrew Hunt. Young, clueless, accessory to burglary but probably not brave enough to pull off a murder."

Dumas nodded. "Then Nye and his girl were probably killed by their co-conspirators. Andrew Hunt could be next."

"They're the only ones currently available," Peller agreed, "but I don't like it. Nye played his part perfectly. He didn't rat out the gang. Why kill him?"

"The reward posting," Montufar said. "Somebody saw it." She folded her arms over her chest and stared at the floor. "Strange place to dump the bodies, though. Eric and I circled the place several times. All we can figure is, they were a bit harder to see on that side of the pumping station than the other. But they weren't exactly hidden, either."

"So somebody wanted them to be found," Dumas added.

"A warning to others," Peller suggested.

"Seems likely," Montufar said. "Speaking of others, do we have anything yet on the three who committed the burglary?"

Peller pulled his family tree diagram from his pocket and unfolded it. "We do. Hunt told me yesterday he was recruited by a distant cousin named Alice Crandall, daughter of James Ferring V."

"What the hell," Dumas grumbled. "Is the whole family involved in this?"

"Half of it, anyway," Montufar said. "So far, they've all been Ferrings."

Dumas looked surprised. "What about Nye?"

Peller leaned back and gave Dumas the same tight-lipped look as before.

Montufar nudged her fiancée. "You suggested it. You find out."

"Joy," Dumas said, but he went straightaway to his desk to get started.

"What's the girlfriend's name?" Peller asked Montufar.

"We don't know yet. I've put in for help canvassing his neighborhood. Wish me luck."

"Good luck."

And she was on her way.

Resisting the temptation to call Chuck Ferring and read him the riot act, Peller resigned himself to waiting for the data to come in. He went to the break room for coffee. He had the place to himself for a few minutes and took his time pouring a cup and adding sugar. The rising wisps of steam occupied his attention while he stirred the hot liquid. When finally he tossed the stirrer in the trash and turned to go, he found Theresa Swan standing in the door. She didn't seem to know whether to join him or flee in terror.

He set his cup on a table and motioned her over. She approached, hesitant, and he pulled out a chair for her. "Looks like you need to sit down."

"Thanks." She sat. He took the chair to her left. She folded her hands on the table and stared at them. "Corina said I should talk to you."

Peller noted the symptoms of fear, guilt, and anger: eyes avoiding him, muscles taught, a slight tremor in her voice. He gave her space to work out her approach.

"Coffee," Swan said. She rose and poured herself a cup, taking her time before returning to her seat. She took a careful sip before starting. "Something happened when I went to The Lodge."

She continued to avoid his eyes as she told the story. Peller listened in silence. She fidgeted with the foam coffee cup, turning it, pulling it close, pushing it away. Occasionally she paused for another drink. She kept her voice flat, even when talking about how she had wanted to shoot Brandon. When she finished, she stared into her coffee. Peller waited for her self-assessment. It wasn't hard to guess what it would be.

"I don't trust myself anymore."

"I know," he said. "But you will."

"How?"

"By reflecting on it. You were hit hard, but you protected yourself and deescalated successfully. You kept your fear and anger in check. Nobody got hurt. That's success."

Swan finally looked at him. "And next time?"

"Well. If you're lucky, there won't be a next time. And if there is, this experience will get you through it."

"How do you know?"

That must have been why Montufar sent Swan to him. She couldn't speak from direct experience as Peller could. He didn't care to talk about it, but he had to give Swan something, so he told it the short way. "The man responsible for Sandra's death tried to goad me into killing him. And I wanted to. It would have been easy. I only had to pull the trigger." He picked up his cup, stared into the dark liquid, set it down again. "I've thought about it a lot since then. Why didn't I do it? If it happened all over again, would I? Emotionally, I don't know. But then I ask myself the logical question." He shrugged. "What justifies pulling that trigger?"

She rotated her mug. "Protecting ourselves or others."

"Which is a judgement call. Fear and anger wreak havoc on judgement. We all know that. But in the moment, we don't think about it. We simply hold them at bay, or we don't. You don't know which you'll do until you're tested. But here's the thing, Theresa. You and I, we've been tested. We know what we'll do, because we've already done it."

Swan pondered that for a few moments. Then she stood and gathered up her cup. "Thank you, Lieutenant." She paused at the door. "Oh, I found Chuck Ferring's father. Andrew owns an auto body shop off Route One in Savage. I'll pay him a visit today."

Peller nodded and, after she left, stared into his coffee. He wasn't sure how much his ruminations would help. He had a healthy dose of self-doubt, himself, in spite of them. But at least she'd know she wasn't alone.

He drank his coffee and tried not to think too hard about the past.

Digging through public records was nobody's favorite job, but Dumas had a leg up. Between them, Jack Collins and Rick Peller had already done a lot of the work. He started at the top of the family tree and worked down, by dumb luck picking the right branch from the start. James and Amanda had six children. Their oldest, James Jr., had five, including the ill-fated George Ferring, who had been killed by his uncle Roger. The third child of that family was Beatrice, born 1919 and died not so long ago in 1998. She had married Peter Nye, likewise deceased in 2001.

Bingo.

A bit more digging proved Troy Nye to be Peter's grandson and thus inheritor of what Dumas increasingly regarded as the Ferring family curse. He took his findings to Montufar and slapped them down on her desk in triumph. "Told you," he said. "Family feud."

She gave him a quizzical look. "Rat's maze, more like. Spell it out for me."

Taking a page from her book, he perched on her desk for a change. "James Jr. and Roger, brothers. One successful, inheriting the family business from dad, the other dishonorably discharged and disgraced. An argument arises, and Roger kills James's son George. Roger is attacked by a mob and is himself killed. Ten years later, Roger's son William vanishes. Fast forward to today, and his body shows up under James' bakery."

"Maybe," Montufar interrupted. "We don't have DNA tests yet. We don't even have a donor."

Dumas gave her a pinched smile but didn't object. "Meanwhile, James Jr.'s grandson Art loses a beloved horse to a so-called hunting accident, and Roger's great-grandson Chucky is vandalized, robbed, and threatened nonstop. Then James Jr.'s great-grandson Troy Nye plays distractor during a robbery at Chucky's and is subsequently shot to death along with his girlfriend. And the cherry on top? James Jr.'s great-great-granddaughter Alice Crandall was a co-conspirator in the robbery. It's a war, James Jr. vs. Roger, echoing through the decades."

"Both of them are dead," Montufar reminded him.

"Their mutual hatred isn't. *Somebody* pulled the trigger that killed Troy Nye, and odds are that somebody is a Ferring."

"One of Roger's descendants?"

"I'd lay money on it," Dumas said. "Didn't Jack say Ruth Vickeridge had children?"

"Two. However…" Montufar waggled a finger at him. "You know what the captain said. Don't you go disturbing that dear old lady."

"Because of her ex-cop husband. Yeah, I know. I'll start on the other side of the family. Maybe Troy Nye's mother can offer some insights."

"What makes you think she'll talk?"

Dumas hopped off the desk. "Her son might be a Ferring," he said, "but she's not. Maybe she'll have some opinions she's been dying to share."

"Under the circumstances," Montufar said in all seriousness, "that's a *really* poor way of putting it."

Holly Ross figured she had two shots at unraveling the Gordian knot that was the Ferring family, people young enough that, with any luck, they wouldn't be invested in the wars of their elders. She started with the younger, Doug Ferring, son of Art Ferring. Doug was thirty-one and working for a medical data processing service on Gateway Drive in Columbia. Ross called ahead and asked to meet him on his lunch break. Ferring tried to wiggle out of it, but Ross turned on the charm and eventually he capitulated, suggesting a fast food joint in the shopping center off Dobbin Road. Ross told him she would be driving a white Ford Fiesta and wearing a dark blue dress. Ferring said he'd find her and declined to give a description. She found that odd but didn't object since he agreed to meet.

Being midday, the place was jammed. She arrived ten minutes ahead of schedule, parked in the last empty space available, and stood behind her car. Ferring arrived right on time. He stopped beside her and put down the power window on the passenger side. "Detective Ross?"

"That's me."

He lucked out; someone pulled out two spaces down, so he parked there and a moment later they were in line together inside. Wearing tan slacks and a green button-down shirt, Ferring looked a lot like his father, but his eyes still had the sparkle of youth. Since seating was at a premium and the weather was nice, they ordered to go—he a double burger and she a spicy chicken sandwich—and carried it outside. There were no tables, so Ross suggested her car. She put down the windows and they settled in with their food.

"You're a detective, huh?" he asked before taking the first bite. "You don't look like a detective."

She laughed. "How should a detective look?"

"More grim, less…" He looked embarrassed but said it anyway. "…pretty." He tried to smile at her. It might have been his first time complimenting a girl.

Ross didn't object. She needed his cooperation. "I'm doing some follow-up work on an old case," she said. "I'm sure you remember your father's horse being shot."

Ferring had just taken a bite of his burger and nearly choked on it. "Damn, that *is* an old case."

"Is it that surprising?"

"Well, yeah, I mean, I thought that was all wrapped up."

That hardly seemed a reason to gag on lunch. "You were in high school at the time, is that right?"

He nodded. "I was a senior. I wasn't home when it happened."

"You must have heard about it, though."

"Nothing the police didn't hear, I'm sure."

Ross lowered her voice even though nobody could hear them. They were surrounded by empty cars. "I'm hoping you did."

Ferring looked confused. "Probably not." He turned his attention on his French fries. "All I know is, a hunter shot Dad's favorite horse, and he spent the next month crying one minute and raging the next. I'd rather not remember."

"What did he say when he was raging?"

Ferring shrugged.

"Come on, Doug. I really need your help."

"I don't know anything."

She put on a damsel-in-distress mask. "Please?"

As much as he might have wanted to date her before, the act didn't work. Ferring's face flushed with anger. "What do you think? He cursed vigilantes and police and the whole world. It didn't resurrect the damned horse. All it did was drive mom and Carol and me insane."

"Vigilantes? Not hunters?"

Ferring jammed his sandwich into his mouth and tore off a chunk. Ross thought he looked a bit like a famished T-rex.

"So he knew it wasn't a hunting accident."

Although not denying it, Ferring focused on his food and refused to answer. He wasn't doing a stellar job of eating, though. Not only would Ross have to vacuum her car, he really would choke if he kept that up.

"Hey, calm down. We're not after your father and certainly not you. But something is definitely strange. If he didn't think it was a hunting accident, why was he so happy to let investigators think it was?"

Ferring stopped attacking his food and got himself under control. "Maybe it was."

"You don't believe that."

"What, you're a mind reader?" He bagged the remains of his lunch. "It was a damn horse fourteen damn years ago. What the hell difference does it make?"

Ross decided to go out on a limb. She knew she shouldn't tell him, but maybe it would shock him enough that he'd say something. "It might be connected to the other crimes that hit your family."

"That's a good one."

"I'm not joking. I'm talking vandalism, theft, and murder."

He crushed the top of the bag shut. His hands were trembling. "I don't have to listen to this." He threw the door open. It struck the car next to them. He barreled out, slammed the door shut, and rushed to his own car. Ross got out and watched him fumble with the key fob, accidentally setting off the alarm before he got the door open. Once he silenced the noise, he threw himself into the car, started his engine, and backed out so fast he nearly hit someone coming up behind him.

Ross watched him zip out of the parking lot, cutting off another motorist on the way. "Wow," she muttered. "That got a rise out of him."

Rounding the car, she looked at the damage on the vehicle next door. A painful dent. She retrieved paper and a pen from her glove compartment, wrote a note, and tucked it under the victim's windshield wiper. The rest of the vehicle had previously collected a constellation of scratches and small dents. With luck, the owner wouldn't think it was worth the trouble.

Andrew Ferring's body shop was doing well, if the collection of damaged vehicles awaiting service was any indication. As traffic swished by on U.S. Route 1, Ferring ran his finger over a blue Camry with an impressive dent in the rear passenger-side door and shook his head. "I don't remember him," he said. "I was only one when he left. They said he wanted to see the Rockies. I always figured that's where he went. Maybe he fell off a mountain." He laughed without conviction.

Theresa Swan saw little of Chuck Ferring in his father. Andrew was thin and of average height with sparse gray hair scattered over his head. His eyes strayed here and there without seeing much of anything. "Who said that?" she asked.

"Oh, everyone. Aunt Ruth, some of my older cousins. I never heard any other story. I think you're wrong about those bones, but I'll do the test, just in case you're right. It would sure make the story stranger, though."

"Why?" Swan had the sample kit in her hand, but she didn't proffer it right away. No sense acting like she was in a rush, even though everyone from Peller down wished they had the results yesterday.

"I can't imagine how he would end up there."

"A lot of Ferrings seem to be wearing targets."

Ferring looked at the sky, contemplating either her remark or puffs of passing cloud, but he didn't offer any insights on either.

"Your son, for example," Swan added. "It's a dangerous family."

He laughed bitterly. "A swarm of mosquitos, that's all. The one who makes me nervous isn't even a Ferring."

"Who would that be?"

Ferring gave her a sidelong glance. "Don't read too much into my ramblings. It's probably my imagination. I don't trust anyone who's too proper." He knocked a stone aside with his foot and watched it skitter over the asphalt. "My father, huh? I don't know. Maybe James knows the truth. If anyone does, I guess it would be him."

The family tree wasn't fresh in her mind, but Swan knew the name had been handed down through five generations. Probably it would perpetuate itself as long as the Ferrings did. "He owns the bakery now, doesn't he?" she asked.

"No, that's his son, James IV. I don't really know him. His father, James III, is my, let's see, first cousin once removed, I think. Last I heard, he was still alive, but he must be close to a hundred years old by now." Ferring shook his head. "Not that it matters. I have no feelings about it one way or the other. I grew up without a father. His bones won't do me any good."

"I don't suppose they will," Swan admitted. "But it would help us with our reports." She held up the test kit. "Shall we?"

Ferring nodded, and she talked him through the collection of cells from inside his cheek. Once she had the swab secured in the phial, she thanked him and promised to let him know the results. He didn't seem to care. He had work to do.

A pair of vacant eyes stared at Dumas from the darkened doorway of the townhouse for a good thirty seconds before a skeletal hand waved him half-heartedly in. His breath coming in thin whistles around the plastic tubes strapped to his face, Peter Nye Jr. maneuvered a portable oxygen tank into the living room and carefully lowered himself onto a dark blue couch. The curtains were shut and no lights were on. It was a sunny mid-afternoon outside but felt like Dracula's crypt in here.

"I'm sick of police," Nye sighed.

Dumas understood. Uniformed officers had brought him word of his son's death a couple of hours earlier.

"Sick in general. COPD. Smoked like a chimney when I was younger. You a smoker?"

"No, sir."

Nye nodded his approval. "Something else can kill you, then. Maybe a bullet, like Troy." He examined his fingers. "What the hell do you want?"

"Just background. It'll help us understand why this happened and find Troy's killer."

"There's nothing to tell. He was born, went to school, got a job, got shot." Nye fiddled with the tubing, adjusting how it draped across his chest. "He was a good kid. Took more after his mother than me. Got good grades, didn't get into too much trouble. He liked to play silly fantasy games. I didn't approve of that. Waste of time, if you ask me. I played baseball when I was in school, back when I had lungs. Do kids still play baseball? Doesn't seem like it."

Dumas wasn't up on the state of the little leagues. "Does he have any brothers or sisters?"

"No. There was another baby, but Maggie—that's my wife—she miscarried, and after that couldn't have no more children. Troy hung around with some cousins on occasion, but we tried to keep him away from them."

Dumas wanted to pursue that, but first he hoped to get Maggie involved in the conversation. Nye was part Ferring, but she wasn't. "Is your wife here?"

Nye shook his head. He still wasn't looking at Dumas. "She's the one puts food on the table these days. I can't."

Then he'd have to wait to talk to her. Might as well see how much the father was willing to say. "You didn't approve of Troy's cousins?"

Another shake of the head. More adjustments to the tubing. "Bunch of hooligans, if you ask me. They weren't even close cousins. Second, third, something like that. Maggie explained it to me a few times, but I never could remember."

"What did they do that was so bad?" Dumas asked.

"When they were younger, just pranks, stuff that got the neighbors mad but didn't do no harm. Later, God only knows what they got up to. One of 'em, Doug was his name, ended up in juvenile detention for vandalism when he was sixteen. Broke some store windows or something." Nye shook his head. "Bad influences. We didn't want Troy hanging around with them."

"Doug," Dumas said as though trying to recall the kid. "His last name wouldn't be Ferring, would it?"

Nye finally looked at him. His eyes were narrowed and his mouth pinched into a thin line. His whistling breath quickened.

"I see."

"You don't see anything," Nye grumbled.

Dumas waited, but no explanation followed. Instead, Nye got lost in his past.

"You try to keep your kids safe. You try to teach them. Sometimes you can't. They don't listen, or danger comes right to your door. It was the same with me. Dad tried, too, but when you're young and stupid, it goes in one ear and out the other. Some of the things I did." He shook his head and fiddled with the tubing again. "I never went to jail, but only 'cause I never got caught. Eventually I grew up and realized dad was right. And I tried to teach Troy the same way. He took after his mother. Thank God, I always said to her, thank God he takes after you." He put a hand over his face and sobbed.

Dumas looked at his shoes and gave Nye time. He had a hundred questions to ask, but none of them were well-formed. Something told him, though, that the frail figure before him knew all the answers he needed. Would he give them up?

After a time, Nye dropped his hand and looked, pleading, at Dumas. "Who killed him?"

Dumas shook his head. "Who would have wanted to?"

"He must have gotten mixed up with a bad crowd."

"His cousins?"

Nye looked at the heavy curtain shrouding the front window. "What did he do?"

Dumas didn't want to say. Nye didn't need to hear such things about his son.

"Tell me."

"We think he was involved in a robbery. He and his girlfriend seem to have distracted the owner while three others ransacked the place."

"What place?"

"A gun shop."

Nye hung his head. "Gun shop."

"Yes, sir."

For a time, there was no sound but the old man's whistling breath. Then Nye leaned back and closed his eyes. "I need to rest. Please go."

Dumas rose, but he couldn't help but think Nye was on the precipice. Just a nudge, and he might yet unburden himself. "All I need is a name," he said.

Nye said nothing. He remained so still that but for his breathing Dumas might have thought him dead. Exhausted and disappointed, the detective made his way to the door. When he opened it, a beam of sunlight streamed in, nearly blinding him. He put his hand up to ward it off.

"I gave you a name," Nye said in the dark.

Dumas dropped his hand as his eyes adjusted to the daylight. "Thank you, sir." He stepped outside and quietly closed the door behind him.

Chapter 16

Montufar returned from the canvas of Troy Nye's neighborhood. The results were fairly unilluminating, although they now had his girlfriend's name: Mia Hambleton. Everyone described Nye and Hambleton as quiet, respectful, helpful neighbors. Nobody much noted their comings and goings, except they both worked day jobs and sometimes dressed up and went out for an evening. They were a stunning couple, he handsome, she beautiful and a bit of a flirt in company that enjoyed that game.

Montufar had just emailed these tidbits to the team when a dispirited Jack Collins arrived. Hoping to cheer him up, she said, "Ella didn't say no, did she? If so, I'll go over there right now and straighten her out."

Collins flopped into the chair beside her desk. "Ha, ha. No, I haven't popped the question yet."

"Why not?"

"You know." He waved his hand vaguely. "Waiting for you and Eric to figure out what you're doing."

Montufar laughed. "Don't wait on us. We never know what we're doing."

Not even a smile.

"Okay, what's wrong?"

"I blew it. A slip of the tongue while interviewing James and Denise Ferring. Now they know I've been talking to you guys."

That wasn't so bad. She gave him a gentle smile. "No worries. You don't work for HCPD, so we can't fire you. Besides, you got some good background on the family. That business with the horse is illuminating."

"I thought your boss's boss didn't like my suggestion."

"She didn't, but she's not the one investigating. You also dug up a lot on Roger and George. I doubt the family would have talked to us about that."

The pep talk worked. Collins sat a bit straighter and looked less miserable.

"Tell me about your visit with James and Denise," Montufar said.

Collins related the details, such as they were.

"So Denise fingered you. That's interesting. How did James react?"

Collins pondered that for a moment. "He seemed distant. When he spoke, it was like a prepared lecture."

"And Denise tricked you."

Collins lowered his eyes and nodded.

"Don't take it so hard. You're trained to do news interviews, not police interviews."

The distinction must have been lost on him. He continued to brood.

Montufar considered this new wrinkle. James Ferring IV, Art Ferring, and Ruth Vickeridge all seemed to have something in common. They had all run away from the family curse. Art and Ruth literally, James figuratively, by focusing solely on his business. Unlike the others, James had Denise to protect him, and she had displayed some cunning in her encounter with Collins. James and Denise likely knew about the body in the basement.

So how would they have known?

She jumped to her feet. Collins rocked back, startled by the sudden movement. "Hang on a sec."

She rushed to Peller's desk and found him jotting notes on a public records search. "Who're you after now?" she asked him.

"Alice Crandall," he replied. "According to Andrew Hunt, she's part of the gang that broke into the Lodge."

While important to Peller's investigation, Montufar didn't much care about Alice Crandall at the moment. "Got a minute?" she asked.

"What's up?"

"Jack had an interesting encounter with James IV and Denise. Bring that family tree."

A moment later, Peller was smoothing the paper on Montufar's desk, and Collins joined them in leaning over it.

Montufar pointed out family members while Collins craned his neck to follow along. "The two key incidents are when Roger kills George in 1937, then someone kills William in 1947 and buries him in the bakery cellar. Eric suggests a family feud. If he's right, the possible suspects in William's death are James Jr. or any of his children: James III, Andrew, Beatrice, and Clara. Clara's the youngest, and she's twenty-four when William dies."

Peller shook his head. "It's not that simple. Even if we assume it's a family affair, any of Roger's siblings or their children could have done it."

"But the body in the cellar suggests otherwise. It likely couldn't have been buried there without James Jr.'s or James III's knowledge."

"Corina," Peller started.

She waved him to silence. "Tell him, Jack."

Collins repeated his story for Peller.

"Suggestive," Peller admitted, "but without a direct admission, it's hard to prove they know anything."

"Real hard," Collins agreed. "How many of James Jr.'s children are still alive? They'd be pretty old by now."

"I found death records for Andrew and Beatrice," Peller said. "Clara might still be alive. She'd be eighty-three this year. James III is probably dead. He'd be a hundred if he was still around, although I didn't find a death record for him."

A new voice intruded. "He's around." Theresa Swan stepped into the cubicle. "I talked with Andrew Ferring. He gave us a sample for the DNA test. We'll have results back in two to four weeks. Uncle James, he said, lives in a nursing home."

"Does he," Peller said. "Which one?"

Swan hesitated. "I don't know. I should have asked."

Montufar didn't criticize her for the omission. Until this moment, nobody had expected James Ferring III would be alive, much less available for an interview. "No problem," she said. "I'm sure you can locate him. When you do, why don't you take Jack along?"

Peller winced. "Corina..."

So did Collins. "Is that a good idea? After all..."

"James III isn't in the loop. He won't know about your little slip. Anyway, you need him for your story, right?"

Collins shifted his weight.

Peller studied Collins with an uncomfortable intensity before speaking. "All right. But be careful, Jack. Don't tip him off."

Still looking uncertain, Collins nodded.

It took Holly Ross some time, but she finally located Carol Mondy née Ferring. She lived with her husband and two children in a large home off state route 94 in the southwestern part of Howard County, an area designated Annapolis Rock. The homes here were widely spaced, the unfenced yards green and populated with trees of modest age. Thick stands of woods wound about the edges of the developments, filled with birdsong. Crop and horse farms were interspersed with residential communities.

The Mondy home was one of the older ones in the area, with beige siding, a wrap-around porch, and a large red shed out back where, Ross supposed, garden implements and a riding mower were stashed. The house itself had two floors and a long drive leading to a three-car garage. It was elegant without being pretentious. She could see herself living there someday, if she ever had the money.

Ross called ahead and learned that Mondy would be working from home and was available to talk. Her husband Rich was away on a business trip and the kids were in school, so it would be the two of them. Mondy answered the door in yellow knee-length skirt and a white long-sleeve T and invited Ross into the living room, which was furnished in blue, gold, and oak. She offered Ross a seat on the sofa and took a facing chair for herself.

"I work from home three days a week," she said. "You picked the right day to come."

"What do you do?" Ross asked.

"I'm a software engineer for a company in Fairfax. You couldn't pay me to make that commute every day, but twice a week is tolerable, if you work odd hours."

Ross couldn't imagine driving to Virginia even once a week. Traffic flowing around the nation's capital was impossible at rush hour and horrid at most other times. "I'm glad it works for you," she said nonetheless. "This seems like a nice place to live."

Mondy nodded. "Oh, do you want coffee or anything?"

"No, thank you. I don't want to put you out. I'm here to talk about the day your father's horse was killed."

Mondy sat a bit straighter, suddenly on alert. "Why?"

Ross made it sound as boring as possible. "I pulled case file clean-up duty. I just need to clarify a few things."

"I'm afraid I don't know anything about it."

"You might, indirectly. This accidental shooting theory. What did your mother think of it?"

"Whatever she thought, I'm sure she told the police."

Ross shook her head. "Your father kept her from talking to the police beyond her initial report."

Mondy's hands gripped the arms of the chair. "What do you mean, kept her from talking?"

"Just what I said. What did she say when the police weren't around?"

"She said nothing to me."

Ross could believe that. Cassie Ferring wouldn't have intentionally crossed her husband. "Your father, then."

Fingers digging into the fabric, Mondy snapped, "It was his favorite horse."

Which didn't answer the question, but at least it wasn't a denial. "A birthday present, right?"

The other nodded.

"Killed on his birthday, too. Strange coincidence."

No answer that time.

"What's wrong, Carol? You look upset."

"What do you really want?"

"Not much, just the truth. Did *anyone* think it was an accident?"

"Yes, everyone did. The police did. My parents—"

"Your parents are liars, and so are you. Look at you. You're shaking all over."

Mondy released the chair and folded her arms over her chest in a vain effort to hide her agitation. "I am not."

"What are you people hiding? Your father knew it wasn't an accident, yet he was angry that your mother called the police. Who killed that horse, Carol?"

"A hunter, damn it, a hunter!" Mondy sprang from the chair fists balled, face red. "Get out of my house."

"Not until you tell me the truth."

"Get *out* of my house!"

Ross stood but kept pushing. "What're you afraid of? It wasn't you, was it? Did *you* shoot Benjamin?"

"No! A hunter did!"

Ross laughed and turned for the door, but she wasn't quite ready to leave. "Not a deer hunter. Maybe a revenge hunter."

"Leave me alone, you bitch!" Surprised, Ross turned back and was greeted by a punch to the gut. She doubled over and stumbled, disoriented, as Mondy grabbed her shoulders and shoved her at the door, screaming, "Get out, get out, get *out*!"

Ross fumbled for her gun, but Mondy threw her smack into the front door. The doorknob struck her hip, and she all but toppled in pain. Then the door was open, and Mondy, hauling on Ross' arm, threw her out. She tripped and fell face-down on the porch. The door slammed behind her. Ross picked herself up and pounded on the door. Parts of her hurt, but the primary injury had been to her dignity.

"Go away!" Carol called from within. "Before I call the cops!"

"I *am* the cops!" Ross bellowed. Her hands hurt. Her knees, too. And her hip and back and a few other body parts she couldn't quite pinpoint. She limped off the porch and back to her car. Nobody was there to see, thank God. She dropped herself into the driver's seat, grabbed the wheel, leaned on it, eyes closed.

Why, she wondered, *was Carol Mondy so furious?*

And more to the point: *What the hell did I just do?*

Peller caught up with Alice Crandall on a school baseball diamond, where she was helping teach a hyperactive gaggle of pre-school girls to swing plastic bats without hitting each other. She was an athletic young woman, twenty years old, with short brown hair and an infectious laugh. The kids clearly loved her and vied for her attention as she marshalled them into some semblance of order and showed them how to hold their bats.

Watching from behind the backstop, Peller couldn't help but smile, but he reminded himself this was a woman who had made off with a haul of weapons and threatened the life of the man from whom she stole them.

Crandall wasn't alone in managing the children. Three other adults, all women older than her, joined the fray. One noticed Peller and approached warily. "Can I help you?"

Peller showed his ID. "Detective Lieutenant Rick Peller, Howard County Police. I'm here to talk to Alice Crandall. That's her, I believe." He pointed.

The woman looked over her shoulder. "Is something wrong?"

"I just need to talk to her, ma'am."

Reluctantly, she nodded and went to tell Crandall she had a visitor. Brushing off her hands, Crandall gave Peller a once-over, then sauntered around the backstop to him, smiling like she was meeting a good friend. "You're a detective, huh?"

Peller introduced himself again.

She nodded her approval. "A handsome lieutenant. I must really rate."

"The ATF posted a five-thousand-dollar reward for you," Peller said. "So yes, I'd say you do."

She laughed. "What did I do to deserve that?"

"Robbed your uncle and threatened his life."

She looked back at the kids. Some of them were calling for her. She waved and smiled. "He probably deserved it. You know how family is."

"Is that an admission or a denial?"

Putting a finger to her cheek, Crandall feigned puzzlement. "I don't know. What makes you think I did this dastardly deed?"

"Video footage and detective work. Your cousin, Troy Nye and his girlfriend Mia Hambleton helped. She was particularly effective at creating a diversion."

Another laugh. "Hot, is she?"

"Not anymore. She's dead, along with Troy. They were murdered yesterday morning. Was that your handiwork, too? Eliminating witnesses?"

The humor drained from her. She took a step back, put a hand to her mouth, mumbled something Peller couldn't make out.

Her reaction was too genuine. The murders were news to her. "If not," Peller said, "you could be next. Care to start at the beginning and tell me what's going on?"

"Troy's dead?"

"I can get pictures, if you want. Start talking, Alice. We can do it here or at my office. Your choice."

She shook her head. "I—I want a lawyer."

"You come from a distinguished family. I'm sure they have one. I'll be happy to wait while you make a call." Peller walked back to his car, leaned against it, and watched from a distance.

At first, Crandall didn't seem to know what to do. She stared at nothing, then put a hand over her face and might have wept. Eventually, she pulled a phone from the pocket of her jeans and fumbled with it while one of the other women approached and spoke to her. Crandall said something, and the woman embraced her, then returned to the children. Once the phone call was over, Crandall slowly came to Peller's side and leaned on the car, too.

"What's the story?" Peller asked.

"Bob McPherson is his name. He'll be here in twenty minutes."

"Extraordinary service," Peller said. "I'll wait. Go ahead and take care of the children until he gets here."

She went, shuffling halfway there, then wiping her face and picking up the pace. By the time she was with the kids, she was once more all smiles, if not as springy. Quite the contradiction, he thought, stealing guns and issuing death threats one day, helping raise a new generation the next. Alice Crandall, Peller decided, was a woman working for causes she believed in. Children he could understand. But what could lead her to persecute Chuck Ferring?

Bat swinging gave way to tossing big plastic baseballs and finally to some actual batting practice, such as it was. The kids seldom hit the ball anywhere, but with careful pitching by one of the older women, they managed to make contact some of the time.

Bob McPherson showed up right on schedule, driving a blue Camry and dressed more for a casual dinner than a meeting with a client. He eyed Peller before going to the diamond. Crandall rounded the backstop and talked with him for five minutes before they approached the detective, who was still leaning on his car, waiting.

McPherson nodded to Peller and introduced himself. Peller reciprocated. "Are you making an arrest?" the lawyer asked.

"Just asking questions at the moment," Peller said. "But more important, your client may be in danger. She's a suspect in a firearms theft, and two of her alleged accomplices have since been murdered. She'd be smart to give full accounting of her involvement, so she doesn't end up dead."

"Don't mince words, do you?" McPherson turned to Crandall. She looked sickly and scared now. "Could you come to my office right now?"

She looked at the children playing and bit her lip. "I guess. They have it covered."

"All right." He returned his attention to Peller. "My client won't be answering any questions until I consult with her, Lieutenant. But I appreciate the warning. I'll make sure she's safe."

Peller didn't answer. He watched McPherson escort Crandall back to the field, where she spoke briefly with the other adults, then they went to their cars and drove off, she following him. He had little doubt she had been involved in the robbery, and equally little she was innocent of the murders. Unfortunately, she had left Peller with nothing but impressions.

Theresa Swan cradled the receiver and rubbed her eyes. "Struck out again," she told Jack Collins. "None of the family members I've been in contact with know or care where James Ferring III lives. Or even if he does live. There's only one thing for it."

Collins, seated beside her desk, looked at the time on his cell phone. The workday would be ending soon. "What's that?"

"Call every senior living facility in the county."

"How many are there?"

Ross glanced at her computer, where a map was displayed, dotted with pins indicating the locations of nursing homes. "A lot. Over fifty, anyway."

"Can I help?"

"Better not. They generally won't confirm a particular individual lives with them, but they'll talk to a cop if she makes it sound important." She gave Collins a lopsided smile. "Even so, I probably won't have an answer until tomorrow. You may as well go home."

"All right." Collins rose and shoved his hands into his pockets. "I'll take the rest of the day off, such as it is." He mimicked her smile but looked more disappointed than happy. Once he was gone, Swan started making calls and crossing facilities off her list.

He was inside, seated in his recliner with that accursed wheelchair parked beside and a blanket thrown over his body. The TV was on, and people were chattering on screen about protests in France. Mr. Jim's tired eyes slid shut, but he listened because it was France. The whole mess had started in France. If only Roger hadn't enlisted. Plenty of other men had been clamoring for the chance to die for their country. They could have done without Roger. He hardly proved the best of them.

That damned French woman!

"You have a visitor, Mr. Jim."

Mr. Jim rolled his head to look. The woman in the doorway was tall, thin, and black. Another woman followed, a white woman with a familiar face, dark hair, and piercing eyes. He harrumphed. "I don't want visitors. I'm watching the news."

"You like seeing family, don't you?" The black woman whispered something to the guest, who patted her shoulder and came into the room. The door closed, leaving them alone.

"How are you, Jim?" she asked as she sat on the edge of his bed.

He wasn't going to fall for *that*. He wasn't like Roger. "Go away. I'm not interested in tarts."

She smiled indulgently.

He didn't like that smile. It meant she was after something. Mr. Jim fixed his tired eyes on the television and ignored her.

"I just wanted to make sure they were treating you well."

He waved her off. "I know what you want. I'm married. I don't have any money. Go away."

She laughed. "I always loved your sense of humor."

He hadn't been joking. Besides, she didn't know him. Or did she? He gave her sidelong scrutiny before pulling the blanket about his neck and focusing fiercely on the TV. "You French women are all alike. But I'm not Roger. I won't desert my post for you."

"They didn't forget your pills, did they?" She looked concerned. "Did you have your pills yet?"

What the hell was she talking about? He was sick of pills.

"I'll just go check." She rose and went out the door.

"And don't come back!" he snapped as the door closed.

The scene on the TV changed to a press conference. The White House seal was behind the speaker, but Mr. Jim didn't recognize the man. Probably some under-secretary of something or other. He listened to the speaker drone on and on, but the words didn't register. After a time, not even the sound registered.

"They forgot, all right."

Startled, he opened his eyes and found a woman standing beside him. Where the hell had *she* come from? More to the point, who was she?

She set a cup of water on his nightstand and handed him a pill. "Here you go."

He held it in his shaking fingers and peered at it. "What's this?"

"Time for your meds, Mr. Jim." She handed him the cup of water. "Bottoms up!"

Automatically, he popped the pill into his mouth. It had a funny taste. He didn't like it. She couldn't make him take it. Tucking it under his tongue, he took the water and swallowed a sip to fool her.

She took the cup back, set it on the nightstand, and adjusted his blanket. "Sleep well, Mr. Jim," she said.

Water ran in the bathroom.

The door snicked shut.

Mr. Jim settled back and watched the news until he drifted off to sleep and dreamed of his fool of a brother Roger walking hand-in-hand with his woman along a riverbank in France.

Chapter 17

As soon as Peller set foot in the office Wednesday morning, Captain Morris called him in. She was clicking her pen nonstop before he even sat down. Her habit of doing that when annoyed, frustrated, or just plain thinking always irritated Peller, but he never commented on it. Best not to further aggravate the boss.

"What's up?" he prompted.

"That's what I'd like to know. Your team has always been steady, if unorthodox at times, but now…" She tossed her pen on the desk and leaned forward. "Chief Jeffries received a complaint."

Peller checked the time on his cell phone. "Already?"

"Last night, in the middle of dinner. He obligingly passed it along to me thirty seconds later."

Ouch. No wonder she was angry. "About what?"

"Holly Ross has allegedly been bullying people."

"What? Which people?"

"Art Ferring's wife Cassie and his children Doug Ferring and Carol Mondy. I've been instructed to instruct her to back off. This is just a warning. Next time, it'll be administrative leave and an internal investigation. In fact, if it hadn't been for the gun robbery and the murders, this whole Ferring business would be shut down. I managed to walk him back, but any more incidents like this, and I'll have to put strict limits on the scope of your investigation. Don't make me do that, Rick."

Given that Ross had been following up on the horse shooting, Peller figured he knew what was going on. The Ferring stonewalling must have morphed into active interference in the investigation. "Who filed this complaint? Art Ferring? If so, I wouldn't trust—"

"No," Morris snapped. "Terrance Vickeridge. I warned Corina about him."

Peller leaned back. "How the hell does *he* know what Holly's doing?"

"He's a detective."

"But not a mind reader. Whitney, he's on the wrong side of the family. Look." Peller took his Ferring family tree from his pocket and spread it on her desk. "Holly was following up this branch of the family. Terry is over there. The two sides of the family—James Jr.'s and Roger's—are at each other's throats. They shouldn't even be speaking, much less cooperating."

Morris didn't bother with the diagram. "I don't care. The Chief's given me my marching orders, and I'm giving you yours."

Peller folded the paper and shoved it back in his pocket. "Somebody's using Terry. Let me talk to him and—"

"No. Keep your distance from him and his wife. They aren't part of this."

"We don't know that."

"We do unless and until we have tangible evidence to the contrary."

"Fine." Peller stood. "I'll put Holly on a leash. But once that evidence surfaces—and it will—I'll personally arrest the whole damn family, Terry included. For obstruction of justice if nothing else."

Dumas knew something had gone wrong the moment Holly Ross slipped into his cubicle and dropped into the guest chair. Not only had her usual optimism gone AWOL, she wouldn't even look at him, and the only word she spoke was, "So..."

He gave her a minute to come up with something more eloquent. She didn't. "Personal or professional?" he asked.

She sighed. "I think so."

"Conference room," he suggested and rose. She followed him in, sank into a chair opposite the window, and waited while he closed the door and sat beside her.

And waited some more.

"I'm no good at talking about my problems, either," he said. "So you have nothing to fear."

That earned him a weak smile. "I interviewed Doug Ferring and Carol Mondy today."

Dumas didn't know the second name, but the first had cropped up the other day in his talk with Peter Nye, Jr. This would be interesting. "Who are they?"

"Art Ferring's children. I thought they might know something about the horse killing."

"Did they?"

"They claimed not, but I'm sure they did."

"Which is a problem because …" He motioned her to fill in the blank.

"I pushed too hard."

Dumas couldn't see Ross beating on anybody, but given how obstinate the Ferrings had been, he could understand frustration and anger boiling over. "How hard?"

"I accused them and their father of lying."

"Is that all?"

"So…"

"Come on, Holly. I can't help if you don't tell me."

"I didn't use force, I just got loud and . . . direct. And I didn't stop when they got mad. Irate, actually. Doug stormed out on me. Carol attacked me and physically threw me out of her house."

Dumas blinked. "She *attacked* you?"

A knock sounded. Ross cringed when she saw a grim Rick Peller watching through the glass. Dumas motioned him in.

Closing the door behind him, Peller took a seat on the opposite side of the table. "From the look of things," he said, "this is why Captain Morris just chewed me out."

Ross pinched her eyes shut.

"Don't worry," Peller said. "I'm on your side so far. What happened?"

"Holly did nothing wrong," Dumas said. "She got a bit strident, but those Ferrings are trying your patience, too."

"I didn't ask you, Eric. I asked Holly."

Ross looked out the window. She wasn't crying. Not yet, anyway. She repeated what she told Dumas and added, "I just wanted the truth. They *are* liars. I just wanted…" She shook her head. "I just wanted to impress—"

"You definitely made an impression," Peller said.

"I'm sorry. I…" She squeezed her eyes shut again.

"You're not officially in trouble," Peller assured her. "Not yet. But we've been warned. Unfortunately, the Ferrings have friends in high places. So here's what we'll do. If anyone calls a Ferring a liar, it will be me. And Holly, I think it best you don't interview them alone."

She looked up, hurt, angry, devastated, God knew what else.

"It's not a judgement on your abilities," Peller said. "It's just a precaution. Something strange is going on in that family, and until I know what, I won't take chances with anyone's career but my own."

Dumas felt the whole business had been strange right from the get-go. Still, this was a new twist, and he didn't understand it. "Strange how?"

"The complaint didn't come from Doug or Carol. It didn't even come from Art Ferring, which you might expect. It came from Terrance Vickeridge."

"What the hell? That makes no sense."

"That's what I told Whitney, but she's on the hot seat, so she doesn't care."

Confused, Ross asked, "Vickeridge is covering for them?"

"Or being used by them," Dumas mused. "Either way, the whole family is cooperating to keep it quiet. Whatever *it* is. He frowned at the table. "Of course they are. There are murderers on both sides of the feud. Expose one, and everything unravels."

"And," Peller added, "they aren't only killing each other anymore. Maybe it started as revenge, but now it's survival. Anyone who threatens the family secret could be eliminated. Mia Hambleton for one. Maybe others."

Ross studied her hands. "No wonder they won't talk. And I blundered in like—"

"It's not your fault," Dumas assured her. "There's an art to twisting people's arms, and these aren't your average people. I told Corina Kevin Graham and I could make Troy Nye talk. We'll never know, but maybe I was wrong."

Peller looked thoughtful. "You could have. He was one of the weak links."

Ross and Dumas both raised their eyebrows.

"People we can pin something on," Peller explained. "Andrew Hunt was one of them. I got him to talk. Alice Crandall might be another. Unfortunately, as soon as I told her Nye was dead, she ran for the family lawyer."

So we need another weak link, Dumas thought. And in fact, he had one. "Doug Ferring."

"He ran out on me," Ross reminded them. "He was furious."

"Yeah, but Nye's father fingered Doug as a bad apple. He did time for vandalism."

"Did he," Peller said. "That's interesting. Wait a second." He gazed at the tabletop, and Dumas knew he was looking again at some scrap of evidence. Peller's memory, if not technically photographic, tended that way. "The letters scratched into Chuck Ferring's car. DC."

Dumas spread his hands and looked at the ceiling. "Doug and Carol."

"And Doug's a convicted vandal," Ross said. "Maybe he's the one who hit The Lodge over and over."

"Unfortunately, he's involved in our political situation." Peller turned to Ross. "Any ideas about that, Detective?"

She looked thoughtful but shifted uncomfortably. "Given the circumstances, I'm not sure I should make suggestions."

Dumas smiled encouragement. "If you have something to say, say it."

"We could..." She twined her fingers together, tight. "We could talk to Terrence Vickeridge."

Peller pointed at Dumas. "You've been giving her lessons in crazy, haven't you?"

Dumas spread his hands in innocence. "You're the one who asked."

Ross bit her lip.

"As it happens," Peller said, "I was thinking the same thing."

In the early morning, a light fog rose from the waterways and caressed the valleys. It burned off quickly, leaving a hotter day than forecast, which was either welcomed or cursed depending on who was asked. Theresa Swan cheered the sudden summer even though she was cooped up inside, calling senior facility after senior facility in search of James Ferring III, age older than dirt, with any luck still alive.

Number fifty-three on her list was the presumptuously named Golden Villa. The receptionist who answered spoke in a chirpy soprano that suggested nothing could be wrong with the world. Swan introduced herself before saying, "We're trying to locate a Mr. James Ferring III. Could you tell me if you have a tenant by that name?"

The chirp fled the receptionist's voice at the mention of police. "Is something wrong?"

Paydirt. She wouldn't have asked if Ferring wasn't there. Swan circled the facility's name on her list.

"No," she said. "We just need to talk to him for a few minutes, if possible."

"About what?"

"A minor family matter. What are your visiting hours?"

The receptionist didn't answer at once. Maybe she was trying to figure out how she'd tipped Swan off. "I'll check with my manager, but you probably won't be able to talk to him."

"Why not?"

"Dementia. He doesn't make sense a lot of the time."

She'd take her chances. "I'll wait while you check."

The receptionist put Swan on hold. Looped music with a cheery lilt played for three minutes before she came back. "You can try to talk to him, but a staff member will have to be present."

Swan would rather have kept the interview private, but at least they weren't asking permission from the family. She made an appointment for eleven o'clock, then called Jack Collins to let him know.

"That's great," Collins replied. "*If* he's more willing to talk than the rest of his family."

"Or able. They say he suffers from dementia."

"Only one way to find out. Give me the address and I'll meet you there."

Swan didn't know if that was optimism or resignation, but the thought of peering into a box sealed more than twice her lifetime ago both thrilled her and gave her a chill.

She hoped Ferring *could* speak coherently…and would.

"I want you to go with me," Peller told Captain Morris.

Her lips pinched in a tight line, she mixed sugar into her coffee and tossed the stirrer into the break room trash can. "I don't even want *you* to go with you."

"I'm going anyway. It would help if you were there. You know Terry. I'm just another detective."

Morris took a sip of her coffee and made a face at it, although Peller couldn't tell whether it was the drink or his intentions provoking her. Maybe both.

"Somebody's using him, Whitney. We have two homicides, and somebody's pulling his strings to keep us off the scent. I doubt he'd appreciate that if he knew it."

"You may as well try to remove his gall bladder as tell him anything. Stubborn doesn't begin to describe him, and men only get worse as they age. I know from personal experience."

Peller cracked a smile. "Me, or Daniel?" he said, referencing her husband the doctor.

"Yes." She turned and dumped her coffee down the sink, which answered half the question. "I don't know, Rick. I don't disagree with the theory, but this is as much politics as policing. The Chief wanted heads to roll. It took me half an hour to convince him to stand down and let me handle it."

"If we don't get to the bottom of this," Peller predicted, "more people will die."

Morris leaned against the counter and shook her head. "Damn it, Rick."

"I'm not making book on it, but I told Chuck Ferring the same thing a few days ago, and now we have a double murder."

"Fine. I'll go, but just to keep you out of trouble. And this will be *my* interview. I'll do the talking."

"Understood," Peller agreed.

"When do you want to go?"

"Now."

Straightening, Morris motioned him to the door. "I'll make a quick call to make sure he's there. You can drive and fill me in on this mess. "

Peller waited outside her office while she made the call. She spoke in a low voice so he couldn't eavesdrop and emerged looking no happier than when she'd gone in.

"He's deigned to listen to my full apology," she said. "But expect snarling and snapping."

"Goes with the territory," Peller replied. "Shall we?"

They left in silent lockstep. The day had grown hot and the inside of Peller's car hotter. He cranked up the air and, as he made his way toward Dayton and the Vickeridge home, gave Morris the full rundown on the case so far. She asked few questions and spent most of the ride looking out the passenger window. When Peller finished, she said, "You all think the skeleton was William."

"Most likely," Peller said.

"Killed why? Roger had already paid the price for killing George."

"Roger was the family pariah. William could have inherited his father's stigma. It's not hard to imagine a fight breaking out, as it did between Roger and George."

"And Troy Nye?"

"That's why I want to talk to Terry."

"You're not talking to him. I am. What do you think he knows?"

Peller turned the air down a notch. "Everything and nothing."

"In English."

"His wife is a Ferring. He probably knows all about the clan, but he doesn't know there's a new killer in their midst. Give him half a chance to think about it, and he might realize who it is. At least, he might narrow the field."

Morris finally looked at Peller. "What if it's Ruth?"

Peller took his time in answering. "It's possible. She lost both her father and her brother to the infighting. But I don't think it's her, for the same reason I don't think it's Art Ferring. They both ran away. If either of them wanted revenge, they would have exacted it long ago. Besides, Troy Nye wasn't killed for spite or revenge. He was killed for a simpler reason."

"Dead men tell no tales." Morris looked out the window again. "The ATF's reward posting made somebody nervous."

Peller nodded.

"And Terry is that somebody's unwitting bulldog."

"Yes." They arrived at the Vickeridge home. Peller slowed and turned into the driveway. "Unless I'm wrong about Ruth," he added. "In that case, Terry's probably her gunman."

Morris drew a long breath and got out of the car.

Golden Villa rather looked as one might expect: a sprawling Romanesque building atop a hill, Doric columns supporting a broad portico, manicured lawn overspreading the slope, old oaks and pines dotting the land, a few white statues and splashing fountains. The only sign that all was not tranquility was the ambulance with flashing red lights just pulling away as Theresa Swan parked. Jack Collins was already there, waiting in the shade of a tree beside the parking lot. He waved when he saw her. She motioned him toward the building, and by the time she got to the door, he was walking beside her.

Inside, the lobby looked only a bit less elegant than the exterior. A maroon floral carpet flowed through the reception area and the glass-enclosed rooms to the side. One of the rooms was occupied, with a small crowd in wheelchairs listening to a younger woman who accompanied her talk with wide hand gestures. Swan and Collins approached the front desk, which was staffed by a middle-aged man with thinning hair. He wore a cheap navy suit.

"We're here to see James Ferring," she said and showed her ID. "I called earlier."

He peered at Swan's photo then at her as though not sure the picture matched the face. "Oh, yes, I was told you'd be coming. Let me just get Ms. Spiegel."

They waited in silence while he went to find her. Swan watched a bent old man with a walker make his way toward the elevator. Though he moved with slow, tottering steps, somehow he stayed on his feet and eventually reached his destination. She hoped to age more gracefully, like her great-grandmother who she could remember puttering around the kitchen into her nineties.

"Detective Swan? I'm Ann Spiegel."

Swan turned and acknowledged Spiegel, a tall, fiftyish woman dressed in a blue pant suit. "We appreciate your help, Ms. Spiegel."

Spiegel looked at Collins. "I didn't catch your name."

"Jack Collins, ma'am. I'm . . . " He glanced at Swan.

Swan figured it was best to keep the media out of it. "Mr. Collins is a consultant who's assisting us."

Spiegel looked puzzled. "Consultant."

"Could we see Mr. Ferring?"

"Of course. This way." Leading them not to the elevator but the stairs, Spiegel took them to a room halfway down a long hall on the second floor, talking the whole while. "We're the most sophisticated facility in Howard County," she boasted. "We have sections for unassisted and assisted living, and for memory care. We have on-premises medical facilities, exercise rooms, a dining facility that rivals most restaurants, high speed internet, and all kinds of programs. The grounds have walking paths, picnic areas, and even a playground for visiting grandchildren and great-grandchildren."

"Sounds like a great place," Swan said to be polite. *And expensive*, she told herself. "How long has Mr. Ferring been with you?"

"Longer than I have. I've been on staff for five years, six in September. I think he's lived here as long as anyone. Unfortunately, the past few years haven't been kind to him. He broke a hip and is mostly confined to his wheelchair now. And his mind isn't what it used to be. He gets confused about where he is and who he's talking to."

They came to Ferring's room, and Spiegel knocked on the door. "Mr. Jim? It's Ann. You have visitors."

Without waiting for an answer, she held a card to a reader plate above the door and the lock clicked open. She opened the door a fraction and, without looking in, said, "Mr. Jim? Visitors!"

"Who is it now?" a quavering voice demanded.

"A couple of visitors. They'd like to talk for a few minutes. Is that okay?"

"Go away!"

Looking apologetic, Spiegel whispered, "He's developed a bit of a temper, too. He didn't used to be so surly." After a quick peek inside, she pushed the door open and motioned Swan and Collins to follow.

James Ferring III sat in a recliner, feet propped up, his wheelchair parked nearby. He was dressed in ill-fitting black trousers and a light green polo shirt. A blue blanket lay in a heap on the floor beside him. He was staring out the sliding door at the wooded land beyond.

"You're not cold, are you?" Spiegel bent down to pick up the blanket.

"No," Ferring snapped. "Where's Roger? He was supposed to be here by now."

"Oh, look at this. Did you spit out your meds again?" Straightening, Spiegel held the balled-up blanket in her left arm and grasped a small white pill between her right thumb and forefinger. She squinted at it. "I'd better find out which one this is. I'll be right back." Dropping the blanket on the couch, she hurried out.

Swan slowly approached Ferring and smiled at him. "Mr. Ferring? I'm Detective Theresa Swan, Howard County Police. This is Jack Collins." She motioned Collins over. He came to her side. "Could we talk to you for a bit?"

"I'm only talking to Roger. Tell him to get in here."

"Actually," Collins said, "it's about Roger."

Ferring stared at the reporter.

"Could you tell us about him?"

Putting a hand to his forehead, Ferring sighed. "Sit down," he ordered.

Swan grabbed a couple of chairs from the kitchen table and placed them in front of Ferring. She and Collins sat and waited.

Fists balled, Ferring knocked the arms of his chair a few times. "Is he coming?"

"I'm afraid not," Collins replied.

Swan wasn't sure that was a good thing to admit, but she had no idea how to approach this, either.

"Damn him." Ferring stared out the window. "We should bury the hatchet. I'm willing. It's his fault, but I'm willing. Why isn't he?"

Collins leaned forward. "What's his fault?"

"That woman. That French woman. It's her fault, turning his head, making him run off like that. It was *war*, damn it! You go AWOL, there are consequences!"

"Dishonorable discharge," Collins said quietly, as though as pained by it as Ferring himself.

Ferring nodded. "Disgraced the whole family. We all hated him. But . . ." He shook his head. "There comes a time when you have to forgive." Facing Collins, desperation in his eyes, he asked, "Don't you think?"

"Yes, I do."

A deep silence fell. Swan watched, an outsider ignored by both Ferring and Collins, sensing that forgiving his uncle's indiscretion might be the old man's dying act. Yet Ferring showed no sign of giving up the ghost. If anything, he seemed to gain a little strength from Collins' agreement.

"Tell him. Maybe then he'll come."

"Okay," Collins agreed. "But there are complications."

"Complications? What the hell can be so complicated?"

"George. William. What about them?"

Ferring's mouth quivered. "That's why he has to come. So it doesn't happen again."

"Those were accidents, though," Collins suggested. "Right?"

Weariness settled upon Ferring. He closed his eyes and pressed his head back against the recliner. "Who knows? George, probably. William . . ."

Swan held her breath. So did Collins.

"I don't know. An accident, an eye for an eye. You're never sure."

Leaning back, Collins looked at Swan. It might have been a confession. It could have been anything.

The door opened and Ann Spiegel joined them, looking shaken. "Detective Swan? Could I speak with you for a moment?"

Swan glanced at Collins, who nodded. The women went into the hall, where Spiegel said in a whisper, "That pill I found? It wasn't one of Mr. Jim's meds."

"What was it?"

"We don't know. It doesn't match anything we currently dispense to anyone." She held up a plastic sandwich bag containing the pill. "We thought you might want to have it."

Swan took the bag and examined the pill. It had no markings she could see. The surface looked slightly dissolved. "When did he have his meds last?"

"This morning at about nine. He gets meds morning and afternoon. The nursing assistant who took care of him this morning said he swallowed what she gave him. And she's sure she didn't give him that."

"Did he have any visitors recently?"

"Not that I know of, but I'll check."

"All right. Once we're done here, we'll meet you at the front desk. Thank you."

Spiegel rushed off. Swan watched her go, then returned to the room, where Collins was carefully shaking Ferring's hand. "We will," the reporter said. "Thank you."

Ferring dropped his hand and closed his eyes. "Goodbye, Terry." He drew a ragged breath before adding. "Don't forget."

Collins made no attempt to correct Ferring's identification. "I won't." He nodded to Swan, and they left the room in silence.

Stopping at the front desk, Swan retrieved a slip of paper from Ann Spiegel, who said, "Only one visitor. Her name is here. I don't have contact information for her, though."

Swan looked at the name printed in careful block letters, all capitals. "Jenna Ferring," she said. "Do we know that name?"

Collins craned his neck to look. "Not that I remember. I'll have to check my notes."

Thanking Spiegel for her help, they went out into the heat of the day and stopped by Swan's car. Collins squinted up at the sky. "Something's up," he said. When Swan didn't immediately answer, he added, "Yes?"

"That pill Ann Spiegel found. She says they can't identify it. They bagged it and gave it to me."

"You think somebody tried to kill Ferring?"

"Maybe. We'll find out what it is, then we'll know. It could be a mistake, I suppose."

Collins shook his head. "I doubt it. Jenna doesn't sound to me like a Ferring sort of name."

Swan didn't know about that, but the mystery pill bothered her. "What did he tell you while I was out?"

With a shrug, Collins diverted his gaze to something across the parking lot.

"Jack?"

"I'm not sure I should say."

"Why not?"

Another shrug. "He's a hundred years old, Theresa. His mind is slipping away, he's being eaten alive by regret, and if it happened after 1950, he doesn't remember it. Let's leave him alone."

"You know Rick won't accept that. Nor will Corina."

"I don't care. I'm not a cop."

He could fight that battle himself. He'd already as much as admitted that James Ferring III had confessed to a crime, and what crime but one could matter anymore? He must have killed Roger's son William.

Had someone feared he would finally talk after so many decades?

"See you back at HQ," she said.

Collins nodded and shuffled back to his car, hands in his pockets.

Chapter 18

Ruth Vickeridge served them tea and slipped away to another part of the house while Terrance glowered at the china cup before him. They were seated at the round oak table in the living room. The sunlight, muted by the lace curtains in the front window, fell in a streak across the table, separating him from Captain Morris and Lieutenant Peller. Morris wasn't smiling, as one might have expected her to do in the presence of an old friend and colleague. Indeed, she looked grim. Peller waited for her to do the talking, as he had promised.

"Yes," she finally said to Vickeridge's unasked question, "Jack Collins is dating the sister of one of our detectives. Corina Montufar is her name. But he came here on an assignment for the *Columbia Flier*, not HCPD. He did talk to Corina after. His research happened to cross paths with a couple of cases we're working. I encouraged him to give us whatever useful information he uncovered. I'm sorry you and Ruth got caught in the net. But how was I to know? Your name isn't Ferring."

Peller noted she was taking the whole business onto herself. He felt he should claim his share of the blame, but this was her show. She wouldn't abide interference.

Vickeridge snorted. "You expect me to believe that? You and your hotshot apprentice?" He jerked his head in Peller's direction but didn't make eye contact. "Success gone to your head, Whitney? Gunning for the chief's job?"

"Doing my own," Morris snapped back. "You know me better than that."

"What I *know* is, our privacy has been violated. Excuses don't cut it. Ruth's done a lot of good, but all those reporters want is scandal."

"I'm not a reporter. I'm investigating a crime."

Slapping the table, Vickeridge barked, "My wife is not a criminal!"

"Who said she was? Don't play dumb, Terry. You know how it works."

"Reporters aren't how it works."

"Neither are the Ferrings."

With a grimace, Vickeridge leaned back, crossed his arms over his chest, and looked away. "You think we don't know that? Ruth's suffered enough at her family's hands. You have no right to dredge it up again."

"When it's about murder, I do."

"Ancient history."

"Two days ago."

His glare snapped to her, hard but uncertain.

Morris nodded. "Double murder. A young couple. Troy Nye, who just happens to be a Ferring relative, and his girlfriend Mia Hambleton. They were involved in a robbery at Chuck Ferring's gun shop. Apparently, somebody wanted to shut them up." She skewered him with a glower. "Probably the same somebody who doesn't want me talking to Doug and Carol."

After a moment, Vickeridge straightened and lifted his cup to his lips. He took a long, quiet drink of tea.

Morris gave him a moment, but when he didn't reply, she went on. "I won't roll over and play dead, not even for you, Terry. So damn it, talk to me. What's going on?"

Tight lipped, he shook his head.

Peller found himself holding his breath until a whisper of movement behind him drew his attention. Ruth Vickeridge had returned. Standing in the doorway to the dining room, she was looking at Terrance with a mixture of admiration and resignation. "I'm not a hothouse flower," she said quietly. "Maybe we'd better tell them." She crossed the room, sat beside her husband, and put an arm about his shoulder. "It's all right. You always said it would blow up in Jimmy's face some day. Today might as well be the day."

Terrence maintained his defiance. "We don't have to say anything. I could get the whole department fired."

Morris didn't back down, either. "So do it. Be a Ferring pawn. You always have been, apparently."

"That is *not* true!"

"Prove it. Tell me what's going on."

Before Peller knew he had it, Terrance produced a small handgun and pointed it, shaking, at Morris's face. Peller about threw himself at Morris to knock her out of the way, but before he could move, Ruth's weary voice intruded.

"Oh, put that thing away, Terry." She gave Morris an apologetic look. "Don't worry. It's never loaded."

Captain Morris ordered pizza and wings delivered for the team. Peller went for the aspirin bottle before the food arrived and the group assembled in the conference room.

Theresa Swan detailed her brief meeting with James Ferring III and the incident with the mystery pill, which had been sent for analysis. "It's either a mistake," Swan concluded, "or an attempt to kill him, which is my bet. His mystery visitor, Jenna Ferring, doesn't seem to exist."

"Any description?" Dumas asked.

Swan shrugged. "In her fifties, medium height, dark hair, nice blue dress with white flowers. She signed in and was escorted to Ferring's room by one of the staff, who left as soon as she went in. Nobody remembers seeing her leave, but she signed out. It seemed an innocent enough visit."

Peller rubbed his forehead. "What did he say, Jack?"

Collins picked up a slice of pizza, settled it on a paper plate, and stared at it as though not knowing what it was for. "He babbled."

"About what?"

"Roger. The war. Primordial feuds." He pushed the plate away.

Eyes momentarily closed, Peller said, "Details, Jack."

"He's a hundred years old," Collins said. "He'll be dead in a year or two."

Before Peller could get angry, Montufar went to Collins' side and set a hand on his shoulder. "We aren't the DA, Jack. We don't make those decisions. Anyway, we know James didn't wheel himself up to Woodstock to kill Troy Nye and Mia Hambleton."

"I just don't see the point," Collins muttered.

"The point is murder," Captain Morris said. "As long as you're eating our pizza, you'll help us."

Collins straightened and gave the pizza an unhappy grimace. He might have been accusing it of betrayal. "Roger fought in France in World War I. He fell in love with a young French woman. Several times he went AWOL to see her, until he got caught. That led to his dishonorable discharge. The whole family felt disgraced. Roger wasn't exactly ostracized, but he never heard the end of it. Finally, he got into a fist fight over it with his nephew George. In the scuffle, he pushed George down a flight of stairs, which killed him. Roger was arrested and charged with murder, but before he could be tried, a mob caught up with him and killed him. The anger and grief outlived him. The family took it out on Roger's children, Ruth and William. Ruth eventually escaped by moving away, but William..."

Collins shook his head.

"James III killed William in much the same way his uncle Roger had killed his brother George. It may or may not have been an accident. Either way, the DNA results will show that the bones were William's. James buried him in the bakery cellar."

In the silence, Peller thought he could distinguish the breathing of every person in the room. "That fits what Terrence and Ruth Vickeridge told us," he said. "Under a bit of duress." He glanced at Morris, who smiled rather like a wolf.

"Which was?" Dumas prompted.

"Bad blood between Roger and the rest of the family erupts into violence from time to time. It's a pitched battle. James Jr. has a lot of descendants, Roger only a few. Over the years, most of them have been involved in everything from minor harassment to destruction of property. They only go to the police if they have no choice, like Chuck Ferring. As a gun dealer, he's required by law to report crimes against his business. But he tried to pin it on unspecified 'anti-gun nuts' as he calls them. If the truth came out, nearly every Ferring descendant would be implicated in something. Even dear, sweet Ruth admitted to not always having been so innocent. That's why Terry didn't press too hard when Art Ferring insisted a hunter had killed his horse. Terry's report said no casings were found at the scene. It wasn't true. He found them and pocketed them, because they were the type used by his son Mark, who was, yes, a hunter. Best to avoid having them examined too closely. Terry complained to Chief Jeffries about Holly's behavior because Art Ferring told him to get her off his family's back."

Montufar sat beside Collins and snagged a piece of pizza for herself. "Alice Crandall, Troy Nye, Andrew Hunt, and two unknown burglars" she said. "Descendants of George's brothers and sisters, attacking Roger's descendant Chuck."

"Yes." Peller pulled out his Ferring family tree and smoothed it on the table. "And now a murderer in the mix."

Dumas considered the pizzas and pulled a slice of pepperoni. "You mentioned weak links the other day. Let's illuminate the situation for Alice Crandall. Someone's popping members of her team, not to mention gunning for her great-grandfather. She's at risk, too. Even her lawyer would tell her to talk."

"Agreed," Peller said.

Montufar jumped to her feet and circled the table to look at the family tree. "Jenna Ferring, the woman who visited James. Given her reported age, she had to be one of these." She pointed to each. "Denise Ferring. Cassie Ferring. Peter Nye Jr.'s wife. Stephen Hunt's wife."

Holly Ross, who had been uncharacteristically quiet, said, "Cassie Ferring isn't a likely killer. She's too easily rattled."

"But Denise is," Collins volunteered. "She's a rock. And smart."

Peller leaned back and tapped a finger on the table before looking at Morris.

"Your call," she told him. "Now that Terry's under control, I'll back you."

"Can you get Kevin Graham?" he asked Dumas.

"Absolutely. Who's our target?"

"Alice Crandall."

Dumas' eyebrows lifted in surprise. "Not Doug Ferring?"

"He's second on your list, but first let's see if Alice will talk. She's got the lawyer by her side, but maybe she'll see reason."

Dumas checked the time on his cell phone. "Too late to get Kevin today. I'll set it up for first thing tomorrow morning." He left to make the arrangements.

"Holly, you take another shot at Cassie. Who's your friend out in Frederick?"

She all but blushed. "Sam Kohler."

"Ask him to be your foil. And forget what I said before. Call her out. See if you can break her." Peller motioned her to go.

Looking rejuvenated, Ross left as quickly as Dumas had.

"Theresa, see if you can track down the other two women. I doubt anything will come of it, but we need to know who they are and if they have alibis for the time of the killings and the mystery woman's visit to James III. Corina, you and I will take on Denise Ferring. You've got the lead."

"Pitting the woman against the woman?" she quipped.

"The smart against the smart, if Jack's observation is correct."

Montufar gave him a twisted smile. "Thanks. I think."

On Wednesday evening, Peller drove to Eagle's Wings Clinic and waited in the parking lot beside his car. Bird calls rang in the distance as a warm wind blew through the trees. The sun, not quite touching the horizon, was losing its potency, but a moderately warm night seemed to be on

                    DALE E. LEHMAN

offer. He waited ten minutes before another vehicle rolled into the parking lot and stopped beside his.

Peller only knew Winston Marley from a handful of phone calls, so his appearance surprised the detective. He was barely five ten and rail-thin with coal black skin, a pencil mustache, and a short Afro haircut. He hopped from his vehicle like a wound-up spring being released, clearly a man of energy if nothing else, dressed in white dress slacks and a bright red button-down shirt.

Extending a hand, Peller said, "Pleased to finally meet you, Mr. Marley."

"Likewise, Lieutenant, and it's Winston, if you please." He laughed as they shook hands. "I feel like I've known you forever, but I must say…" he gave Peller a careful once-over. "I was expecting a uniform. I must have been thinking T. J. Hooker."

"I never watched him," Peller admitted. "To me, William Shatner will always be Captain Kirk. Anything you want to ask before we go in?"

Marley's face turned somber. "I wouldn't know where to start. I'll just talk to the lady and see what happens."

Peller appreciated his use of the term. "Follow me," he said. They passed through the doors emblazoned with the bald eagle in flight. Once fitted with green paper bracelets by the young brunette keeping watch over the entrance, they received unnecessary directions to Shania North in room two-thirty-seven. Peller led Marley down the bright but cheerless corridors, past the portraits of the facility's donors and leaders, and to their destination.

Peller knocked on the door, which stood open a crack.

"Come in," Shania said, her voice as timid as ever.

She sat in the same chair as before, but now she was dressed in her street clothes, the TV remote in her hand. She brightened and clicked the device off when she saw Peller.

"You look like you're ready to walk out of here," he said.

She shrugged. "They let me put this on today. I guess I'm mostly better."

"That's good to hear." Peller motioned Marley forward. He advanced with some hesitation, watching Shania's eyes. "This is the man I told you about. Winston Marley, Shania North." He stepped back, but they only nodded to each other. Snagging a couple of chairs, Peller put one in front of her for Marley and the other beside her for himself. She would be nervous; with luck, his presence would make it all right.

Marley sat and nodded to her. "Pleased to meet you," he said.

She forced a smile. "Hi."

Clasping his hands before him, Marley gave the room a once-over. "This looks like a hotel. When they yanked my appendix three years ago, I had to stay in a hospital room."

Shania didn't quite laugh, but Peller saw a rare sparkle in her eyes.

"They treating you okay?" Marley asked.

"Yeah." She looked down and drew a breath. "Rick says you knew Jay."

Peller hadn't expected her to be so direct. He hoped it was a good sign.

"I did, Marley said. "A little."

"Did he..." She bit her lip.

Marley cocked his head and smiled at her. "Yeah, he mentioned you. Several times."

Peller wanted to protest that Jayvon had said nothing incriminating.

Shania stretched her thin arm out to Peller. He took her hand in his. "What did he say?" she asked. Her grip tightened. Not that she could muster much force.

From the way she avoided Marley's eyes, Peller figured Shania was probing, trying to determine what he knew about her. Did she want him to know, or would she rather he remained ignorant of her background?

Marley considered his answer before speaking, possibly understanding he was on precarious ground. "Not much, and I didn't ask. Wasn't my business. But I could tell he was worried about you and wanted to help. Maybe that's why Rick and I are here now. Maybe Jay's still trying to help you."

Peller noticed Marley had picked up on Shania's name for Jayvon.

"Jay's dead," Shania said with a longing that Peller understood. It was the same longing he felt for Sandra. Shania's hand tightened on his again.

"Death is just a doorway," Marley said gently. "He's still with you."

"Maybe." She released Peller, fumbled for a tissue from a box on the nightstand, and dabbed at her eyes. "Maybe I'm not worth it."

Marley leaned forward, elbows resting on his knees. "Sure you are."

"You don't know me. Jay didn't tell you. He wouldn't. Rick wouldn't, either." She glanced at Peller, who shook his head.

"True," Marley told her, "but I know one thing. You're a human being, created noble, God's shadow on Earth." His voice was still quiet, but it carried a conviction Peller felt as powerfully as an electric shock.

Shania seemed puzzled by the statement. She looked into Marley's eyes for a long time, scarcely breathing. Then she looked away. "You just don't know me."

"Jay thought you were worth it. So does Rick. That's got to mean something."

Shania plucked another tissue from the box and crushed it with her fingers. "Why did Jay talk to you?"

Marley sat upright again. "To learn about my religion. I'm a Baha'i."

She absently shredded the tissue and balled up the pieces. "Momma was a church-goer. Always took me when I was little. Didn't do me no good, I guess." She looked at Marley warily. "Was that Jay's idea? Get me to church, save a whore's soul?"

Marley didn't react to the word. He might not even have heard it. "He was searching for his own answers, but sure, you were on his mind, too."

She worried at the shreds of tissue before extending her hand and dropping them in the vicinity of the waste basket. Some of the scraps fell in. Others fluttered to the floor. "I wish he was here."

Marley lowered his eyes and nodded, whether from empathy or exhaustion. Maybe both. Peller thought him a good man but out of his depth. He'd likely never done anything like this before.

She wiped her eyes. "Why'd he get himself killed?"

"He didn't," Peller told her. "He was just in the wrong place at the wrong time."

"Funny answer for God to give him."

Marley spoke in a quiet, reverential tone: "I call on Thee O Thou Who slayest the Lovers, O God of Grace to the wicked."

Peller and Shania exchanged a glance.

"It's from a Baha'i prayer," Marley explained. "The Long Healing Prayer."

Shania wiped her eyes with her fingers. "How long?" she asked.

They didn't leave until just after nine o'clock. Peller drove straight home but once there found himself restless. He wandered aimlessly through the house, looking at nothing in particular, encountering for the ten thousandth time his collected memories of Sandra and their son Jason and wondering why time had devoured that life before they'd had a chance to finish living it. In the living room, he paused before the family photos hanging on the wall and looked into Sandra's eyes as she smiled for the camera with an infant Jason in her arms.

He told people, told himself, that Shania was the daughter he never had, but maybe that wasn't it. Maybe it was because they had both lost the battle with time far too early.

Time doesn't win, he thought he heard Sandra whisper. *We have eternity.*

"But I have such a long way to go to get there," he whispered back.

You don't know that.

Whether Sandra or his imagination said it, it was true. He never expected to be swept away by a flood and brought within moments of death. Why had God saved him and not Sandra? Why had He brought Peller to Shania in time to save her but not her boyfriend Carnell?

Why was Peller playing Job, asking questions to which there could be no comprehensible answers?

Shania, at least, had found some comfort in the prayer Marley recited, reading it from his cell phone, and for that Peller was grateful. For himself, it seemed to raise more questions than his mind could juggle. But it did bring eternity a bit closer, even if his life didn't feel any more in focus.

He sat on the sofa, took out his cell phone, and placed a call. Eyes on that photo of Sandra and Jason, he waited for an answer.

When it came, it was hesitant. "Hi, Rick."

"Hi Joan. I . . . well, I called to apologize."

The whisper of Churchill's breath was his only answer.

"For ruining Friday evening," he explained.

"No, I . . . it was my fault. I shouldn't have gotten so upset."

"I don't blame you. I'm probably obsessed with helping Shania, but I—"

She cut him off. "How did it go? Did the guy show up?"

"Yes. He did a great job. Shania's invited him to visit again."

"With you?"

"No. I'll check up on her next week, after she's released, but I think they'll do better without me in the way."

Churchill was silent for a moment. "That sounds . . . positive."

"Yes," Peller agreed. "About us, then. Care to try again?"

"I'd love to. Friday?"

"Friday," he agreed.

"Okay." Another brief silence ensued before she asked, "Rick?"

"Yeah?"

"*Is* there an us?"

He looked at Sandra's photo. Her smile conveyed encouragement. "I don't know yet," he said. "Maybe there could be."

"Okay." The word sounded surprisingly content. "See you Friday. Sherlock."

Chapter 19

It proved easiest to assemble Thursday morning at Bob McPherson's office near U.S. 29 and Little Patuxent Parkway, in a tree-sheltered collection of one-story commercial buildings. The brown brick offices hosted primarily doctors, a few lawyers, an accountant, and a deli to feed them. Rows of evergreen shrubs marched around the edges of the well-kept lawn. Officer Kevin Graham barely looked at the development before remarking, "Bet they charge a pretty penny for rent."

Dumas considered the property. "Looking to invest?"

"Never be a landlord, mon. Too many headaches."

"Unlike dealing with criminals, huh?"

"Much worse." Graham, a big man who hailed from Jamaica, had been on the force a long time, longer than Dumas. He had been one of the first officers Dumas met when he came to Howard County, and Dumas often pulled him in on interviews.

They headed up the walk toward the lawyer's office. "How would you know? You ever try it?"

"My brother-in-law did. He bought a small apartment building and about went mad with deadbeat tenants complaining about each other and tearing the place apart. He finally sold it to some other sucker."

Dumas opened the door and motioned Graham in. "I guess that won't be my second career."

The lobby was small but neat, with a few well-polished desks, black filing cabinets, and photos of hills, streams, and farms. A young man in a dark suit, bright red tie, and military haircut looked up as they came in. "Sergeant Dumas?" he asked.

"In person," Dumas replied. "This is officer Kevin Graham."

"Mr. McPherson is expecting you." He rose and led them down a bright corridor, past offices and conference rooms, all of which were empty. The silence suggested they were alone, but at the end of the corridor he motioned them into a conference room stuffed with a huge table and its attendant chairs. Already in attendance, McPherson sat beside Alice Crandall, who was dressed in a light blue blouse. More than a little nervous, she avoided looking Dumas and Graham in the eyes.

The cops sat opposite suspect and attorney. Nobody spoke for a long moment. Dumas focused on McPherson, Graham on Crandall. McPherson arched his eyebrows but refused to go first.

"Here's what we know," Dumas finally said. "On May thirtieth, a gun shop called The Lodge was robbed during business hours. Three hooded burglars gained access through an unlocked back door. Guns and ammunition were stolen, and a threatening note was left. Surveillance video suggests that one suspect was a woman. The door was intentionally left unlocked by an employee. When confronted with the evidence against him, said employee named your client as the individual who recruited him for the task."

When Dumas paused, Graham interjected, "In other words, Alice, you're looking at felony theft and possession charges. That's serious jail time."

"We know the possibilities," McPherson said blandly.

"You also know," Dumas continued, "that two of Alice's accomplices have been murdered."

"So Lieutenant Peller said."

Eyes focused on the tabletop before her, Crandall clenched her fists.

"Who might've done that?" the detective asked.

McPherson glanced at his client but didn't give her time to speak. "We don't know."

"So speculate."

"That would be pointless."

Graham turned his emotionless gaze on McPherson. It had no effect. "Come on, mon, she must have some idea. Her family's been fighting an internal war for decades."

Ignoring him, McPherson asked Dumas, "What do you want?"

"The truth would be a good start. The names of her accomplices, the location of the stolen property, what the threat was about, and who might have killed Troy Nye and his girlfriend."

"Is that all?"

"As I said, it would be a good start."

"In exchange for what?"

"It's pretty hard to ignore stolen guns," Graham commented.

Dumas nodded. "That, it is."

"In exchange for what?" McPherson repeated.

"I'm not the DA," Dumas said, "but cooperation might make for a lighter sentence."

Crandall looked up, her eyes fiery. "It might get me killed, too!"

"Then help us identify the killer," Dumas told her.

"I don't know! It could have been any of them. Chuck, his kids, that Vickeridge gang. Any of them! I didn't know this would happen. You think I knew Troy would die?"

"No," Dumas said. "I imagine it seemed like a prank at the time."

She leaned forward, arms splayed out across the table as though reaching for something just beyond her grasp. "Yeah, I'm just a thrill-seeking kid. Chuck Ferring getting my dad fired has nothing to do with it."

"Alice," McPherson warned. She pulled her hands back and sank in her chair.

"Revenge?" Dumas asked. "Yeah, that makes sense, given your family's history. But doesn't your dad work for your grandfather at the bakery?"

She glanced at the attorney, who shrugged. The secret had already escaped. "No. He's never been interested. He'll inherit the business, but he doesn't want it. He worked as a loan officer until last year."

"What happened?"

"Chuck's wife Jenna accused dad of sexual harassment. It wasn't true. She pretended to want a loan and made an appointment with him just to get him."

Dumas looked up sharply. "Jenna Ferring?"

Alice nodded.

"How old is she?"

"I don't know. About Chuck's age, I guess."

The alleged Jenna Ferring who had visited James III was a good twenty years older than that. Had someone tried—rather clumsily—to implicate the real Jenna in attempted murder? Dumas jotted a note and continued, "So your dad was fired."

"Allowed to resign. The company didn't want a scandal, and the so-called victim signed a non-disclosure agreement in exchange for a modest payoff. Dad found another job in a couple of months, but it was hell on him. On the whole family."

Graham nodded. "So you plotted revenge."

"You're making assumptions," McPherson said quickly. "There are two other burglars. You have no reason to think Alice planned the crime."

"We got a witness," Graham snapped. "The inside man says Alice recruited him."

Dumas watched Crandall's reaction. The comment had been spoken to McPherson but directed at her, and it hit its mark. She pinched her lips in anger.

"Even if true," McPherson said, "that doesn't make her the mastermind. And a lot more is going on in Alice's family than what happened at The Lodge. It's turned deadly and she's a potential victim. Doesn't that overshadow her small part in it? We can do this one of two ways. You can proceed against her with the flimsy evidence you have, or we can agree to some reasonable protections in exchange for whatever information she can provide. Consult with the DA and let me know." He leaned back and drummed his fingers on the table before folding them over his stomach.

Dumas smiled a thin smile. Deals weren't his provenance, nor did he care for them. Alice Crandall was a thief and probably a vandal, and she had threatened a man's life. Yes, she worked with children and was young enough to command pity from some people, but he well knew how far wrong youth could go. Long ago, he had sent his own cousin Phillip to prison rather than see him open the family's front door to drugs and violence, an act for which his uncle Ethan exiled him.

"Tell me two things before I go," he said.

"Such as?"

"How did you spend Tuesday night, Alice?"

Crandall frowned. "Why?"

"Just answer the question."

She looked to McPherson, who nodded. "I was at home. I share an apartment with a college friend. We had dinner at about six. We watched a movie on cable. I probably checked my social media accounts before going to bed."

"I'll want your address and your roommate's name and phone number."

Crandall sighed but pulled the information from her cell phone.

Dumas noted it down. "Second thing. Where are the stolen weapons?"

"We aren't answering that without a deal," McPherson said.

"Don't sell them," Graham warned Crandall. "That adds a few more ugly charges to your list."

"Are you done?" McPherson asked.

Dumas pushed his chair back and rose. "No. We'll be back." Motioning Graham to follow, he left without saying when.

Cassie Ferring might have expired in the doorway when she saw Holly Ross and Sam Kohler standing there. Her knuckles turned white as she squeezed the doorknob to keep from falling over. "What do you want?" she said, breathless.

"We have a few more questions," Ross said.

"Why all the fuss over a horse? It was fourteen years ago!"

"Because two people have been shot dead. Or aren't they worth the fuss, either?"

Ferring put a hand to her mouth and stepped back. "Oh my God. Who?"

Kohler inched forward. "May we come in, ma'am?"

He sounded far more sympathetic than Ross. Ferring blinked at him, then nodded slightly. "Yes, of course."

She led them to the living room, to the same seats they had occupied during their last visit. Distracted, she offered them coffee, but they refused.

"Do you know Troy Nye?"

"My aunt Beatrice married a man named Nye."

"Troy was his grandson. He was killed Tuesday night, along with his girlfriend, a young woman named Mia Hambleton. Both were shot dead and dumped by a sewage pumping station."

Ferring put her face in her hands and weaved as though about to pass out. "Oh my God."

"Where were you Tuesday night?"

Ferring gaped at Ross. "You think *I* killed them?"

"I think you lied about the horse, so you'd definitely lie about murder."

"Please, I . . . " She looked desperately to Kohler.

Leaning forward and motioning her to calm down, Kohler said, "It's all right, Ms. Ferring. We'll help you if you help us. Just tell Detective Ross what you know, and everything will be okay."

"But I don't know anything! Tuesday. Tuesday. I was here, with my husband. He came home from work, we had dinner, watched some TV, and that was all."

"Just the two of you?" Ross asked.

"Yes, it usually is. We don't have company often. I don't even know Troy Nye. Why would I want to shoot him?"

Ross gave her a severe look before replying. "He was involved in a robbery. He was probably killed to make sure he couldn't talk."

"Robbery?" She looked from one detective to the other. "So he was a crook. Why are you asking me about him?"

"He was a Ferring," Ross said. "And he robbed a Ferring. Chuck Ferring. Know him?"

"Oh God." Ferring clasped her hands in her lap and looked away. "Oh God."

"I'll take that as a yes. What the hell is going on?"

Voice quavering, she muttered, "What will happen to me? What do you think they'll do to *me*?"

Kohler moved to a seat beside her. His voice calm and quiet, he said, "We'll protect you. I promise. We won't let anything happen to you."

He was terribly good at that, Ross thought. He always had been. She could almost wish they hadn't gone their separate ways.

But Ferring wasn't having any of it. "You don't understand this family. You don't know what they'll do."

"Then tell us," Ross insisted.

"The horse . . . it was . . ." She covered her face with her hand again. "Mark Vickeridge. Probably. That's what Art said. It was probably Mark."

"Why?"

Dropping her hand, Ferring finally looked at Ross. "Somebody smashed up Mark's car. He accused Art."

"Was he right?"

She shrugged. "Who knows? All I know is, Art and I both wanted to get away from his lunatic relatives. That's why we came here, and it's been wonderful. Until you showed up."

As if I started it, Ross thought. "When's the last time you had contact with any of them?"

Looking away again, Ferring shrugged.

"Recently?"

Another shrug.

Kohler tried to look her in the eyes, but she turned further to avoid him. "Ms. Ferring? Who did you talk to?"

"Nobody," she mumbled. "Nobody. I was just upset after your last visit. I just needed..."

"Who did you talk to?" he all but whispered.

She sighed. "Just Denise."

In a chambray shirt, faded jeans, work boots, work gloves, and a pair of protective goggles, Denise Ferring was in the bakery's storefront clearing away debris while a gang of three young men worked construction in the back section, an area that hadn't been touched by the flood. Peller and Montufar stood in the doorway, watching, apparently invisible to the workers, who paid them no mind. Montufar had only seen a few photos, mostly of the basement where the bones had originated, but clearly more was going on than mere repair.

Tossing an old chair into a pile of debris and cast-off furnishings, Ferring looked up and finally noticed them. She peeled off the googles and gloves and came over to greet them. "We're not exactly serving right now," she said with a friendly smile, "but what can I do for you?"

Montufar showed her ID. "Detective Sergeant Corina Montufar, Howard County Police. This is my boss, Detective Lieutenant Rick Peller. Sorry for the intrusion, but we need to ask a few questions."

"You want my husband, I suppose."

"No, ma'am, we're here to talk to you."

She arched her eyebrows but didn't object. "Then I guess we'd better go up to the apartment. The ambiance is better."

Montufar smiled at the joke. "I'm sure it'll improve down here. What are you doing, remodeling?"

"That's right. It seemed a good time to make some changes. The place needed a facelift. Come on, this way."

She led them around the building to the back, where a long staircase led to the apartment above the shop. Once inside, she took them through the well-appointed living room to the kitchen in the back. Although small, it had top-of-the-line chrome appliances and a small round table that could seat four in a pinch.

"I'd offer you the sofa," she said, "but I'm filthy. It will be easier to clean up the mess out here."

"Quite all right," Montufar said. She noticed Peller's eyes flitting about the kitchen. So did Ferring, although she didn't comment on it. "Do you know Troy Nye?"

"Troy Nye. I know the name. Beatrice and Peter's grandson, I think? I probably met him at a family gathering once upon a time."

"He was murdered Tuesday night."

Ferring leaned back, eyes wide. "Murdered?"

"That's right."

Whatever was going on in her head, Denise Ferring didn't show it.

That look of astonishment notwithstanding, she maintained the calm of a mountain lake, waiting for something further: details, and explanation, an accusation. Montufar gave her nothing and outwaited her.

"I wish I could say that's terrible," Ferring continued. "It's not that I'm cold, I just don't know him, so I can't feel much one way or the other."

"He was family," Montufar said.

"It's a big family, and I suppose you know it's not always been a close or happy one. Your reporter had that much figured out, didn't he?"

Although she felt some embarrassment at encouraging Jack Collins to entangle himself in this mess, Montufar wasn't about to dwell on it. "We believe Troy was killed by a family member. Who would have wanted him dead?"

Ferring laughed and shook her head. "I couldn't tell you that. As I said, I didn't know him."

"When did you last see him?"

"I really have no idea. It's probably been years."

"How did you spend Tuesday night?"

Ferring flashed that astonished look again. It was too perfect, too practiced. It had to be fake. "Why?"

"That's when Troy was killed."

"Oh, you think *I* did it."

"I don't think anything right now. I'm just gathering information."

"I spent Tuesday night right here with my husband. We had a very romantic evening. Frozen pizza. Discussing plans for the remodel. Watching the news. Steamy stuff."

Montufar didn't react to the sarcasm. "Did you know your father-in-law killed his cousin William Ferring and buried him in the cellar here?"

Denise Ferring hadn't expected that. She blinked and allowed a small sound of surprise before shaking her head. "Is that who was down there? We'd heard stories, of course, but . . . no, we had no idea."

"What would it be worth to someone, I wonder, to keep it from becoming known?"

"It was a long time ago," Ferring objected. "Jimmy's got one foot and half of the other in the grave."

"We've spoken to him," Montufar said. "We know his condition. And his guilt. But back to Troy. What was his guilt, aside from aiding in a burglary?"

"Burglary?"

"Everything's a surprise to you, isn't it?"

"Only things I don't know. And I told you, I didn't know Troy Nye. At most, I met him a time or two years ago."

Peller, who had been all but forgotten, rose and walked to the refrigerator. "Mind if I get some water?" he asked.

Distracted by the movement, Ferring turned in her chair. "Um." She pointed to the cabinet to the right of the appliance. "Glasses are right there."

"Thank you." He opened the door, took out a glass, and used the water dispenser on the refrigerator to fill it.

"There's a theory," Montufar went on. "The burglary was part of a long-running spat between Roger Ferring's descendants and the rest of the family. According to this idea, Troy was killed because if we caught up with him, he might say too much and lead a number of family members to prison."

As she spoke, she noted that Peller furtively examined the contents of the counter before returning to the table: a block of knives, a food processor, a toaster, a small tray with three prescription bottles. He sat and sipped at his water, listening to the conversation.

"Based on other evidence," Montufar continued, "our list of suspects is short."

Ferring's eyes narrowed. "A woman about my age," she guessed.

"You should have been a detective."

"Are you arresting me?"

"Not at the moment."

"Do you have a warrant?"

"I don't need one to ask you questions."

She nodded at Peller. "Does he need one to search my kitchen?"

"If we need to search your kitchen," Peller said, "we'll get a warrant. But you said I could have the water." He raised the glass in mock salute. "For which I thank you."

Ferring rose. "This has been fascinating, but I really should get back to work. Next time you show up, I'll have my lawyer to hand."

The detectives stood, too. "That would probably be sound," Montufar said. "You may need a lawyer. We'll show ourselves out."

Down the stairs, around to Main Street, and onward to Montufar's little red sports car, neither spoke a word. Only once they were on the road, she driving too fast for Peller's comfort, did she ask, "What did you see?"

"Simvastatin, vitamin D, and quinidine."

"Simvastatin treats high cholesterol. I think quinidine is a heart med."

"Yes, for arrhythmia."

"You think she gave something to James III?"

"Maybe. I can see her as a poisoner."

"But not shooting two people at close range."

Peller shook his head. "She's hard to figure, but no, I don't think that's her. She'd be the boss. Someone else would be the triggerman."

"Like who?"

Peller looked out the side window. "Hell if I know."

Chapter 20

Cruising east on Interstate 70, Holly Ross called in, but neither Peller nor Dumas were there, so she asked for Theresa Swan. "Any luck with the old ladies?" she asked.

Swan's voice sounded distant and a bit disjointed over the cell connection. "Yeah, I found them both. Barbara Nye was in the hospital that night, recovering from a cholecystectomy. Know what that is?"

"No clue."

"Neither did I. It's a gall bladder removal."

"Spell it."

"No." Swan laughed. "Kate and Stephen Hunt are on vacation in Florida. They left Saturday. What about Cassie Ferring?"

"She finally admitted the horse killing wasn't an accident. Terry Vickeridge thought his son Mark might have done it."

"Ouch."

"Listen," Ross said casually, "I could use some backup."

"For what?"

"I got to thinking. Cassie implied the whole clan is nuts and liable to do anything. Did she mean Doug and Carol, too?"

"Her own children?"

"Yeah. What say we go rogue and press them?"

Swan didn't answer at once, but that wasn't surprising. She had more to lose than Ross if things went wrong.

"Maybe they don't know anything," Ross added. "But they were definitely on edge last time around."

"What if they complain again?"

Ross didn't know, but she wasn't about to let what-ifs stand in her way. "Lieutenant Peller will back us up. He let me off my leash with Cassie. He wants the job done and doesn't much care how we do it."

"That's not entirely true," Swan objected.

"I don't mean pistol-whipping. I just mean he'll be okay with a bit of pressure."

"I guess I'd better come along, if only to keep you out of trouble."

Yes! Ross silently cheered. "I'll stop by HQ and pick you up. We'll start with Carol and see where it leads."

"All right. I'll be waiting."

It took Ross half an hour to get back and another half hour to reach Carol's place. They turned in the driveway and got out. Swan closed her door gently and drew in a deep breath. "I could live out here," she said. "It's so quiet."

"They pay you that much?" Ross quipped. "I want a raise."

"Go on, burst my bubble."

Before they could approach the door, Carol Mondy came around the side of the house in cutoff jeans and a powder blue t-shirt smeared with soil. She was carrying a trowel and small tray of greenery in black plastic nursery pots. She squinted at them and, recognizing Ross, grew angry. "Why are *you* here again?"

Ross gave her a sarcastic smile. "We have a few more questions."

Mondy set the tray on the ground but kept the trowel in hand, clutching it like a knife. "I'm surprised they let you out so soon."

"Oh, your daddy tried to sideline me, but my boss saw through him. We're pretty sure we know who shot his horse and why. Question is, why does he want to hide it?"

"It was a hunting accident." Mondy said it slowly, spacing the words out as if explaining to a small child. She pointed the trowel at Ross. "Get off my property."

Swan took a half step forward and put up her hands in a plea for calm. "Take it easy, ma'am. We just need your help."

"Yeah? And who the hell are you?"

"Detective Theresa Swan." She flashed her ID. "We already know quite a lot about your family's history. Roger Ferring's background, his altercation with his nephew George, his son William's disappearance. There's a lot of bad blood between Roger's descendants and the rest of the family, isn't there?"

Looking down at the plants, Mondy took a long breath, but her resolve didn't break. "My parents got away from all that. They wanted their children to do the same. It's nothing to do with us anymore."

"Maybe," Ross said. "Maybe not. Troy Nye's been murdered. You know Troy?"

Lips pinched tight, Mondy shook her head.

"Met him once at a family reunion, maybe?"

"No."

"Worked with him on the Lodge robbery, maybe?"

Her head snapped up. She pointed the trowel again. "Get *off* my property!"

Ross casually closed the gap between them, but there was nothing casual about her reply: "Stop lying and maybe I will."

She barely knew what happened next. Mondy lashed at her, and a moment later Ross was on the ground with pain lancing the side of her face and blood on the grass. There was a thud, an exhalation, and Swan's voice, dark and clear: "Don't even twitch." Ross didn't know who Swan was commanding. She rolled onto her side and propped herself on her elbow. Gun drawn, Ross stood over Mondy, who was half curled up and gasping for breath. The trowel, streaked with blood, lay three feet away.

Swan kept her eyes on Mondy. "You okay, Holly?"

Ross grunted and got to her feet. Gingerly, she probed the side of her face. Her fingers came away red and sticky. "So long as I don't bleed to death."

"I could arrest you for that," Swan told Mondy. She lowered her weapon. "But I won't if you start talking. Sit up and stay sitting." She glanced back at Ross and said, "I got this. Go spend some quality time with your first aid kit."

Ross dragged herself to the car and sat on the passenger side. She pulled down the visor and opened the mirror on the back. She looked like a vampire had attacked her. "Nice job, Holly," she muttered. "Next time, try punching out a drug lord." She took her first aid kit and some napkins from the glove compartment and went to work. The wound turned out to be surprisingly short but deep enough to suggest a trip to the doctor. She got the bleeding under control and slapped a pair of adhesive bandages over it.

In the yard, Carol Mondy sat cross-legged in the grass, talking without enthusiasm at the lawn while Theresa Swan stood over her, hands on hips, listening and occasionally asking a question.

Ross hoped this might constitute a feather in her cap, but she had a feeling it wouldn't go over that well with her superiors.

Swan offered to take Ross to urgent care. She declined, after which the drive to Doug Ferring's place of employment was strangely quiet. Swan expected Ross to ask what Carol Mondy had said after the altercation, but no. Nothing. That wasn't a good sign. Ross wasn't generally reticent.

She didn't know what to say to her colleague, but best not to let it fester. With two miles to go, Swan pulled off the road into a church lot and put the car in park.

They both stared out the windshield.

"This isn't Doug's workplace," Ross said. "Not even close."

"I know."

They kept on staring.

Swan wondered how Montufar would handle this, what she would say.

Ross looked out the side window for a change. "What did Carol tell you?"

"When Mark Vickeridge killed Art Ferring's horse, Art decided enough was enough. He moved family and business to Frederick County. Six years later, Carol and Doug were out on their own. They returned to Columbia for jobs. They got to talking one evening about the family feud and their father's horse, and the next thing they knew, they were plotting revenge. Chuck Ferring's gun shop was the easiest target. Their father either found out or suspected what was going on and blew a gasket. He threatened to off them himself unless they dropped the vendetta."

"Such a loving father."

"Carol puts it down to grief. At any rate, they dropped out, but not before passing the baton to a younger generation of Ferring cousins."

"Like Alice Crandall," Ross suggested.

"Exactly."

"What about Troy Nye?"

"Carol swears she doesn't know anything about that. She's been a good girl ever since daddy threatened her life."

Swan turned to Ross, who hadn't taken her eyes from the side window. The case was only half the story. They needed to get the other half out in the open. "We're always at a disadvantage," she said. "You know that."

Ross finally looked at her. "We shouldn't be. We're cops, too."

"Female cops. People assume we're weak. Weaker than men, anyway."

"Yeah. She wouldn't have attacked Rick or Eric."

Swan recalled the customer at The Lodge. Her stomach knotted up. "Probably not."

Ross looked away again, anger and embarrassment fighting for ascendancy.

"It's okay. You pushed the right buttons, at least."

"Did I? She talked to you, not me."

"Only because I pointed a gun at her and threatened to arrest her." Choking back a bitter laugh, Ross nodded. "Thank you, by the way."

"No problem. I should probably thank you, too."

"For what?"

Swan set her hands to the steering wheel and squeezed it. "I had an incident of my own. A customer at the Lodge threatened me. I nearly blew him away. It wasn't a good feeling."

Ross put a hand on Swan's shoulder.

"This time," Swan continued, "I just did my job."

"We're a mess," Ross said.

"A little, yeah."

"I really wanted to impress the boss. You know?"

Swan did. "Howard County doesn't give us young detectives many chances to shine. Or to get smacked in the face with a garden trowel."

Ross touched the wound and smiled in embarrassment. "Maybe that's a good thing."

"You did fine. I'll tell them so."

"Thanks again." Ross waved toward the road. "Enough self-pity. Let's get this over with."

Swan put the car in gear and got back on the road. In due course, they arrived at the medical data processing facility on Gateway Drive where Doug Ferring worked. The one-story building of white stone had smoked glass windows along the front and dual flagpoles flying the U.S. and Maryland flags. The parking lot, which stood only half full, wrapped around the back. Swan parked near the entrance, across from a row of empty handicapped parking spaces.

Inside the lobby, a redheaded receptionist in a white dress sprinkled with blue flowers greeted them. Ross asked to see Ferring. The receptionist, eyeing the bandage on Ross's face, called for him but a moment later depressed the switch hook. "He doesn't seem to be at his desk. Let me try his cell number." She dialed and waited, then shook her head and hung up. "I'm sorry, I can't reach him right now. Is he expecting you?"

"No," Ross said. "It's a surprise visit." She slid her ID across the counter.

The receptionist read it. "One moment, I'll try his manager." She placed a third call and got a response. "Hi Walt. There's a detective from the police department up here looking for Doug Ferring, but I can't reach him. Okay, thank you." She hung up and said, "Walt will be here in a minute."

Ross thanked her, then she and Swan backed to the opposite wall to wait. It was only a moment before the door swung open and a heavyset man in gray trousers and a black short-sleeved shirt came in. His thinning brown hair was streaked with gray, and he looked troubled, whether because the police were there or because he'd been having a bad day to start with. With a glance at the receptionist, he pointed to the detectives, and she nodded.

"Walt Kendall," he said, thrusting out a hand. Ross accepted the handshake first, then Swan. "I'm Doug's manager. I'm afraid he's not here. Is there anything I can do?"

"I don't suppose you know where he went," Ross said.

"Sorry, no. He got a phone call, said there was an emergency, and rushed out."

Ross looked at Swan, who muttered, "Carol." It figured. His sister warned him the cops were on their way, and he bolted. Why?

Ross gave Kendall her card. "If he shows up, give me a call. We need to speak with him."

"About what? Is he in trouble?"

"It's a family matter," Swan said. "We just need to talk to him."

Kendall tucked the card into his breast pocket. "All right, I'll let you know if he shows up." His tone suggested he might not, depending on what Doug told him.

Outside again, Swan asked Ross, "Where does he live?"

"He's got an apartment around here somewhere. I have a note." She got out her cell phone and flipped through her notepad app. "In Owen Brown, off Cradlerock Way."

"Want to try it?"

"May as well."

Swan set course for the address. "You sure you don't want to see a doctor?"

Ross shook her head. "Maybe after we talk to Doug."

"He can wait, Holly."

"Yeah, but he might hit me with something sharp, too. No sense going to the doctor twice."

Swan laughed and shook her head, but Ross hadn't entirely been joking.

Peller, Montufar, and Dumas returned to Northern District Headquarters and compared notes while waiting for Ross to return. Montufar had picked up her voice mail and relayed the message Theresa Swan had left. "Theresa says the women have solid alibis. Also, Holly asked her help in interviewing Carol Mondy and Doug Ferring again."

"Uh-oh," Dumas muttered.

Peller winced. "Well, you can't fault her initiative. Let's review what we've got. Eric?"

"No big surprises from Alice on the burglary. She's scared. She doesn't contest being involved but denies all knowledge of the double murder. McPherson wants to deal, maybe, if the offer is heavy enough."

"Does she have anything worth trading?"

"Nah. Names of accomplices, whereabouts of the goods. That's about it. Kevin and I could get it out of her if the lawyer wasn't there."

Peller nodded. "We'll see what the DA's office says, anyway. They'd like nabbing the whole ring, even though it's of little consequence. If they rob anyone in the future, it'll only be Chuck again."

"Speaking of whom," Dumas said, "guess who Jenna Ferring is? Chuck's wife. But she's too young to be the woman who paid James III a visit, isn't she?"

"That little incident is getting interesting," Montufar said. "Hang on, I've got the list of James's medications here. She turned to her computer and typed. "Nope, he's definitely not on quinidine. He takes digoxin." Switching to her web browser, she looked it up. "That's a heart med, too, also used to treat arrhythmia. Oh, look at this." She ran a finger along the words, not quite touching the screen. "There's a nasty interaction between digoxin and quinidine, potentially fatal in as little as twenty-four hours."

Peller and Dumas both leaned in to read the information.

"Potentially," Dumas said. "That's a dicey way to attempt murder."

Peller straightened. "But if you have the stuff on hand, it would be easy enough to try, and in a guy his age, who would have questioned it? Pass that along to the lab, Corina. Ask them to test for quinidine. If it's a hit, we'll get that warrant Denise wanted."

Dumas re-read the drug information. "You think she tried to kill the old man?"

Montufar pushed back from the computer. "She's the only one who could have. Her husband will give her an alibi, but that doesn't mean much if the drug turns up."

He pondered that for a moment. "And Troy Nye?"

"That," Peller said, "is still up in the air. I was hoping Holly might find something useful on that score. From what she said, Cassie Ferring would break under a little pressure, assuming she knows anything."

"Assuming," Dumas agreed. "But that's a big question mark."

Captain Morris intruded in evident distress. "Rick," she said, hanging on to the cubicle wall. "We have a hostage situation."

Peller stood. "Where?"

"An apartment building in Owen Brown. The building's been emptied and the SWAT team is on site, but I want you down there, too. All three of you."

"Why?"

Morris drew a breath. "It's Doug Ferring. He wounded Theresa and has Holly."

Chapter 21

The mind does strange things under stress. When the second-floor apartment door opened and Ross saw Doug Ferring shaking like a cornered mouse, gun in hand, a sense of detachment washed over her. *That's it,* she thought. *I'm fired.*

A frenzied back-and-forth ensued, with Theresa Swan trying to talk Ferring down and Ferring growing more agitated by the second. An explosion echoed through the hall, a few yelps and screams came from other apartments, and Theresa, with a spray of red erupting from her left shoulder in slow motion—or so Ross saw it—whirled and toppled while fumbling for her own weapon. Then cold metal pressed against Ross's neck. Ferring grabbed her arm and pulled her inside, kicking the door shut as they stumbled together into his incongruously dark apartment. No lights on, all the curtains shut.

"I've got to get out of here," he mumbled. "I've got to get out of here." His terrified eyes flitted over everything as though expecting a secret passage to reveal itself. But with a wounded cop on his doorstep and people no doubt already calling the police, where could he go? He shoved her into an easy chair and, still pressing the gun into her neck, used his free hand to frisk her. Finding her weapon, he confiscated it and tucked it into his belt, then stood back. "I've got to get out of here." He backed away, still searching for that magic escape hatch.

Half sunk into the chair, Ross tried to pull herself up, but he screamed for her to hold still and pointed the weapon, using both hands in a vain effort to aim straight. He was quivering all over.

Ross slowly put up her hands. "All right," she said, voice shaking as much as her captor's body. "I'm cooperating. I'll do as you say."

"You'd better." Sirens wailed in the distance, growing louder. Police, ambulance, fire trucks, all converging on them.

"Just don't kill me. Cop killers don't make it to court."

"God," he breathed. He searched the room once more but didn't take his eyes off her for more than a moment at a time. "I've got to get out of here."

"I don't think we can," she said, allying herself with him. "They'll be here any moment. We're trapped."

"Damn it. *Damn* it! Why did you have to come here?"

"To ask about the horse." She couldn't help it. She laughed. "The *horse*. My God." Risking a look around the apartment, Ross found it a dismal place. The spare furniture looked to be second-hand. Clothing was tossed all about. Doug Ferring didn't seem to know about laundry hampers. The smallish kitchen just off the living room was piled with dirty dishes. The trash can overflowed.

"Damn horse," he muttered. "Who the hell cares about a dead horse?" He lowered the gun a hair, but Ross didn't like her odds of successfully disarming him, so she kept still. "I should tie you up," he said. "What do I have to tie you up with?"

"Rope?" she said unhelpfully.

"No."

"Twine?"

"No." He waved the gun carelessly. "I don't have anything."

"Don't worry about it," she said. "I won't cause any trouble. I'll do as you say."

Ferring blinked at her. "You will?"

"I will. I promise."

"Of course. I have both guns." He patted her gun and looked suddenly confident. "We'll just be quiet. Nobody will know we're here. When they go away, we can get out."

Desperation, Ross thought, *must breed stupidity*. But that didn't alter the fact that he did have both guns.

Noises sounded in the hall. Heavy footsteps. Voices. Ferring turned the gun on the door. "Don't move," he whispered, "or I'll kill you anyway."

"Okay," she whispered back. She eyed the door, tense, ready to throw herself to the floor and crawl out of harm's way if anything happened.

The noises subsided.

Doug, breathing heavy, still shaking, stared hard at the door. Minutes passed. A lot of minutes.

Someone knocked, not too loud, not too rapidly. Doug flinched but stood his ground and, more importantly, didn't pull the trigger.

"Doug?" a voice called. "My name is Rick. I think you have a friend of mine in there."

Ross, who had been holding her breath for the past twenty seconds, exhaled. The danger hadn't subsided, but knowing Peller was there brought a curious sense of relief. It would be okay. Maybe she could even keep her job.

"Doug? Can we talk?"

"No!" Ferring screamed and blew a hole in the door.

Montufar drove on the theory she could get them there fastest. Horn blaring, tires squealing, vehicle flying around traffic, they arrived as Theresa Swan was being wheeled out of the apartment building to a waiting ambulance. Peller and Dumas made for the front lines while Montufar stopped to check on her protégé's condition.

Swan, wincing from the pain but otherwise lucid, spoke first. "Do I get a medal for this?"

"You should," Montufar said. "What happened?"

"No clue. We knocked on the door, Doug Ferring opened it, and here I am. He's got Holly."

"Is she okay?"

"I think so. I wasn't entirely together, but I didn't hear any other shots."

Montufar touched Swan's hand. "Don't worry. We'll get her out." She turned to go.

Swan reached for her with her good arm. "Hey, one other thing."

Returning to her side Montufar asked, "What's that?"

"We talked to Carol first. She attacked Holly with a trowel. Cut her face, but not too bad. She must've warned Doug after we left. But his reaction . . . it's messed up. He came out shooting before we said a word about why we were there. It's not Holly's fault."

Montufar patted her hand again. "Don't worry about it." She watched the paramedics load Swan into the ambulance, then went into the building, up to the second floor, and into the thick of things.

The first responders had begun the evacuation process, and by the time the SWAT team arrived, the residents were away from the site. Stairwells at both ends of the second-floor hall were blocked off and guarded. Montufar found Dumas at the north end of the hall, silently watching the proceedings along with the others. The hall itself was empty save a lone figure standing to the side of an apartment door: Peller, who had donned riot gear minus the weaponry.

"What's he doing?" Montufar whispered to Dumas.

"Doug?" Peller's voice sounded more distant than it was. "Can we talk?"

A gunshot blasted through the door. Everyone jumped but held their positions. Peller looked back at his colleagues, exasperated.

"Letting Holly know we're here," Dumas whispered. "And negotiating, if possible."

"Doug isn't in a negotiating mood."

Dumas nodded.

"What if he doesn't get in the mood?"

"The SWAT team considered using apartment balconies for access, but nobody wants to go in guns blazing with Holly in there. It could be a long day."

Peller tried again. "I just want to talk, Doug. I don't have a gun."

A voice from inside yelled something, but Montufar couldn't make out the words.

"You don't want to hurt anyone, Doug," Peller said. "That's not your style."

Another gun blast blew a fresh hole in the door and pock-marked the wall on the other side.

"Looks like his style," Dumas mumbled.

The SWAT team's commander, Lieutenant Pete Addington, came up the stairs, mouth twitching. "Any luck?" he asked.

Dumas shook his head.

"Ferring closed all the curtains," Addington said. "We can't see to take him out. We'll either have to get in or convince him to come out."

"He's not exactly cooperating."

Peller said something nobody heard and got an angry if indecipherable response.

Montufar didn't see how the situation could improve unless Ferring ran out of ammo. Unfortunately, they didn't know the extent of his stockpile. "What's his weapon?" she asked

"Probably a thirty-eight handgun," Addington said. "According to Detective Swan."

"So five to eight rounds in the chamber. He's taken three shots already."

"Five seconds to reload," Dumas added. "If he's good at it."

"And doesn't have a speed loader." Addington shook his head. "The risk to your colleague is pretty high."

"He didn't kill Theresa," Montufar said. "Either he doesn't want to kill a cop or he's not a very good shot." The men look skeptical. "I'm just laying out the parameters," she added. Their skepticism didn't alter. "So we can think about it clearly."

"Clearly." Addington shook his head. "Operations like this are never clear."

Ferring fired another shot through the door.

Fists balled and jaw locked, Peller looked about ready to kick in the door himself.

"Hey," Ross said gently. "Be calm. Don't get riled. We need to think."

Doug turned on her, gun clasped with both hands but as unsteady as ever. His face had taken on a reddish tinge. "Think about what!"

Slowly, she raised her hands and patted the air. "Just . . . just take it easy. If you're all worked up, we won't figure a way out."

"A way out." He laughed bitterly. "There's no way out of this. For either of us. I can't let you go or they'll bust in and get me. They're *not* gonna get me! I won't let them." He turned back to the door and fired just for the hell of it.

"Come on, Doug," Peller called, "this won't help." He sounded angry, which probably wasn't a good thing.

"You have extra rounds?" Ross asked. "You must be about empty."

Doug sneered at her. "Don't try to be smart."

"I'm just saying. We need ammo to get out in one piece."

"Get up." He motioned with the weapon. Ross slowly stood. "To the bedroom."

She walked ahead of him down a short hall, past the bathroom and a small spare bedroom. She noticed in passing that he had a cluttered desk and a drum set in the darkened room. His bedroom was at the back, an explosion of clothing, music magazines, and odds and ends scattered about. *Star Wars* posters were stapled to the walls.

"Sit on the bed," he ordered.

She didn't care to. The sheets looked like they hadn't been changed in three months. But he had the gun, so she did as she was told, touching as little as possible. He went to the dresser and opened a bottom drawer. From it, he took a box of thirty-eight rounds and rattled it.

"See?" he gloated. "I got three more boxes of these."

"Okay," she said, feigning relief. "That will hold them off for a while."

From outside, Peller's voice called, but Ross couldn't make out the words.

Doug rattled the box again and frowned at it. "Why would you be happy about that?"

"I don't want to get shot. So long as you're in control, I'll be safe. Right?"

He opened the box and took out a handful of rounds, which he dropped in his left trouser pocket. "I'm not in control."

With four boxes of ammo, he could be, at least for a time. "Tell Rick you want a car brought up to the door. Then everyone clears off. Nobody follows you. You can drop me off wherever you want and take off. Leave the state. Disappear."

"He won't do that."

"Sure he will. He doesn't want me hurt, either. He's my boss. My boss's boss, anyway."

Doug examined his weapon. His hands were steadier now, his expression pensive.

"Doug?"

He licked his lips. "They'll try to follow. You have to stay with me."

"For how long?"

"I don't know. Forever, maybe."

Ross figured anything that got him to open the door would be a step in the right direction. "All right," she said. "If you think it's necessary."

Surprised, Doug almost smiled at her. Almost. Then he narrowed his eyes. "You know you're only alive because I need a shield."

"I know. I'd like to stay alive, though, so I'll be your shield as long as you need one."

He nodded warily. "You really came here because of the horse?"

"Yes. Why did you think?"

He regarded the gun.

"Oh, Doug," she said as though sorry for him. "It was you?"

Nodding, he motioned her to stand.

She complied. "I'm sorry. We didn't know. Really, we didn't. We thought it was Denise." Which they didn't, not entirely, but maybe the false accusation would get at least one Ferring to talk.

"Nah. She talks big, but she's weak on the inside. Somebody else had to do it." He pointed out the door, and they returned to the living room.

Peller was trying to talk to Doug again, but again Ross couldn't understand him.

"You want to tell him what you want?" she asked, "Or should I? I can let him know you haven't hurt me. That will count for something."

Doug considered it for a moment. "Yeah, okay."

Ross faced the door but didn't approach it. If things went wrong, Doug might shoot it again, and she didn't want to be in his way. "Rick?" she called. "You still there?"

"Yes, Holly. Are you okay?"

"I'm fine. Doug won't hurt me so long as nobody gets jumpy."

"Glad to hear it. What's the deal?"

"He wants a car parked at the entrance. Leave the keys in it, motor running." She glanced back at Doug, who nodded. "All police withdrawn from the area. He'll be taking me for a ride. So long as nobody follows, I'll be fine." Hoping a bit of improvisation would be safe, Ross added, "He's really sorry about this, Rick. It was a misunderstanding. He doesn't want anyone else to get hurt."

Doug nodded at that, too, and gave her a tight-lipped smile.

"Misunderstanding?" Peller replied. "What happened?"

"We came talk about the horse. He thought it was about . . ." She lowered her voice. "Oh. I probably shouldn't say that part, huh?"

"No," Doug affirmed. He pointed the gun at her, and this time he was rock-steady.

"Okay," she whispered. To Peller, she said, "About something else. It doesn't matter now. Just get the car, Rick, and tell everyone to leave."

"I'll see what I can do," Peller replied. "Doug, I need you to keep your word. Don't hurt Holly, and everything will be all right."

Ross motioned Doug to keep silent, then said, "He says we'll keep our word if you keep yours."

A moment of silence told her Peller understood. "Agreed," he promised. "I'll be back shortly."

Uttering an exhausted sigh, Ross spread her hands. "Now we wait," she said.

Doug's lips were pinched tight. "Why," he asked, "did you say 'we'?"

"We're in this together," she said. "You and your shield." She smiled mischievously. "Kind of exciting, right?"

Using the gun, he motioned her back to the chair. "Not really."
She sat, he stood, and they waited in prolonged silence.

Chapter 22

Peller parked the car, a slightly-used gray Honda Accord with a GPS tracker secreted under the hood, as close to the door as possible. Leaving the key in the car and motor running, he signaled the withdrawal, and all units dispersed. An uneasy quiet fell over the neighborhood save the sound of the engine and his footsteps ascending the stairs one last time.

Before they left, he told Montufar and Dumas what he had learned: Doug Ferring had killed Troy Nye and Mia Hambleton. He panicked when Theresa Swan and Holly Ross showed up, thinking they had pegged him for the murders. Ross was trying to manipulate him, apparently with some success. With any luck, Doug would release her once in the clear. Peller told Montufar to bring Captain Morris up to speed and request the FBI be alerted. They would track the car, but at some point somebody, likely outside Howard County, would have to arrest the armed and dangerous Doug Ferring. With luck, he would release Holly before then.

Resuming his position to the side of the door, Peller knocked. "Doug? It's Rick again. The car is ready. All police have withdrawn except myself, and I'm on my way out. Promise me you'll keep your end of the deal. Don't hurt Holly, and let her go as soon as possible."

"Letting her go wasn't part of the deal!" Doug yelled back. Peller braced himself for another gunshot, but none came.

"Not as such," he admitted, "but you can't keep her forever without hurting her, and if you hurt her, all bets are off."

He thought he heard Holly's voice, low, calm, and then Doug's more strident reply, but he couldn't make out words

"I'll be fine, Rick," Ross called. "So long as you've done your part."

He wasn't too sure of that, but he dared not argue. "All right. I'm gone."

Peller hurried to his truck and back to headquarters, hoping Ross knew what she was doing.

Ross didn't think they'd ever get out of the building. Quivering like a cornered mouse, Doug Ferring refused to open the door for a good fifteen minutes. "The car will run out of gas before we get out there," she told him.

"He's lying," Ferring insisted for the sixth time. "They're waiting for us."

"I know Rick. You can trust him."

"You can't trust cops."

Ross was back in the chair, Ferring standing, moving aimlessly about the room, gun in hand but at least no longer pointed at her. "Look out the window," she suggested.

"No! They'll shoot me!"

"Then damn it, let *me* look out the window."

"Don't tell me what to do! You're not my mother!"

Thank God for that.

He shook the gun at nothing. "What if they didn't fill up the tank? Maybe we're supposed to get in the car and run out of gas."

"Why bother?" Ross snapped. "It would be easier to let us starve to death in here."

Ferring looked at her, horrified. "Would they do that?"

"No. They gave us a car."

"Why?"

"So you wouldn't hurt me." She drew out the words as though explaining to a stupid child.

He mulled it over for another minute. "Check the windows," he decided. "But just look. No hand signals or anything. I can kill you whenever I want."

"Sure, commit suicide. Once I'm dead, so are you." She rose and went to the end of the curtain. Nudging it aside with her index finger, she peered out. Not that she could see anything but trees and the freshly-mown lawn and other buildings. Nothing stirred. The world held its breath. "Clear," she said.

"They're hiding," Ferring insisted. "They must be."

"I'll check the hall, too." Without thinking about the consequences, she strode to the apartment door. If he shot her, at least this would be over.

He watched her pass by. As she set her hand to the doorknob, he warned, "Don't."

She turned the knob.

"Don't!"

"Quiet," she commanded. The door slipped open an inch. She set her eye to the gap and looked into the relative light of the empty hall. "Clear," she whispered.

Ferring had come up behind her. He set the gun to the back of her head. "It better be."

"It is." She pushed the door wide open. "See?"

The gun moved away. "It's a trap," he whispered.

Ross exhaled in exasperation. "I thought you were a killer."

He pushed her into the hall so hard she nearly hit the floor. "Shut up and move."

At last. She hurried to the stairwell and without looking descended, taking the steps two at a time. Ferring followed, apparently no longer concerned about cops hiding in the shadows. The car was waiting for them, as Peller had promised. Ferring opened the driver's door and with the gun waved Ross in. Keeping the weapon trained on her, he rounded the car and jumped into the passenger seat. "Go."

"Where?"

"Out of Maryland."

"Which way?"

"The short way. North."

Ross drove. "We'll take ninety-seven north," she said. "We'll be in Pennsylvania in about an hour. Does that work?"

"Fine."

"Then you can let me go. You can pick up any of several interstates in Harrisburg and vanish."

He pressed the gun into her arm. "You're going with me."

Ross had no idea how to get him past that, but maybe after an hour of driving, in the imagined safety of a different state, he'd calm down and listen to reason. At the very least, he had to sleep sometime.

They left the houses and townhomes of Columbia behind, turned west on Interstate 70, and exited north on state route 97, speaking not a word to each other. Ferring kept the gun cradled in his lap as they drove the two-lane road through the rolling farmland, into and through Westminster, and out the other side. Once in the northernmost reaches of Maryland, they encountered little traffic, just an occasional car or SUV following at a distance, passing the other way, or disappearing over a rise up ahead.

"It was pretty easy," Ferring said for no apparent reason.

Ross glanced at him. "What was?"

"Killing Troy and Mia. They didn't know it was coming. I walked up behind them and shot them, first her, then him. I just moved my hand from here to there." He demonstrated, pointing the gun at the left side of the glove compartment, then the right. "Squeeze, squeeze, done."

"Weren't you nervous?"

"A little. I'd never killed anyone before. But they deserved it. Aunt Denise said they betrayed us. We could go to prison if they talked to the cops."

"You could go to prison for killing them, too. Didn't you think of that?"

"Aunt Denise said we'd never be caught."

Aunt Denise must be pretty damn persuasive, Ross thought. "Where did you do it?"

"Near where we dumped them, on the road into the Howard County Conservancy. It was just after sunset. They were closed. We didn't go too far up the road, 'cause they have video cameras on the buildings There are a couple of big trees close to the turnoff. Denise told them to meet her there. She told them about the reward for their capture and said she could help them stay in the clear. She got them back under the trees where nobody would see them meet, and I was waiting for them."

"And she was there?"

"Oh, yeah. She couldn't pull the trigger, but she wanted to watch."

"What was it like?"

Ferring gazed at Ross, puzzled. "You never shot anyone?"

"No."

"You will. Then you'll know."

She hoped not, although she might be willing to start with a Ferring.

"It was a shock," he admitted. "The blood. The way they fell. But when I saw them lying there..." He grinned. "It felt good. Powerful."

Being Doug Ferring, Ross supposed, had been like being a gnat until that moment. Now he knew he could snuff out a life.

"Troy was always so smart, and I was always so dumb. And that woman of his." Ferring made a face and shook his head. "She should have been a whore. That's all she was good for."

"Did you sleep with her?"

"Hell, no."

"Then how do you know?"

Turning in his seat, Ferring fixed Ross with a murderous glare. "I just do. But she's not so sexy now, is she?"

Ross figured there was a dark history between Doug, Troy, and Mia. Probably she had pushed Doug off an emotional cliff while Troy laughed. Doug Ferring seemed the sort others would laugh at. But not anymore. He was a killer now, a man to be feared.

"I guess not," she said. "Having a hole blown in you makes you far less attractive."

"That's right." He settled back again. "You're at least smart enough to know that."

"And to know who has the power."

Ferring smiled. After years of insignificance, validation must feel good. "I think I like you. What's your name again?"

"Holly."

The road surface morphed from old to older. A sign welcomed them to Adams County and announced Littlestown in two miles, Gettysburg in twelve.

"I'm hungry, Holly." He stretched his legs as much as he could.

"We're in Pennsylvania," Ross said. "Should we stop in town?"

"Sure. What's there?"

"No idea. I've never been to Littlestown. But there ought to be a fast food place."

Ferring tucked away the gun and watched the scenery go by. They might have been a couple on vacation. The road cut through a hilly landscape with houses separating pavement from farmland beyond. Fields gave way to more housing and businesses as they entered town.

But he wasn't just looking out the window. He was focused on the side mirror. "That car has been behind us for miles."

Ross looked in the rearview mirror. A nondescript gray sedan followed at a distance. She couldn't tell the make or model, nor could she see the driver clearly. "It's nothing," she said. "Just somebody going our way."

"How do you know?"

She didn't, but Ferring wouldn't know more than he'd seen in cop shows on TV. "We're out of Maryland. Even if the Carroll County police tailed us, they couldn't have followed us across the state line."

Ferring watched the car anyway, as did Ross. As they got farther into town, it turned off on a side street, and they were joined by other cars. The highway became Main Street and carried them into the business district. Ross pulled into the first fast food drive-through she saw. "Who's paying?" she quipped.

Ferring laughed. "You know what? I'll pay. You've had a long day, haven't you?"

"Yeah. I wouldn't mind going home after lunch, either."

He told her what to order and dug a debit card out of his wallet, then thought better of it and handed her cash instead. At the speaker box, Ross placed the order and pulled up to the window to wait. The window was closed. Inside, shadows rushed about. Muffled voices just penetrated the glass. Everyone inside the building seemed to be moving away from them. A sense of unease gripped her. It was as logical a place to trap Ferring as any, but he still had his shield—her—and the gun and enough rounds loaded to do some damage. Who the hell would risk an ambush under those circumstances? She kept her eyes on the drive-through window so as not to alert him to the danger.

An unmarked car drove slowly by then cut left and stopped, blocking their path. Another came up behind, and a third halted with its engine by their front passenger door. Wide-eyed, Ferring fumbled for the gun with one hand and grabbed a fistful of Ross's hair with the other.

"Doug Ferring," a bull horn amplified baritone called. "Put down the weapon."

Oh, God, Ross thought. *Don't they know he'll kill me?*

He yanked Ross against him and pressed the barrel to her throat. "Go away!" he screamed. "Go away or I'll kill her!"

He will! she pleaded in silence. *Back off! He will!*

Two uniformed officers with ballistic shields raised rounded the front of the car to their right. There might have been more behind, but Ross couldn't see. Ferring hauled on her hair so hard she thought he'd yank it right out. Dizzy from the pain, she choked down her fear and forced herself to stay still. One wrong move by anyone, and he'd fire. The gun pressed into her throat, all but choking her.

"Damn it! Damn it!" He turned and twisted, trying to take in everything at once, searching for a way out. He was shaking. The gun twitched madly over her skin.

Ross shook, too, as much as Ferring. "Stay cool," she whispered desperately. "Don't shoot. You need me alive, Doug. I'm your shield. I'm your friend, Doug. Please, Doug, please, you need me alive!"

The shielded officers flanked the passenger door but didn't attempt entry. It was a waiting game now, waiting for a terrified animal to see reason and let his executioners take him.

Someone was going to die. Her, Doug, someone. Probably both of them. Who ordered this? What had they been thinking? Ross pinched her eyes shut and waited for the inevitable.

"Doug," the amplified baritone called. "Let her go. There's no other way. Put down the gun and exit the vehicle. We won't hurt you if you don't hurt her."

"What can we do?" Ferring whimpered. "Holly, please! What can we do?"

She ought to hate him, but his fear was hers now. They were in it together, doomed together. Death was the only way out. "I don't know," she whimpered. "I just don't know."

His tormentor called again. "Come on, Doug, put the gun down and get out of the car."

"Damn," he muttered. "Damn. I'm sorry, Holly. I'm sorry."

"It's all right," she said. "Do as they say. It will be all right."

Metal slid down her throat and pressed into her sternum.

"I can't. I'm sorry."

The pressure shifted wildly as the gun barrel slipped uncontrollably around her chest.

"I know, Doug," she said. "I'm sorry, too."

His eyes were squeezed shut. "I'm sorry, Holly. Really, I am." He set his forehead against hers.

"I know."

An explosion filled her ears. Pain seared her, then another explosion, and blood, blood everywhere, and a jumble of voices and hands pulling her from the car and sirens screaming and the world descending into dark.

Chapter 23

Denise Ferring opened the door and gave Peller a sarcastic smile. "You got that warrant, didn't you?"

Peller held up the paper for inspection. She motioned him in without looking at it. He went straight to the kitchen, but the medications weren't where they had been before. Turning, he leaned back on the counter and crossed his arms over his chest. "Where are they?"

"They're Jim's, and he's away on a business trip. He took them along, of course."

"I'll get his medical records, if necessary. I expect Alice Crandall will talk eventually, and we'll soon have Doug Ferring in custody."

Denise shrugged and went to the coffee maker. "Can I get you something, Lieutenant?"

"Just the truth."

"Truth is a big word." She got a mug and made herself a cup of something, then sat at the table and motioned Peller to a chair.

He remained standing, watching her, waiting.

"My husband is a good man, but he comes from a psychotic family. Not clinically, of course. They just have this *idée fixe* regarding the family honor. Roger Ferring committed the cardinal sin of shaming the clan. Worse, it was over such a little thing. He fell in love."

"Love wasn't the issue," Peller said. "Going AWOL was the issue."

"Some might call it romantic."

"Most didn't."

Denise drank her coffee. "The rest was everyone making sure nobody forgot who the villain was. For most of the family, that was Roger. For Roger and his descendants, it was everyone else. Arguments, slander, vandalism, even killings were just footnotes to a love story gone wrong. And the only thing everyone agreed on was this: no matter what happened then or happens now, it stays in the family."

Roger's love must have been some woman, Peller reflected. "What was her name? What became of her?"

"Roger never spoke of her, not even at his court martial. He kept it to himself, married someone else, had two children, ended up dead. That's the family story, anyway."

She seemed willing to talk, so Peller kept her going. "Did you know about the body in the cellar?"

"We did. And yes, we knew it was William. My father-in-law told us one dark and stormy night." Her voice deepened dramatically as she said this, and she laughed. "He's been living in the past of late, asking for Roger, promising to bury the hatchet as he puts it. Remorse is eating him alive, and there's nothing he can do but die."

"Is that why you tried to poison him? Pity?"

She took another sip to make Peller wait for the answer, but his patience was up to the challenge. "God, no. I don't pity him. He's half the problem."

Which wasn't quite the confession Peller hoped for. "So you wanted to silence him before, in his dementia, he let something slip."

"You really want to arrest me, don't you?"

"Yes," Peller admitted. "I do."

"On what charge? Or will anything do?"

"Attempted murder and incitement to commit murder. You tried to kill James Ferring III, and you recruited Doug Ferring for the murders of Troy Nye and Mia Hambleton."

"If I did those things," she said with a demur smile, "I should get a medal for preventing further mayhem. At some point, this needs to stop, don't you think? The family ought to know someone is ready to turn them over her knee when they get out of line."

"So you're just being a responsible mother to the clan."

"I didn't say me. I said someone."

Peller finally crossed the room and sat, leaning on the table, eyes meeting Denise's. "Cassie will talk once she learns we have her son Doug in custody for murder."

Denise shook her head. "I like Cassie. She's a nice girl. But she's not very bright. She doesn't know anything useful. And quinidine, as you must know, isn't hard to come by. So what if my husband takes it? That's what you call circumstantial evidence, right?"

"How do you know I'm interested in quinidine?"

"Come on. I saw you looking at the bottles, and nobody gets a rise out of vitamin D. If you want to arrest me, you'll have to do better than that."

"That's why I'm looking forward to speaking with Doug."

The threat didn't rattle her in the least. Denise took another drink of her coffee and smiled into the mug.

Captain Morris called Dumas and Montufar into her office. When they got there, her elbows were on desk, her head in her hands, her eyes shut tight. Dumas nudged the door shut. "What happened?" he asked.

Morris looked up and composed herself. "First, Holly will live. Either Ferring was a rotten shot, or he didn't really want to kill her. He messed up her left shoulder pretty good, but the doctors say she'll recover."

Dumas frowned at the floor. "I shouldn't have let her . . ."

"Stop right there," Morris snapped. "It's not your fault. That's an order."

He might have laughed in other circumstances, as she well knew, but right now he could feel only guilt. He'd failed to protect Ross, failed to guide her, failed to . . . whatever. He'd failed, that was all, and she paid the price.

Montufar took his hand. "Captain's right," she said. "Holly wanted to make a name for herself. I'd say she did. She talked Ferring out into the open, and we got him." She raised her eyebrows at Morris for confirmation.

"More or less. He killed himself."

Dumas shook his head in disgust. "Damn it. We needed him to confirm Denise's role in the double murders."

"Obviously that's off the table." Morris picked up her pen and clicked it a few times. "I talked to the DA's office. We're in agreement that under the circumstances, we want everything Alice Crandall knows. They'll prosecute but agree to alternative sentencing in exchange for full cooperation. She won't have to do jail time. The same for her accomplices. Those that are still alive, anyway." She dropped the pen. It clattered on the desktop.

As deals went, Dumas supposed, it wasn't horrible. "I'll deliver the glad tidings."

Morris nodded. "Just make sure she understands that if we catch her withholding anything, those little leaguers will be in the majors before she sees them again."

Montufar leaned back and regarded the ceiling as though reading a message written on the tiles.

"Uh-oh," Dumas mumbled. "We're in trouble. She's thinking again."

She nodded. "Thinking Denise is about to walk."

"Why?" Morris asked.

"The one person who could testify against her is dead. Alice Crandall didn't know about the murders. Rick said she was stunned when he told her Troy had been killed. I wonder if Denise picked Doug hoping it would end this way."

"Hoping?" Dumas asked. "Or knowing?"

"Hoping. She hoped the drug interaction would kill James III, but she didn't know. She takes risks, probably calculated, but risks."

Morris picked up the pen again but didn't click it this time. "So?"

Rising, Montufar said, "I think I'll have a talk with Chuck Ferring."

"About what?" Dumas asked.

"About what happened to Theresa, for one thing." She slipped out without waiting for either questions or approval.

Morris and Dumas stared into the empty door frame and the office beyond. "What was that about?" the captain asked.

"No clue," he replied.

She shook her head. "Your marriage is going to be an adventure, isn't it?"

Dumas didn't bother answering.

Chuck Ferring had never seen Montufar, so her arrival caused him no distress. He was busy arranging a display in the back and only glanced up at her arrival. Tara Saunders was on duty, too, and greeted her presumed customer, eager to sell something.

"Sorry, but I'm not here to make a purchase," Montufar said. "I'm here about Brandon."

At the name, Ferring stiffened. "What about him?"

Saunders winced but said nothing.

"Word is, he threatened one of my detectives." Montufar approached Ferring and offered her ID.

Ferring pinched his lips.

"I'm doing a preliminary investigation to determine whether Detective Swan stepped out of line."

"No," Ferring said quickly. "Brandon started it, and she handled it..." He searched for the word among the guns. "Appropriately."

"Glad to hear it. What was Brandon's problem?"

Ferring looked away, embarrassed, but Saunders had no problem naming it. "He's a racist. Probably a Klansman. He shouldn't be allowed in here."

"I'll handle this, Tara. Find something to do."

She gave him a petulant smirk and stalked into the back.

"I told him to leave," Ferring added. "He did."

"I suppose having a gun trained on him helped." Montufar examined the wares in the display case.

He had no reply to that.

"One other thing. I have news on your grandfather. We're still processing the DNA sample your father provided, but we have independent confirmation that the skeleton—you heard about the skeleton?" She looked up, eyebrows arched in query.

"Yeah," Ferring grumped.

"It is in fact your grandfather's remains."

"Great. Is that all? I have work to do." He shuffled some papers as though that constituted work.

"Pretty much." Montufar said it, but she made no move for the door. She continued looking at the weapons as though pondering a purchase after all.

"Well, then," Ferring said, obviously hoping to see no more of her. He looked at the case, too, inspecting the display. Maybe something needed rearrangement?

"Could I ask something personal?"

He sighed.

"Your father said something strange."

"My father says a lot of strange things. Or at least I always thought so. Now that I'm older, not so much."

"He said your family was a swarm of mosquitos."

Caught by surprise, Ferring laughed.

"He said the one family member who made him nervous wasn't even a Ferring, someone too proper." When Ferring didn't take the bait and offer up a name, she said it herself: "Denise, I suppose?"

The name killed his mirth, and he turned his attention back to the display case. "What's your question?"

"Why does he fear her?"

"Paranoia, probably."

"And you?"

"I barely know her."

"What about Troy Nye? You know him?"

Ferring shook his head.

"No, you wouldn't. He and his girlfriend Mia Hambleton distracted you the night of the break-in. They couldn't have gotten away with it if you knew them."

Ferring gave her a genuine look of confusion but kept his mouth shut.

"Troy was part of the Ferring clan, too."

"Was?"

"He's dead now. Murdered, along with Mia. She wasn't a Ferring. She just had the misfortune to be involved with one."

"I—" Ferring stacked up his papers, shaking his head.

"Tell me about Denise, Mr. Ferring."

"You think she…" His hands trembled. He shoved the papers aside. "It wasn't done with one of my guns, was it?"

"We'll know soon enough. We know who killed Troy and Mia. He took a cop hostage and, in the end, shot himself. We also have one of the thieves and will soon have the others."

Ferring nearly collapsed on the counter. Leaning heavily on it, he took a few ragged breaths. "This damn family," he muttered. "We can't ever move on. That's all I ever wanted. I just wanted to move on."

"Tell me about Denise," Montufar repeated. "Then maybe you can."

Ferring straightened, drew a long breath, and motioned toward the back. "My office," he said. "I don't have a choice anymore. I'll tell you everything."

Chapter 24

Events moved faster than the lab work, but eventually everything came together. Alice Crandall, on the advice of her attorney, took the deal for alternative sentencing. She gave up the names of her accomplices and the location of the stolen weapons, which she'd stashed in her father's attic. He didn't know they were there. She counted on ignorance in another way, too: her accomplices were her younger brother Steve and Andrew Hunt's younger brother Bill. Alice made Bill swear not to tell Andrew about the plot. All pled guilty as part of the deal, so none went to prison, but neither did they continue lives of crime. Peller counted that as a success.

Alice's testimony solved another riddle, too. Troy Nye and Mia Hambleton were rank amateurs in it for the thrill. Mia's flirtatious nature fit the bill perfectly, and Troy enjoyed the role-playing. It was like being in a game, pretending to shop for a weapon to wield in the next dungeon. Alice didn't warn them about the cameras. They were clean, so how could the cops identify them? That mistake made their first offense their last.

The mystery pill proved to be quinidine. When James Ferring IV returned from his business trip, Peller swooped in and seized samples of Ferring's prescriptions. His quinidine came from the same manufacturer as the dose James Ferring III spit out. They also found the nursing home employee who escorted Denise Ferring to James III's room the night before the pill was found. She testified at the trial but hedged on the identification under severe cross-examination. In the end, the jury didn't buy the state's case for the attempted murder charge.

But Denise didn't walk, thanks in large part to Holly Ross. Ross and Theresa Swan recovered from their wounds and in due course received the department's Purple Heart. Ross was also awarded the Bronze Star. At the trial, she testified to Doug Ferring's confession and his implication of Denise Ferring in the murders of Troy Nye and Mia Hambleton. Her account, crucial in Denise's conviction on incitement to commit murder, was strengthened by Chuck Ferring's long-delayed tale of family infighting and Denise's manipulation of Doug over the years. Ever the outcast, Doug's only friends were his sister Carol and aunt Denise. Denise at first tried to steer Doug straight but later wielded him as a threat to force family miscreants into line.

With his wife behind bars and his son less interested than ever in the family business, James Ferring IV sold the Colonial Bakery, which thrived under its new management, benefiting from the notoriety of scandal.

That left James Ferring III. The DNA sample provided by Andrew Ferring sufficiently matched the bones Detective Ross had dubbed Napoleon to demonstrate a close relationship. Between that and the statements on record, nobody doubted William Ferring had been buried under the bakery. The centenarian could have been sent up for involuntary manslaughter, but given the state of his mind and body, no charges were filed. He passed away a year later, never having achieved his much-desired reconciliation with his uncle Roger. Not in this life, at any rate.

Peller and his team were relieved to be done with it, though other work remained. Dumas and Montufar had a wedding to orchestrate and Ozzie White to worry over. Theresa Swan and Holly Ross had to heal and work through the mental trauma of their experiences. And Rick Peller himself . . .

Well. Three of the four women in his life still needed attention.

"Sorry I'm late," Joan Churchill said when Peller opened the door. She stood on his porch, glowing in the light of the lowering sun. She wore a yellow and pale orange dress with dark lines swirling about the fabric.

Peller's breath halted, just for a moment. She was as beautiful as the sunset itself. "That's all right. I imagine traffic was awful."

"Worse than awful. So, can I come in?"

"Oh, yes, sorry." He held the door wide and let her pass by.

She waited while he closed the door, then they moved together into the living room and sat on the sofa. They had been there but a moment when the photo gallery on the opposite wall caught her attention. She rose and crossed the room. "This is wonderful," she said.

Peller joined her and began identifying the photos. Sandra. Rick and Sandra's wedding. Newborn Jason. Sandra and Jason when… Jason and Sandra when… Rick and Jason, Rick and Sandra and Jason when…

"None of the grandkids?" she asked.

"Not here. I have those in photo albums. We put this display together on the tenth anniversary of buying the house. It was quite a project. We had photos scattered all over while trying to pick the right ones and organize them."

Joan looked and looked and looked. "Ever change any of them?"

Peller shook his head and smiled at young Sandra, the first picture he had taken of her. They had still been in Lockport, New York then. She smiled back, ageless, beautiful, exactly the way he always thought of her.

"Why not?"

He shrugged. "We never wanted to. And after she died…" He lightly set his finger to Sandra's cheek. "I haven't changed a thing in the whole house. I've kept everything the way she wanted it."

If Joan thought that strange, she didn't say so. Her eyes wandered among the photos for a time, then she turned to Peller. "I burned my photos. Both times, the day the divorce came through. I got rid of anything that might remind me of the pain. But the memories didn't go away. I couldn't get rid of it, after all."

"Wasn't anything worth keeping?"

"That's the worst part. A lot was."

A pity we can't have the one without the other, Peller thought.

And Sandra countered, *Then how could you appreciate the good parts?*

Peller took Joan's hand in his. "Enough of that." He led her back to the sofa. "I have a confession to make."

She cocked her head, curious.

"We aren't going to be alone this evening."

"Oh?"

"There's someone I want you to meet."

"Who's that?"

Now that it came to it, Peller was afraid to tell her. Before he could summon the courage, the doorbell rang. "Ah," he said. "That would be them." Releasing Joan's hand, he rose and went to the foyer to admit them. Joan followed.

On the porch, Shania North looked uncertain. Winston Marley stood beside her. "Hi, Rick," he said. "How's it going?"

"Just fine, Winston. Come on in." Peller and Churchill moved aside to let the guests enter. Peller closed the door, drew a long breath, and said, "Joan, this is Winston Marley, and this is Shania North."

Marley extended his hand to Churchill, who hesitated before shaking it. Then she turned to North and looked her over. It was hard to tell what she was thinking. Timidly, Shania extended her hand, and Joan took it with the gentleness required for a wilting flower.

"Hi," North said.

Churchill bobbed her head. "Hi. Rick's told me a lot about you."

North glanced at Peller, uncertain.

This might have been a bad idea, but it was too late to turn back. "You're all getting a taste of my culinary expertise tonight," Peller said to deflect the tension. "I've ordered crab cakes from our local deli."

Marley laughed. "You scared me. I thought you were going to say you had frozen pizza in the oven."

Peller motioned them into the living room. North and Marley sat on the sofa, he and Churchill on the loveseat. An awkward silence settled over them. North clasped her hands in her lap and kept her eyes on them. Marley looked the room over much the way Peller would a crime scene. He nodded at the photos on the wall. "Quite a display," he said. "Who are they?"

"My late wife Sandra and my son Jason," Peller said. "I'm in some, too, but I took a lot of them myself."

At Sandra's mention, North looked up. She squinted at the photos, then stood and approached them. She studied them, lips pursed, eyes more intense than Peller had ever seen them. Churchill and Marley watched her, too, as though she was on stage performing a play and they the audience. Once North put a hand to a frame and adjusted it slightly.

"Does it help?" she asked. "Seeing her?"

"Sometimes," Peller said. "Sometimes it hurts."

She shuffled sideways to get a better look at one of the photos.

"I don't got any pictures. None of Carnell. None of Jay." She turned to Churchill. "Are you Rick's girlfriend?"

Churchill squirmed and looked to Peller for the answer.

Peller didn't know what to say.

North returned to the sofa and looked at her hands again. "I don't know what I'm doing, either," she said. "Win says pray about it. I'm trying." She looked up, but not at Peller. Her eyes met Churchill's. "We gotta keep trying, right?"

Churchill nodded. "Right," she said. "I guess that's all we can do."

A Personal Postscript

I hoped *A Day for Bones* would be released in 2021. The manuscript was ready, but cirrhosis began to take its toll on my wife and editor Kathleen. As her illness progressed, it became clear she wouldn't be able to work her magic on my words, so I enlisted my daughter Andrea for editing, and she did a fine job.

In March 2022, Kathleen was evaluated for a liver transplant. She seemed a good candidate until a heart catheterization yielded devastating news: she had an eighty percent blockage in her right cardiac artery, plus pulmonary hypertension. A transplant was out of the question; she would likely die on the table.

The following months were a roller coaster of hospitalizations and increasingly bad news tempered by occasional good news, but there was no changing the outcome. Kathleen wanted three things: to live until our 45th anniversary on June 20th, to be home surrounded by her family and friends, and to die in my arms. Although the last two days of her life were spent in a hospice facility, she largely got her wishes. She passed away the morning of June 27th, 2022, her hand in mine, my voice in her ear.

A Day for Bones is only the second of my books that Kathleen didn't edit, the other being *Space Operatic*. (Andrea also edited that novel.) I've often said that without her, I'd never have written anything publishable, and it's the truth. Where writing is concerned, she was more than just my editor. She was my mentor, from whom I spent 45 years learning. I never considered a work complete until she was satisfied. In our final years, we co-authored a work just for fun, and I learned so much as I watched her write and rewrite. With all that, you'd think I could now write with confidence, yet suddenly I feel I'm working without a net. I hope I don't fall.

As for the Howard County Mystery series, I once told Kathleen I thought *A Day for Bones* might be the last installment. She concurred but a few months later handed me the gist of yet another crime for Rick Peller and company to solve. I expect I'll write it for her, and so our story will go on after all.

~Dale, June 29, 2022

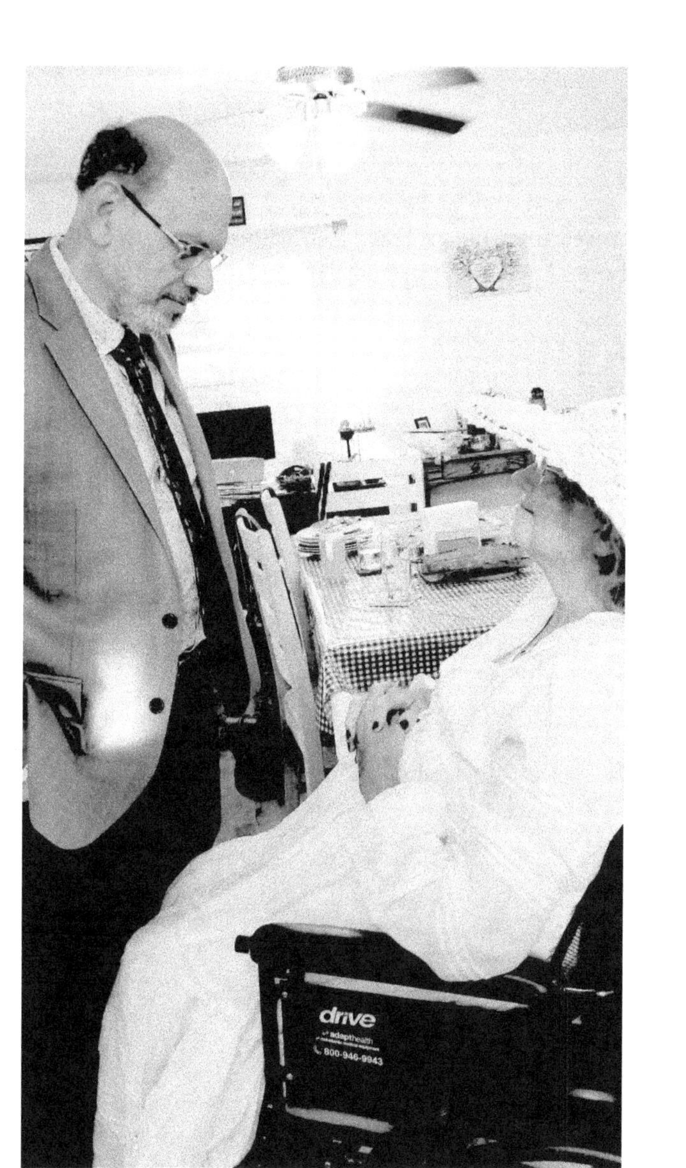

drive
adapthealth
800-946-9943

Thank you for reading! Please leave a short, honest review wherever you bought this book. I greatly appreciate it, and it will help others discover my books.

Further Reading

Rick Peller, Corina Montufar, and Eric Dumas return in more Howard County Mystery novels, available in print and ebook through your favorite bookseller:

The Fibonacci Murders (HCM #1)

"I start with zero. Nobody dies today." The strange note delivered to Rick Peller proves to be a warning shot. He, Corina Montufar, and Eric Dumas are soon pursuing a cunning killer basing murders on the Fibonacci series, a mathematical sequence in which each number is the sum of the preceding two. And the only thing Peller knows for sure is that the series never ends.

True Death (HCM #2)

Four years ago, Rick Peller's wife Sandra died on a country road. The driver who rammed her car vanished without a trace, leaving police stunned and baffled. Now, a bungled robbery raises new questions. As Corina Montufar and Eric Dumas investigate, Peller's memories awaken, triggering a series of insights that shine new light on Sandra's death.

Ice on the Bay (HCM #3)

A veterinary technician vanishes without a trace. A arson in an exclusive area bears the marks of an arsonist currently serving a prison term. A murder victim leaves behind an address book full of suspects. While temperatures plummet, cold cases collide with new crimes, and somewhere a killer with blood as icy as the waters of the Chesapeake watches and waits.

9 781958 906002